The
October
Circle

Also by Robert Littell

THE DEFECTION OF A. J. LEWINTER
SWEET REASON

The October Circle

Robert Littell

1976

Houghton Mifflin Company Boston

Library of Congress Cataloging in Publication Data

Littell, Robert, 1935-
The October Circle.
1. Czechoslovakia Republic—History—Interven-
tion, 1968-   —Fiction.   I. Title.
PZ4.L7720c3 [PS3562.I7827] 813'.5'4 75-26955
ISBN 0-395-21502-1

Printed in the United States of America

C 10 9 8 7 6 5 4 3 2 1

For Jonathan October
and Jesse August
and that old gang of mine

"We hover like falcons, motionless on political currents, facing into the stream but not progressing against it; making slight adjustments in the angle of a wing; above all comfortable; above all apathetic. Every now and then we narrow our beady eyes and swoop down, spittle streaking from our beaks, for a juicy intellectual kill."

> The Flag Holder, in one
> of his less guarded moments

Contents

Cast of Characters

The Flag Holder, Lev Mendeleyev
The Racer, Tacho Abadzhiev
Mister Dancho, a magician
The Dwarf, Angel Bazdéev, a retired clown
Atanas Popov, a collector of broken images
Octobrina Dimitrova, a painter of still lifes
Valentine (Valyo) Barbovich, an opera singer

} *Members of the October Circle*

The Rabbit, Elisabeta Antonova, the Flag Holder's mistress
Melanie Daisie Krasov, an American
Poleon, a motion picture director
Poleon's ex-wife
The Mime, thought to be Dreschko, a Spanish Civil War comrade
of the Flag Holder's—but no one is certain
The Scream Therapist, Hristo Evanov
Kovel, the Dwarf's taxi driver
Georgi, the Flag Holder's son
Comrade Minister, the Second Secretary of the Communist Party
Katya, the Minister's wife
The Witch of Melnik, a seer
Major John, a Greek bureaucrat with an unpronounceable name
Gogo Musko, an ex-soccer star who runs the Milk Bar
Marko, a journalist
Punch, a portrait artist who has switched to landscapes
Rodzianko, a television actor
Maya, a teen-age admirer of Mister Dancho's
Velin, Octobrina's brother, a translator
The Lamplighter, a printer who published an underground news-
paper during the war
The Trainer, Petar

Ivkov, the director of a funeral parlor
Blagoi, a cook
The Tomato, a traffic policeman
Stuka, a waiter
Baby Face, a police official
Green Socks, an internal security agent
Trench Coat, an internal security agent
The Prosecutor
The Defense Attorney
The Lady Judge
A Police Informer

The Fat Lady
The Juggler
The Tattooed Man   *The Dwarf's circus friends*
The Fire Eater
The Lion Tamer

Sacho
Tony   *The Racer's racers*
Evan
Boris

August 1948

The Past Imperfect

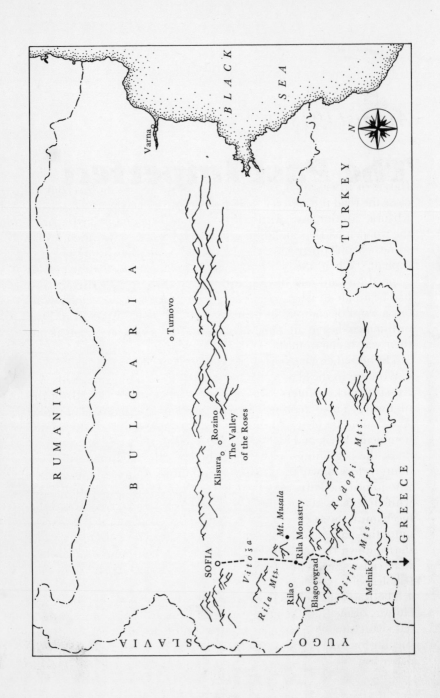

DRIFTS OF HEAT stirred, piling up against the jeeps that had come to close the road through the Valley of the Roses between Rozino and Klisura. Motionless, sweat-stained, the militiamen sulked against the wooden barriers and followed with their eyes the approach of a truncated pickup truck through the wavy air that hung over the asphalt. When the truck became whole again, the lieutenant stepped forward and flagged it onto the detour. The driver, who had heard about what was to happen on the road, turned off without a word of complaint. At dusk, the air cooled quickly and the militiamen began making book with the collective farmers on their way home from the single bar in Rozino.

The odds they gave were seventy-five to one against.

Working in the glare of an antiaircraft searchlight mounted on a Russian truck, painters redid the white line down the middle of the highway. Three representatives from the International Timing Association, fat men with suits and smiles cut from the same cloth, hammered black-and-yellow-striped poles into the spongy earth to mark the beginning and the end of the official kilometer. Two hours before dawn the District Communist Chief, a rose-grafter who joined the Party after the Russians came, not before, tested the white line with his forefinger, judged that it was dry and waved the mechanical sweeper — the only one of its kind in the country — onto the pavement. Brushes whirring, it jerked into life and started down the line. Behind it, swinging their lanterns as if they were censers, came a dozen workmen checking for oil slicks and pebbles.

The Racer arrived as dawn cracked the slate sky over the roses. He was of medium height, lean and leathery. He was wearing a red sweat suit with a green number eight on the back, and was sucking on rock candy that the Trainer supplied from a brown paper bag.

The Trainer cleared his throat. "I will inspect the line myself," he announced.

The Racer shifted his weight from one foot to the other nervously. "I'll come along."

"Better to wait," advised the Trainer.

"Better to go," insisted the Racer.

Single file, they walked the line as if it were a tightrope stretched between Rozino and Klisura. Lost in fear, the Racer went first, striding along with his hands burrowing into his jumper pockets. The Trainer, who limped from a war wound, followed, his eyes fixed on the ground.

Sunup brought with it the perfume of roses from the surrounding fields and a fine, mistlike dew.

Frowning, the Trainer held out his palm to the dew. "Perhaps we should call it off," he suggested. "The road is wetter than we calculated."

The Flag Holder, who was there to drive the big Mercedes with the sheet of Plexiglas bolted on to the rear bumper, agreed. "Another day," he said quietly, and then drew himself up and put the thought more formally. "It is my opinion that you should wait for another day."

The Racer, who had six weeks to go until his nineteenth birthday, stood silent, considering the matter. Finally he shook his head. The dew would lubricate the pavement and cut friction, he said. He would go ahead, he said, as long as no wind came up.

No wind did come up.

It was light now and families from the rose collectives began to gather under large black umbrellas along the embankment that ran parallel to the highway. The peasants were not sure what they had come to see. An ancient woman with red-rimmed eyes and no teeth told a child with braids that there would be a parade, though why a parade would be held on this lonely stretch of road she could not say. An old man with sucked-in cheeks and a hacking cough spit up phlegm and said in all probability a dignitary would pass before them, perhaps a Turk. But one among them who could read, a middle-aged man whose back was bent from carrying huge baskets of petals, said they had come to see a man die.

The militiamen who had been sleeping stiffly on the seats of buses parked in the Rozino schoolyard filed onto the road, formed ranks and trotted toward the highway to take up positions every hundred meters. A teen-ager from Rozino, the nephew of the District Communist Chief, brought up the strange bicycle with the long chain and the enormous rear gear. The Trainer received the bicycle from him and pinched the front wheel, and then the rear wheel, between his thumb and forefinger to test the pressure. The wheels were without treads to reduce friction; the rims were made of wood to prevent overheating.

The District Communist Chief who joined the Party after the Russians came approached the Flag Holder, who held Party card number four, and raised a finger to attract his attention. His gold teeth flashed when he opened his mouth to speak. "You are invited to begin when it pleases you," he advised.

The Trainer measured the progress of the sun, still low over the roses, and studied the dew-moist surface of the highway. Then he looked back at the sun again. If he waited, the sun would burn off the worst of the dew. But it would also burn off the morning coolness, which was essential if the Racer's body heat was to be kept within tolerable limits.

The District Communist Chief coughed discreetly. The Trainer arrived at his decision. "We will commence in five minutes," he informed him.

Chain-smoking Rodopies, a strong Bulgarian cigarette that the peasants thought more effective against germs than asafetida gum, the Flag Holder beckoned the Racer onto the embankment.

"Have you selected a name for the baby?" the Racer inquired.

"Georgi," the Flag Holder replied. "I'm going to call him Georgi, after Georgi Dimitrov."

The Racer nodded approval and turned to look out over the land. As far as the eye could see, the fields were all roses. In the distance, a line of women swept across a field plucking petals and deftly dropping them into the burlap bags tied to their belts.

"Do you remember the grade-school teacher from Blagoevgrad," the Flag Holder reminisced, "the one who blew off his leg with his own grenade and tried to hurry and die so we could get away? He was born here in the valley. He used to tell how the women collected the petals before the sun rose up and burned off the dew. They were paid by the kilo, you must understand, and the petals weighed more with the dew on them. The women would joke

— the grade-school teacher said you could hear their voices calling back and forth in the darkness long before you could see them — they would joke that they were harvesting dew."

The Flag Holder lit another Rodopi on the embers of the one in his mouth and sucked the new one into life. With the first deep puff he broke into a spasm of coughing. "I must give these up," he rasped, and then mocked himself by adding:

"Again."

He motioned with his cigarette toward the women in the field. "We Communists are on to their little tricks, of course. We still let them start before sunup because the petals have more perfume when they are wet, but we deduct the weight of the dew from the weight of the petals." The Flag Holder pulled morosely on his cigarette. "In our lust for forward motion, we have forgotten to honor the humanness of backwardness."

The Racer looked across the fields to the low, worn, wooden sheds where the rose petals were stored. The side of one had buckled inward, and the roof looked as if it could go at any moment. After a while the Racer said:

"Where is the forward motion of which you speak? Are you sure you are not confusing motion with movement?"

The Flag Holder smiled — though only those who had known him before the Germans captured him would have recognized it as a smile. "I'm not *sure* of anything. In this imperfect world, all a man of logic can do is repeat what Ptolemy said: 'The sun rising in the east *seems* to move across the sky.'"

The Trainer called up from the foot of the embankment, "See — the dew seems to be burning off."

The Trainer's use of "seems" made them both grin, but then the grins evaporated, like the dew. "You are a fool to attempt this thing," the Flag Holder said quietly, "but I honor you for it." The cigarette stuck to his lower lip and bobbed as he talked. "I wish you long life and many children," he added formally — even now he was not able to find an intimate tone.

The Racer waited for him to say something more. When he understood that nothing more would be said, he nodded and turned and scrambled down the embankment. The Racer's friends clustered around to wish him luck. Dancho, a pink-skinned partisan comrade who was beginning to make a name for himself as a magician, embraced him warmly.

"Say the word," he forced himself to joke, "and I'll tag along on the handlebars."

Valyo Barbovich, a young opera singer, laughed uneasily. "The last thing he needs is excess baggage."

"Much luck to you," said Angel Bazdéev, a dwarf who was already well known as a circus clown.

The Racer smiled tensely. "All right, let us start," he called. He bent quickly, easily, from the waist, almost as if he were hinged, and undid the ankle zippers and stripped off the sweat suit. Underneath he wore red shorts and a green T-shirt with the number eight in red on the back.

The Flag Holder revved up the big Mercedes. The Trainer climbed in alongside the Flag Holder, hauling his bad leg in after him, and the Mercedes started down the highway. The Racer pulled on his crash helmet and tightened the strap until it bit into his chin. Then, as Dancho and the Dwarf steadied the bicycle, he climbed on and reached over to tighten the straps that locked his toes into the pedals.

A motorcycle rumbled alongside and the driver pushed the Racer onto the highway; with the special gear, 130 teeth connected to a sprocket of 15, the Racer could not start the bicycle by himself. At thirty-five kilometers an hour his legs were barely moving. At seventy kilometers he began to hit his stride. At eighty kilometers the Racer nodded and the motorcyclist swirved away and the big Mercedes veered into place in front of him, the Plexiglas wind screen on the rear bumper inches from the front wheel of the bicycle.

There was no margin for error. Riding in the vacuum of the Plexiglas, curved gracefully over the handlebars, head down, arms thrust forward, feet pumping, the Racer began to accelerate. He had to go as fast as the Mercedes, no faster, no slower. Faster and his wheel would touch the Plexiglas. Slower and he would fall back into the slip-stream. Either one would kill him.

Inside the Mercedes the Trainer stared at the special speedometer mounted on the hood, and glanced back at the Racer. The man on the bicycle nodded imperceptibly.

"Another increment," the Trainer told the Flag Holder. "But for the love of god, be gradual."

At 120 kilometers an hour the Racer began to gulp for air. At 150 the heat hit him, engulfed him, smothered him, hammered at his temples. At 170 a point of pain in his thigh muscle brought tears to his eyes and he had to blink them away to see the Plexiglas.

Ahead the first black and yellow marker came into view.

"Faster," hissed the Trainer, his eyes glued to the speedometer. "Still faster."

Hurtling along behind the Mercedes as if he were part of the Plexiglas, the Racer worked his legs until they appeared almost motionless. Sparks of sunlight glinted off the ticking spokes. Sweat stains spread under his arms and down his back. The Racer was in full flight now, soaring fifty-eight meters a second — faster than free fall in space — pushing himself to the limit of pain, torturing himself across a frontier he thought he could never cross, pushing against the limit again, riding on the mirror of moistened road, sucked ahead by the pane of Plexiglas, gulping air, afraid he would ignite from the heat, afraid he would disintegrate from the pain, afraid most of all of the fear, thinking god whom I don't believe in help me to keep going please. Riding faster than his thoughts, the Racer abandoned himself to speed, lost himself in speed, became speed. A spoke in the front wheel snapped. Smoke seeped from the wooden tire rims. A fine spectrum-colored spray arched up from the rear wheel as the Mercedes and the bicycle leaped past the second marker.

The Trainer caught his breath and stared at the stopwatch in his damp palm. "Seventeen point five eight seconds between poles." He looked up at the Flag Holder and whispered hoarsely:

"It is done. A record for the world to beat! Two hundred kilometers an hour."

They slowed down as carefully as they had accelerated. When the Mercedes reached forty kilometers an hour, the Racer dropped back and raised his eyes and saw the triumph on the Trainer's face. Suddenly he thrust his right fist deep into the sky.

From the side of the road a flash bulb froze the instant of exhilaration.

August 1968

The Present
Ridiculous

1

"Fst."

Mister Dancho freezes, cocks an ear, listens . . . decides his imagination is working overtime and goes back to tugging on his cuffs so that they protrude from the sleeves of his blazer.

"Fsssst."

There is no mistaking it this time. Mister Dancho's eyebrows dance as he takes in the lobby. The only one in sight is the old woman who checks coats in the winter and spends the summer keeping out from under foot so that the restaurant's director won't get it into his head to lay her off. Right now she sits tucked away in a nook behind the empty coatracks, staring with total absorption into a pocket mirror propped up on a ledge, carefully lining up the tweezers and pruning with short snapping motions hairs from her chin.

"Fsssssssssst."

Mister Dancho wheels. The skirt of his blazer flares. "What in — "

The door marked "Sitters" opens a crack and a single heavily made-up eye peers out at him.

"*You!*" Dancho whispers, darting through the door and catching the woman inside in his arms. Wordlessly, they embrace.

After a while the woman sighs:

"These six weeks have been an eternity."

"My dear Katya," Mister Dancho murmurs, arranging his facial expression as if he were setting a table, "how I've waited for this moment." He holds her at arm's length and stares unblinkingly into her eyes. "There is no logic in this, you understand." A thought strikes him. "Where is your husband?"

"Not to worry. The Minister is off to Moscow — something to do with Czechoslovakia. He won't be back till tomorrow, maybe even Tuesday." She looks up at him with anxious, moist eyes.

Mister Dancho is obviously relieved. "On the other hand," he goes on, "we can spend a few stolen hours together. This is no small thing, because there is much emotion between us." He breaths heavily, as if breathing is an effort. Then he says gravely:

"I stand ready to try, on the condition that either one of us has the right to call it quits if the" — he searches for a delicate word — "*liaison*" — and watches carefully to see what effect it will have on her — "produces more pain than pleasure."

She winces at the word "liaison" (Dancho, who is not without experience in such matters, has the impression she feels she ought to), then leans against him and breaths into his ear:

"I'll risk everything."

"My darling," Mister Dancho exults. He draws her palm to his lips, which are as soft as a child's. "I'll be at Club Balkan later . . ." he implores, and she seals the rendezvous with a smile. Before it fades, he has slipped out of the ladies' room.

For Mr. Dancho, entrances and exits are the parentheses between which he invents himself, and so he gives them as much attention off stage as on. Pausing just outside the threshold of the dining room, he pats his lips with a monogrammed handkerchief, tucks it into his breast pocket so that the tip spills out haphazardly, adjusts his cuffs again, rearranges his facial expression and plunges through the curtain into the waves of sound the way a fish returns to water — a quick splash and he is off and running as if he has never been away.

"*Dobăr večer*, Mister Dancho! *Kak ste?*"

"*Salut*, Dancho — how was London, England?"

"Our conquering Dancho returns! But you must take a drink with us."

"Welcome back, Mister Dancho! Did you convert the Queen to Communism?"

Shaking hands left and right, pecking with his child's lips at rouged cheeks angled up to him, Mister Dancho drifts from table to table in crosscurrents of conversation. Behind him, waiters in wrinkled black jackets race into and out of the steam-filled kitchen through a swinging door that squeals on its hinges like a cornered cat. At one booth, six actors are arguing over a cure for migraines. They have divided into two camps, the herbalists and the acupuncturists, and appear ready to go to war over the point. Nearby, two adjacent dinner parties are joining forces, the men scraping tables and chairs together while the women hold high the drinks as if they are afraid of mice or flooding. The waiter for the station looks on sullenly, not lifting a finger to help, concerned only with how he will sort the checks. A woman who is table-hopping backs into Mister Dancho, turns, brightens and plants a wet kiss on his lips. Raising her eyebrows, she smiles and moves on, sure that Dancho's eyes will follow her. Knowing she is sure, he looks away, his fingers scraping the excess wetness from his lips.

A darkly handsome young actor grabs Dancho's arm as he passes. His name is Rodzianko, and he is the star of an immensely popular television series in which Bulgarian intelligence agents foil the American CIA every Monday between 8:00 and 9:00 P.M. (In the most recent episode, Rodzianko was abducted to Greece. "How many counterespionage operatives in Bulgaria?" the CIA interrogator demanded. "Eight million — our entire population!" Rodzianko replied arrogantly.)

"Just the man I've been looking for," Rodzianko insists now. He pulls Dancho's head toward him and, lowering his voice to a stage whisper, gives him a hot tip on the Paris stock market.

"My dear fellow," Dancho bellows over the din, "how can I show my appreciation? I'll cable my broker first thing in the morning."

Rodzianko looks at Mister Dancho in astonishment. "You'll *cable* your broker? Just like that?"

"I'll use a code, naturally," Mister Dancho shoots back, inventing himself as he goes along. "I'll tell him: 'Don't buy such and such.' He'll understand."

Mister Dancho sidesteps a waiter hurtling across the room with half a dozen plates of *kebapčeta* balanced on an arm, then stops to chat with a middle-aged portrait artist who has recently divorced his wife and married his mistress, who happens to be the granddaughter of an alternate member of the Presidium.

"Business is booming," yells the artist, whose name is Punch. He is very drunk. "Never had it s'good. I'm into landscapes nowadays, you know. Day doesn't go by but I get a commission from one of those neopreposterous tourist traps on the Black Sea."

"I thought they went in for portraits," Mister Dancho ventures.

"Portraits! Portraits have to be changed every time someone in the superstructure sneezes. But a good landscape, Christ, you can get ten or fifteen years' wear out of a good landscape." The artist swivels in his seat and thumps the back of a man at the table behind him. "Did you catch that? Mister Dancho here thinks I could give 'em portraits. That'za laugh!"

Dancho leans closer to the painter. "Would you do a portrait for me?"

The painter sees he is serious. "Sure, why not. Who you have in mind?"

"Alexander Dubček."

"Alex — " the painter roars with laughter.

At the far end of the table, directly opposite the portrait painter, sits a beautiful television actress with a scrubbed Slavic face — full pink cheeks and large brown eyes. Rumor has it that she is the illegitimate daughter of the Soviet marshal who led the Russian armies that "liberated" Bulgaria in the closing days of the Great Patriotic War. Mister Dancho looks the television actress in the eyes and she stares back, a belligerent smile forming on her lips.

"Give us a trick," Dancho's artist friend calls.

Never lifting his eyes from the actress's face, Dancho strides over to her and dips two fingers into her low-cut bodice. Someone at the table gasps. The actress doesn't bat an eyelash, but the man sitting next to her starts up angrily. An older man next to him puts a restraining hand on his elbow and whispers something and he sinks back — perhaps a shade too eagerly, Dancho judges. From between his fingers Mister Dancho begins to extract lengths of silk. With a flourish, he shakes the fabric loose and holds it up for everyone to see.

It is made up of small Czechoslovak flags sewn end to end.

An uneasy murmur goes round the table as Mister Dancho laughingly beats a retreat.

"It's all good fun, friends," the former portrait painter, suddenly sober, assures everyone. But a thin man with a Party pin in his lapel says quietly:

"Bastard — someday one of them will go too far."

The old waiter Stuka approaches Mister Dancho. There is a suggestion of a shuffle to his walk, an almost imperceptible hunch to his shoulders, a hint of vagueness to his speech. Stuka, who can still spend eight hours a day on his feet thanks to the lace-up high shoes with built-in arches that Mister Dancho once brought him from West Germany, bows and points toward the thick red curtain that divides the private room from the main dining room of the restaurant, which is called Krimm.

"They are all here, all except the Dwarf and the one you call the Rabbit. And Valentine, who is off singing in Italy."

Mister Dancho reaches into Stuka's breast pocket and produces a thick wad of American dollar bills, a currency it is illegal to possess.

"Ha! You devil, Stuka," Mister Dancho whispers, as if excited by the find, "hoarding hard currency again!"

Dancho smiles warmly and Stuka, shaking his head happily, reaches into his own breast pocket to see if Dancho has left any of the bills behind. As usual, he has. Stuka starts to protest, but Dancho motions him to remain silent and parts the curtain to peek into the private dining room.

Nothing has changed. ("Nothing ever changes," the Flag Holder is fond of saying, "except our point of view.") The table is cluttered with overflowing ashtrays, abandoned dinner plates and half-empty bottles of mineral water and red wine from Melnik, a small town near the Greek border that cultivates vines imported from Bordeaux. A single glass of cognac, full to the brim, rests — as always, untouched — before the Flag Holder.

In theory, the room is open to the public. In practice, only a handful of people would have the nerve to use it without an invitation from one or another member of the "October Circle" — an informal group that takes its name from its only female member, Octobrina Dimitrova, who was born on the October day the Bolsheviks stormed the Winter Palace and named Octobrina to honor the revolution. The four people who are in the room now, sitting in straightbacked chairs beneath blown-up photographs of themselves, are all charter members. For them the room is a home away from home. Small, windowless, it is dominated by a heavy wooden table and a massive sideboard ("A period piece," the Flag Holder calls it, "Stalin Gothic!") in which the restaurant's accounts are stored.

Looking through the peephole he has created in the curtain, Mister Dancho cannot make out who is speaking. But he knows from the way everyone hangs on his words that Popov must be reading his list.

"One plastic contraceptive coil, manufactured in France by the look of it. One Communist Party card, undated but unlaminated, which indicates it is fairly old, in the name of Nadezhda Alexandrovna Dreschkova. Do you recognize the name, Lev? She was the wife of the poet Dreschko, who hanged himself when they confiscated his manuscripts." Popov lets his breath whistle softly through his teeth, a sign that he is rummaging in his brain for a misplaced detail. "Sssssssss. There was a Dreschko who fought in Spain with you, wasn't there, Lev? I ask myself if he was any relation?"

"The Dwarf knew him too — he was in the circus before the war," the Flag Holder replies thoughtfully. "I seem to recall he had a younger brother who wrote poetry."

"Must be the same family," Popov guesses. "Whatever happened to him?"

"He worked with Georgi Dimitrov in Moscow for a time, then he just disappeared. Dimitrov once told me he made discreet inquiries, but he never received an answer. From this Dimitrov assumed that Dreschko died in Siberia."

Popov stares, with unfocused eyes, at the table. Then he snaps his head. "Let me see, where was I? Sssssssss. Ah, one electrical bill in an unopened envelope, addressed to 'Resident, eighty-four Stalin Boulevard, Sofia,' postmarked eight January nineteen fifty-four, with the words 'Deceased' and 'Left no forwarding address' written across the face of the envelope. One plastic reproduction of our statue to the unknown soldier, with the gold paint peeling away; I wrote a poem once — is it possible you remember it, Octobrina? — about a man who tells the authorities he knows the name, rank and serial number of the unknown soldier."

Smiling inquisitively, Octobrina Dimitrova shakes her head no, and the Flag Holder asks:

"And?"

Popov looks puzzled. "And what?"

"The man who knows the name, rank and serial number of the unknown soldier," the Flag Holder replies politely. "What happens to him?"

Popov's throat rattles gleefully. "Why, he's shot for trying to deprive the state of its heroes, and buried in an unmarked grave, that's what happens to him. A few decades later, some Reformers came along and put a marker on the grave announcing the presence, in the earth below, of the remains of the *unknown prisoner!*" Popov looks down at his ledger. "Where was I? Sssssssss. Ah, yes, one broken violin with a single string on it." Popov's eyes wander off to one side, trying to recall the details of another story. "There was a well-known Russian violinist in the thirties who only gave concerts in towns without newspapers. It was at the height of the purges and he was afraid a review would draw attention to him at a time when it was dangerous to draw attention to oneself. One day a critic from *Pravda* happened to hear him play and wrote a rave review. When the violinist heard he had a review in *Pravda*, he dropped dead on the spot. Heart attack. They swear it's true. Does it ring a bell, Valentine?"

"Valentine's not here tonight," Octobrina reminds him gently.

"Ah, yes, so you said, so you said. No matter. Where was I? Sssssssss. Ah, here" — Popov taps his ledger excitedly — "here's an exceptionally interesting item. One . . ."

With four stubby fingers wedged between his high starched collar and the ever-present red welt on his bony neck, Atanas Popov works his way down the list, which is written, as always, in a pocket ledger in a tiny, meticulous handwriting. His breath whistling through his teeth like a slow leak in an inner tube ("Sssssssss"), his brow furrowed and his good eye bulging behind the thick pince-nez, he struggles to read each entry. Occasionally his fingers abandon their post under the collar to edge the pince-nez down to the tip of the misshapen nose (it was given considerable attention by several interrogators before his "rehabilitation") where it acts as a magnifying glass. When he finally makes sense of the handwriting, Popov's small, agile head bobs excitedly — "Ah, yes, that's it" — and he plunges on.

Popov is half-deaf and half-mad, though at any given moment nobody can say which dignity (the Flag Holder insists on equating insanity with "dignity" rather than "indignity") has the upper hand: people accuse him of being insane when he has merely turned down his hearing aid (Swiss manufacture, a gift from Mister Dancho); the all-union psychiatrist who examined him after he cast the only dissenting vote at an important Party meeting neglected to commit him because he thought he was merely hard of hearing. And so Popov remains at large, shoring up against his ruin, in the

strident tones usually used by people who have trouble hearing themselves, his daily heap of broken images.

". . . One copy of the German edition of *Das Kapital;* Tacho
here is too young to know this, but the first country in the world to
translate Papa Marx was Mother Russia. Ha! Translations are
the kiss of death. They say poetry is what's lost in translation
That's what they say. As for me, I've been published in translation only. Which is probably why the handful of people in the West
who have an opinion of me have a low opinion of me. Where was I?
Sssssssss. Ah, yes. One packet of Rumanian headache supposi-
tories, empty, marked 'Not to be used after January 10, 1937.' That's
a coincidence. Mandelstam wrote a poem entitled 'January 10,
1934.' Hmmmmm. One fragment from an icon, dating — judging
from the absence of any halo over the head of the infant Jesus —
from the Second Bulgarian Kingdom; you have only to glance at
an icon to realize that iconoclasm is the only reasonable way of life.
Ha! What do you say to that, Lev? Ah, here's my last but not
least. One carton of bankbooks listing, in an anal handwriting
common to the English upper classes, deposits and withdrawals
for nineteen twenty-nine from the Balkan branch of Barclays.
Sssssssss."

Popov looks up from his ledger in time to see Mister Dancho
thrust aside the curtain (another entrance!) and sweep into the room.

"Friends, Romans, comrades — " he cries, flinging his arms
wide as if he intends to embrace everybody at once.

"I don't believe it!"

"Is it you, Mister Dancho?" exclaims Popov, his good eye bulging
behind his pince-nez.

"We didn't expect you until — "

"Dear Dancho, a thousand times welcome!"

One by one, with great warmth, Mister Dancho embraces his
friends. Then, settling his bulk into a vacant seat beneath a blown-
up photograph of himself as a young man taking a curtain call on
some long-forgotten stage, he points a playful finger at the Racer.

"Tacho, dear boy, you have changed — for the worse, *bien
entendu.* You never used to button the top button of your shirt.
If you do that, you must wear a tie like the Flag Holder here. What
is it? Trying to look like the perfect proletariat? Or perhaps it
is just age — "

Popov interrupts in accented English:

"He grows old, he grows old, he shall wear the bottoms of his trousers rolled. Ssssssss." He reaches into his side pocket, turns down his hearing aid and sits back with a distant smile on his lips to watch the mouths move.

"Tell us about London, England," demands the Flag Holder, whose name is Lev Mendeleyev.

"And be sure to give us the unexpurgated version," urges the Racer, whose name is Tacho Abadzhiev.

"Dear Dancho, don't mince words with me," Octobrina Dimitrova teases. "Tell us of your conquests."

"There was a German girl," Mister Dancho concedes. " 'I'll do anything,' she whispered, so I tried everything I'd ever tried. 'I mean absolutely anything, anything at all,' she panted, so I tried everything I'd ever read about. 'Hey, I'm serious, really, anything under the sun,' she moaned, so I dipped into my imagination and invented a few things. She licked her lips. 'Listen,' she begged, 'there's nothing I won't do, absolutely nothing.' "

"What did you do then?" the Racer demands impatiently.

"Why, I packed away my magic wand and beat a retreat, naturally. What else could I do?"

Mister Dancho joins his friends in laughter; he has an endearing way of laughing at his own stories. He is beginning to get into the spirit of things, rocking back and forth and gesturing extravagantly as he talks. "There was another girl, what the British call a bird. I rented a Daimler and took her to dinner at an old inn on an island in the Thames. There were scratches on the bar from the spurs of the Crusaders. We drank from pewter mugs and ate dinner in a corner of the garden next to a bed of forget-me-nots. Can you visualize it? At one point the bird looks up at the sky, a breathless expanse of stars, and says: *'Looks just like a bloomin' planetarium.'* " Shaking his head with exaggerated sadness, Mister Dancho repeats the line. " 'Looks like the planetarium!' "

"Dear Dancho," sighs Octobrina, "for you sex is mere recreation, something you do to keep your weight under control. Will you ever settle down and get married again?"

Mister Dancho and the Racer ooh and aah at the suggestion, and Popov, tuning into the conversation, says:

"You think wives are bad. Widows are worse. Remember what

Stalin said about Krupskaya. 'We'll have to appoint another widow
for Lenin' is what he said. Ha! That's humorous. *Appoint
another widow!*" Popov's face suddenly tenses. "It was the only
joke Stalin ever made. Ssssssss." Leaning back, he turns down
his battery and removes himself from the conversation.

"I've had my fill of living with women," Mister Dancho announces
jovially, but everyone understands he is speaking out of bitterness.
"Living with a woman is the process of peeling away masks. When
you start out, you pee in private so as not to spoil your image. Before very long you discover you are peeing with the door open,
scratching your arse, farting freely." Mister Dancho summons a
memory. "One day I peeled away a mask too many. And so she
peeled away another one of her masks — that particular one was
undying affection — and left me."

Octobrina smiles. "If you peel away enough masks you get to
the real you."

But the Flag Holder shakes his head. "There is always another
mask underneath. We are constructed like onions — all layers,
no core."

"Seriously, though, Dancho," Octobrina implores, "what's
London, England, like — what's it really like, I mean?"

Mister Dancho picks absently at a cuticle. "My dear Octobrina,
you will know everything you want to know about London, England — indeed, about the English — when I tell you that in
Harrods, which resembles our ZUM in the sense that a diamond
resembles cut glass, you will find a sign that reads in its entirety:
'Please *try* not to smoke.' "

"Oh, that's lovely," marvels Octobrina. " 'Try not to
smoke!' "

"I attempted to purchase the sign in question for our friend here"
— Dancho indicates the Flag Holder, who is puffing away like a
chimney — "but they apologized profusely and said it was most
unfortunately not for sale. The salesman — who resembles our
sales clerks in the sense that a Maserati resembles a Moskovich —
the salesman actually offered to telephone the sign maker to see if
some accommodation could be worked out. But as I was leaving
shortly, I decided to take home the story in place of the sign."

They banter back and forth, skirting the subject foremost on their
minds almost as if they are afraid to put a curse on it by talking

about it. The silences grow longer and more awkward. Looks are exchanged. Finally Mister Dancho cannot stand it any longer. "You've followed what's happening?" he asks guardedly.

"Sometimes," the Racer says carefully, "I listen to the news and pinch myself to make sure I'm not dreaming."

"Who among us would have reasoned that such a thing was possible?" Popov demands, turning up his hearing aid.

"It is a new beginning," Mister Dancho agrees excitedly. "If the experiment is successful, it will spread."

"The wind will carry such ideas like seeds," exults Popov.

"It's true," the Racer laughs. "It could happen here."

"The Flag Holder will be our Dubček," exclaims Mister Dancho. He spills wine into a glass and leaps to his feet.

"To the Dubčeks," he cries, his glass thrust high, "theirs and ours."

"The Dubčeks," the Racer joins him in a toast.

"The Dubčeks," Popov echoes.

The Flag Holder rises slowly. "To friend Dubček," he says softly, holding aloft his glass of mineral water.

They all turn toward Octobrina, who remains seated. "You're all fools," she sneers. "I don't permit myself the luxury of hope."

"What you don't permit," Mister Dancho chides gently, "is the luxury of admitting you hope."

"Come on, Octobrina," the Racer coaxes.

With a snort Octobrina climbs to her feet. "To Alexander Dubček," she toasts grudgingly, "the plastic surgeon who is trying to put a human face on Socialism." And she mutters under her breath:

"He will be the death of us all."

Solemnly, they drink his health and settle into their seats again. The Flag Holder punches a Rodopi between his lips. As he fumbles for his lighter, Mister Dancho holds out his empty hand and, with a twist of the wrist, produces a flaming match.

"Let us hope," Octobrina says sourly, "that friend Dubček doesn't wind up as a chapter in Lev's book." She is referring to the Flag Holder's work in progress (it has been in progress for the better part of a decade), a history of nonpersons in the Communist movement.

The Flag Holder's face twists into a smile. "Let us hope," he repeats.

"How is it going, your book?" Dancho inquires.

The Flag Holder pulls on his cigarette reflectively. He is wearing an old corduroy jacket and a hand-knitted tie (imported: a gift from Mister Dancho) knotted carelessly, with the narrow end hanging lower than the wide end. The bottom button of his shirt, the one just above his belt, is open, revealing the skin of someone who never exposes himself to the sun. The cuffs of his shirt and his collar are frayed. His hair, the color of sidewalk, is cropped close to the scalp, making him appear younger and more vigorous than he is.

The Flag Holder operates from under a carefully cultivated turtle's shell of formality, to which the only threat (as he sees it) is spontaneity. His first reaction to anything is usually a reflective silence. (When he is moody, which is often nowadays, the silence can be a prelude to long periods of introspection.) When finally he joins a conversation, he speaks the way he writes: selecting his words cautiously, the way you select footfalls in a newly seeded garden. He never raises his voice and seldom gestures; he believes that words should carry an impact based on their precise meaning and not on the emphasis you give them. With people he doesn't know well, he is meticulous about keeping his distance, which he feels is essential to human intercourse. Even his closest friends are kept at arm's length. There are only four people in the world he addresses with the familiar "thou" — his son, Georgi, the Racer, Mister Dancho and the Rabbit, Elisabeta Antonova, who is his mistress.

In overall physical appearance, there is something "hewn" about him despite his exceptional height; Octobrina came closest to putting her finger on it when she likened him to a "knife-sharpened pencil." Her description made the rounds, and eventually turned up in one of the public school biographies that describe the Flag Holder's exploits during the war.

The Flag Holder is painfully self-conscious about his hands, which he keeps out of sight whenever he can. The few who are able to get a look at them see immediately what is wrong. He has no fingernails.

"As a matter of fact," the Flag Holder replies, "I discovered a new nonperson just the other day. Does the name Joseph Konstantinovich Livshitz ring a bell? He won a Stalin prize in the late forties for his novels about the war. A translation of one of them appeared in England, and some damn fool made the mistake of sending him the money it earned. Livshitz was arrested as an enemy agent and sentenced to twenty years of hard labor. His Stalin prize was revoked. His books disappeared from the library shelves. His name was removed from *The Great Encyclopedia*. His birth certificate and later his death certificate vanished. People who had known him were carted off to prison camps. He ceased to exist."

"Where did you find him?" Octobrina inquires, as if Livshitz is a warm body about to be presented in evidence.

"In the archives at the Centre. It seems that at one point during the war Livshitz hid out with his family on a farm. He drummed it into their heads never to let on that they were Jewish. One day a Fascist sympathizer stopped by for lunch. He asked Livshitz's little girl where she wanted to live when she grew up. Palestine, she said. Everyone held their breaths. The Fascist asked why Palestine? The little girl said because Jesus was born there."

Stuka shuffles into the room with a pot of tea and a tray full of cups and saucers. As he parts the curtain to enter, the din from the restaurant intrudes, and fades again as the curtain falls back into place. Octobrina pours. Mister Dancho takes a jar of confiture from the sideboard and mixes a spoonful into his tea. The others use lump sugar — oversized cubes wrapped in cheap paper with the name of a tourist hotel on the Black Sea printed on it. The Flag Holder drinks his tea Russian style, straining it through a lump held in his mouth.

"Lev and his nonpersons," snorts Octobrina, fussily flicking ashes from her black lace shawl (Spanish: a gift from Dancho) with the back of her hand. "It's more than flesh and blood can stand." Octobrina is old before her time and bone dry and brittle like a fallen leaf or a fallen angel. When it comes to people or politics, she is a kettle at perpetual boil: the water sizzling inside, the tin cover rattling overhead. When it comes to material things, she exhibits a carefully nurtured ineptitude: she is awkward when ordering in restaurants, graceless when introducing people, forgetful about paying bills. When she pays for something out of pocket, she cups her hands and holds out whatever coins she finds in her purse. (Dancho occasionally tests her by taking a few coins too many, but if she is keeping count, she never lets on.) She smokes American filter cigarettes through a long ivory holder, gripping the holder between her thumb and third finger and barely putting it in her mouth. In the winter she smells of moth balls, in the summer of lilacs. She smells of lilacs now.

"Dear Lev, you permit that book into circulation and they'll make a nonperson out of you."

"They'll have their work cut out for them," the Racer retorts lightly.

"But no," cries Octobrina, stabbing the air furiously with her holder, "you don't understand them, you don't understand them at all. Push them too far and they are capable of anything."

Mister Dancho nods toward the blown-up photograph of the Flag Holder, which shows him with a flag pole thrust high leading a partisan unit into Sofia in 1944. "Be reasonable, Octobrina, they can't touch him and you know it."

"Our pictures," agrees the Racer, "are our protection."

"Not Octobrina's," notes the Flag Holder. "At least not the ones she is painting these days."

"Out on another artistic limb?" chides Mister Dancho, and he shakes his finger at her as if he were scolding a schoolgirl for trespasses against the curriculum. "What are you up to now?"

Octobrina takes a series of quick puffs on her holder and peers mischievously at Mister Dancho, her head cocked to one side so that she presents him with a three-quarter profile; as a young girl of twelve she had been introduced to Mayakovsky, who told her she had a beautiful profile, and so she is forever presenting it to people. "I'm not *up* to anything," she declares in a tone of voice that makes it clear she is up to something. "I've started a new phase in my artistic cycle. I'm experimenting with still lifes."

"You mean apples and oranges and grapes!" Mister Dancho rolls his eyes in mock horror.

"You don't understand, you don't understand at all. I'm working with still lifes of animate objects. My still lifes are life abstracted down to its motionless essence. On my canvases, things exist not with respect to their movement, but only in the contrast between their stillness and their potential for movement. Do you see it? I'm trying to capture the tension generated by the dialectical contradiction between the word 'still' and the word 'life.' "

"I smell political comment," declares Mister Dancho, flaring his nostrils and sniffing the air.

"You smell correctly," observes the Racer.

"You smell politics everywhere," Octobrina protests, but she is secretly pleased. "If man is a political animal — "

"Does anyone doubt it?" the Racer puts in.

" — then for me, his significance lies in the contrast between his potential for political action and his political inactivity."

"She means *our* potential for political action and *our* political inactivity," the Racer sums up.

"They'll never let you exhibit," Mister Dancho tells her flatly. "They'll see through your still lifes in a minute."

Octobrina remains unfazed. "What makes you think I want to exhibit? As a matter of fact, I'm working in white, and a painter who works in white has to reckon on what time will do to the color — tone it down, mellow it, yellow it. I have no intention of showing my whites until they're at least five years old. Perhaps five years from now white still lifes will be just what our constipated cultural counselors are looking for. Who can say what history has in store for us?"

"History," comments the Flag Holder, the Rodopi bobbing on his lower lip, "is a sponge that soaks up events as if they were spilt milk."

"I see you haven't lost your talent for coining phrases that stop conversation," groans Dancho, suddenly downcast. He smiles weakly. "Don't mind me. It's the postpartums. Happens every time I get where I'm going."

Octobrina tugs at his sleeve. "Dear Dancho, you are a moody soul. You are protected by layers of appropriate emotion which you unfold and use and crumple and toss away as if they are disposable paper handkerchiefs."

"Cheer up," the Racer cries. "I'll tell you about Octobrina's escapade at the Artists' Union."

Octobrina gleefully supplies the details. "Some hyena raised the criticism that too much religious hocus-pocus was creeping onto our canvases under the guise of historical themes. I simply pointed out that the first thing that Lenin did upon taking power was to make the sign of the cross. And for good measure, I told them that Georgi Dimitrov died with his mother's crucifix in his hands." She laughs happily. "The uproar would have warmed the cockles of your heart, dear Dancho."

"How do you know such things?" Mister Dancho marvels.

"I don't — I make them up!"

"Wait, there's more," the Racer insists. "The Dwarf got into hot water for asking his circus comrades to adopt a resolution calling on all fraternal Communist parties to respect the independence and integrity of other parties in the Communist family."

"The Dwarf is a lovely person," the Flag Holder says.

"Needless to say," the Racer continues, "his motion was not seconded, much less voted on. As for me, the All-Union Sports' Directorate just circulated another petition against Solzhenitsyn. I was the only member who didn't sign on the dotted line."

"Tell what happened," Octobrina demands, clapping her hands together happily.

Tacho smiles sheepishly. "The Chairman, who is a pompous ass, tried to embarrass me into signing by asking me to explain myself at a public meeting."

"So you explained yourself," laughs Mister Dancho.

"So I explained myself," Tacho admits. "I told them that since Solzhenitsyn's writing is banned in Bulgaria, I have never had the opportunity to read him, and since I have never read him, I couldn't very well condemn him."

"And what did he say to that, your chairman?" Dancho inquires.

"He didn't say anything," the Racer concedes, "but I had the impression he was filing something away in his mind."

"Tell about the circular, Lev — " Octobrina prompts.

There is a chorus of encouragement. "Out with it," orders Dancho.

"It came about this way," says the Flag Holder, drawn almost against his will into the game. He pauses to light a Rodopi from the butt of an old one. The first deep puff makes him cough; he sips mineral water to set it straight. "I received a circular for senior Party people ordering recipients to keep an eye peeled for evidence of mental instability on the part of other senior Party people."

"Don't tell me you — " Dancho's arms open wide.

"I submitted a dossier on each of the members of the Presidium, citing various actions or comments attributed to them and analyzing the mental condition of which this was a symptom."

"You go too far," Octobrina warns.

"My poor efforts pale beside your leaps of imagination," Mister Dancho declares.

"And what poor efforts do you speak of?" the Racer wants to know.

Mister Dancho tugs modestly at his cuffs and tells them how he dipped into the bodice of the television actress "to pull out — "

"American dollars," guesses the Racer.

"Too obvious," cries Octobrina. "Something more devious. Ah, a *samidzat* written on toilet paper — "

"A Swiss bankbook," ventures the Flag Holder.

Mister Dancho cannot contain himself. "*Czech flags sewn end to end!*"

"Oh, dear Dancho, how could you?" sighs Octobrina. "And in front of everyone."

"In London, England," Dancho continues, "someone at an embassy reception noticed that the Soviet Ambassador and I had small pins in our lapels and asked if we belonged to the same organization. The Ambassador showed his. It was a small likeness of Lenin. I showed mine. It was a small portrait of — "

"Stalin," Octobrina tries.

"Mao?" guesses the Racer.

"Me!" explodes Mister Dancho, and he thrusts his lapel forward with his thumb so that everyone can witness his audacity.

Tapping his knife against an empty wine glass, Tacho calls the meeting to order and says formally:

"I propose we award our friend here the golden sickle of achievement."

Octobrina nods happily. The Flag Holder looks on the way an adult watches children at play — trying to keep his distance, but aching to join the fun.

"How do you know he's not exaggerating," scoffs the Rabbit, pushing through the curtain into the room. She goes straight to Mister Dancho and plants matter-of-fact kisses on both his cheeks. "Stuka told me you were back."

She kisses Octobrina and squeezes her hand, and then hugs Popov and the Racer before slipping into the seat next to the Flag Holder, whom she greets by resting her hand lightly on his thigh. He shifts in his chair; physical intimacy is not something he is comfortable with.

"I'm not exaggerating, little Rabbit," Mister Dancho protests, but Elisabeta waves away the comment. "The whole business is

immature, if you ask me," she frowns. "Grown men playing with"
— she looks at the Flag Holder — "fire."

"How can you sit there and say that?" Mister Dancho retorts
belligerently, and Lev tries to smooth things over:

"If we are immature, Elisabeta, more power to us."

"Immaturity," snaps Octobrina, parroting the Flag Holder's
style of speech, "can be seen as the refusal to pocket those portions
of the personality which rub society the wrong way."

"Just so," agrees Lev, annoyed.

"Have it your own way," Elisabeta yields grudgingly, "but I
still say you're playing with fire. This simply isn't the moment . . ." She shrugs and lets it drop.

Octobrina asks Elisabeta if she has eaten.

"Someone fetched sandwiches to the ministry," the Rabbit tells
her.

"What news?" asks the Racer.

Popov turns up his hearing aid. Octobrina leans forward in
her seat. The Flag Holder stops smoking.

Elisabeta speaks quietly. "It doesn't look good. The Boss was
summoned to Moscow this morning — "

"The Minister went with him," Mister Dancho interjects.

"How do you know that?" Elisabeta fires at him in astonishment.
"You only just arrived."

"I heard it," Dancho replies evasively. "What's the difference
where?"

The Racer and the Flag Holder are staring at each other grimly.
"Maybe it's consultations," the Racer suggests, but Elisabeta shakes
her head:

"They are not in the habit of consulting us; they *inform* us. Be-
sides, some of our army people went along too. No, no. Something's definitely up." She fiddles with an earring. "There is a
rumor making the rounds that the Soviet Politburo's already voted
seven to four to use force, with Kosygin, Suslov, Podgorny and
Voronov on the dove side."

Elisabeta plucks an orange from the bowl in the middle of the
table and begins peeling it. Her long, thin fingers work quickly,
stripping back petals of skin, then tucking the ends under so that
the final product looks like the bud of a large orange flower. She
raises her eyes and silently offers the open orange to Mendeleyev

— the offer is intended, and taken, as an expression of intimacy — but he shakes his head imperceptibly, and so she attacks it herself.

After a while the Racer asks:

"Is there more?"

The Rabbit nods as she swallows a section of orange. "We put together a sheet of excerpts from Pravda for internal circulation. Believe it or not, they're comparing the situation to Hungary in fifty-six."

"They're priming the pump," concludes Octobrina. "I warned you not to get your hopes up."

"It's all a bluff," asserts Mister Dancho. "Don't you see that? In the end, Czechoslovakia isn't that important to them."

"It's important to us," observes Octobrina, "and that makes it important to them."

"The wind will carry such ideas like seeds," declares Popov, who is having difficulty following the conversation.

"It's important," the Flag Holder insists. The cigarette bobbing on his lower lip is burning dangerously near the skin, but he doesn't appear to notice it. "What's happening now has nothing to do with Hungary. That was a crisis of Stalinism. This is a crisis of Leninism — the first in the history of the Movement. In the end, Dubček and his Czech comrades are challenging three things that Lenin superimposed on classical Marxism: democratic centralism, the monopoly of power of the Communist Party and the ideological dogmatism with which that power is exercised."

Lev suddenly becomes aware of the cigarette and plucks it from his mouth. "If the Czechs succeed, they will have redefined Communism — they will have created something called Socialist Humanism." He hesitates, then continues almost in a whisper. "I share Octobrina's fears about hope. After all these years — "

"Why torture ourselves?" Octobrina cries.

"Why torture ourselves?" the Flag Holder repeats. "And yet . . . and yet . . ."

There is a long silence.

"There's another side to consider," Octobrina says finally. "Changes like the ones Dubček is proposing tend to be open-ended. What if our Russian friends are right? What if Dubček doesn't stop at some vague finish line called Socialist Humanism? What if he reforms himself right out of the bloc?"

" 'The worst workers' party,' " Popov quotes, " 'is better than none.' "

"Marx?" guesses Octobrina.

"Engels?" guesses the Racer.

"Not at all," snaps Mister Dancho. "It's Lenin."

Popov shakes his head and supplies the source. "Rosa Luxemburg," he says, delighted to have stumped them. "Sssssssss."

"What if it does lead to a restoration of capitalism?" Octobrina insists. "What if?"

"No adventure is without risks," the Flag Holder tells her.

"Risks are what the Russians won't take," Octobrina bursts out. "Why are you all so blind? They'll crush the Czechs under their heels."

"It's not that simple," the Flag Holder observes. "If they use force, they'll alienate every Communist in the world. Think how the French or the Italian Communists would respond to an invasion of Czechoslovakia. The Russians will be totally isolated."

"The Russians won't dare to use force," Mister Dancho assures Octobrina, "for fear the Czechs will fight."

Octobrina throws up her hands in frustration. "Oh, they'll fight all right — to the last drop of ink!"

"The Czechs don't have to fight," the Racer points out. "They only have to convince the Russians they *intend* to fight. Tito did that in forty-eight and it kept the Russians out."

"Tito convinced the Russians because he *was* ready to fight," Octobrina reminds him.

"But surely the Americans will intervene, or threaten to intervene, which will amount to the same thing," the Racer suggests. "The Americans have democratic traditions — "

"No, no, never," Octobrina retorts.

"Octobrina is right about the Americans," the Flag Holder confesses. "We must understand that, in some respects, Czechoslovakia is more of a threat to America than Russia ever was. Up to now, the world has had to choose between Stalinism and Capitalism, and the Americans have had no real competition. But imagine if the world had a third choice — Marxist Humanism! No, no, the Americans are dead set against Dubček."

"Everybody says that Capitalism and Communism are moving toward each other," the Racer observes. "In a sense, this confirms it."

"With our luck," Dancho says, "they'll pass each other and keep going, leaving us with two extremes."

Octobrina sighs and follows her own trend of thoughts:

"Nothing moves us greatly, that's the heart of the problem. We pay textbook attention to our lives. We treat our bowel-moving and our lovemaking as if they were punctuation. We embrace our children with parentheses. We package whatever bits and pieces of self-knowledge we come by, as I'm doing now, in corrugated metaphors."

"We hover like falcons," the Flag Holder says quietly, staring into the stillness of his untouched cognac, "motionless on political currents, facing into the stream but not progressing against it; making slight adjustments in the angle of a wing; above all comfortable; above all apathetic." He looks up. "Every now and then we narrow our beady eyes and swoop down, spittle streaking from our beaks, for a juicy intellectual kill."

"What an image," Octobrina cries excitedly. "That would make an absolutely wonderful still life."

"Well, I think it's not quite fair," Mister Dancho starts to say, but Popov, in a world of his own, interrupts:

"We cleanse our souls the way we clean our windows," he recites, articulating each word as if he is composing, "with the curtains already hanging on them." His voice peters out and he looks around and smiles foolishly.

"Who said that?" Octobrina inquires.

"I wasn't quoting anybody. I said that."

"Oh, Atanas, it was very lovely," Octobrina tells him.

"We cleanse our souls," Popov begins again. "Sssssssss." He can't remember the rest.

"That's all right," Octobrina covers his hand with hers. "I remember that it was very lovely."

Later, while Stuka bends over the sideboard moistening his pencil point on the tip of his tongue and adding up the bill, Mister Dancho comes back to Dubček:

"If he is as important as we think, Lev, then he must do everything to survive. No holds barred."

The Flag Holder considers that for a moment. "Perhaps" is all he says.

Dancho is ready to let it drop, but the Racer presses Mendeleyev.

"You say do everything to survive," the Flag Holder says. "It

seems to me that even Dubček — that especially Dubček — must draw
the line somewhere. You must fight the demons without becoming
the demons you fight. This is central to the struggles taking place
in the world today. When you adopt the enemy's tactics, or his
weapons, or even his double-speak, even if you win, you lose —
because you are the enemy. This was the error Lenin made." A
thought occurs to Mendeleyev. "Malraux once asked Nehru: 'What
has been your most difficult task?' And Nehru replied: 'To make
a just state with just means.'"

"You're saying the ends don't justify the means," the Racer interjects, following the conversation intently.

"I'm saying that ends and means are the same thing."

Stuka folds the check on a plate and places it on the table. Each
member of the Circle calculates his share and puts the money on the
plate; Dancho, gallant as always, insists on paying for Octobrina.
The four dinners and wine and tea and the Flag Holder's cognac
come to fifteen leva. With one leva for Stuka, the total is sixteen.

"My very dear ladies and gentlemen," Octobrina announces, "we
can't change the world, but if we hurry we can still catch the last
trolley." It is ten to two, and the trolleys stop running at two.

"I think I'll meander over to Club Balkan," Mister Dancho says
casually. "How about it, Tacho?"

On weekends the Hotel Balkan keeps an upstairs bar open until
four, when the trolleys start running again. It is always full of
foreign tourists and well-heeled Bulgarians. The prices are steep,
but the liquor is imported.

"Why not?" Tacho agrees amicably.

The main dining room is empty except for two waiters clearing
the last tables; they are required to set them for lunch before they
are allowed to go home for the night. In the lobby, another waiter
is talking into the wall telephone.

"Hold on a second," he shouts. Letting the telephone dangle,
he blows his nose into an enormous handkerchief and inspects the
results. Then he picks up the telephone. "Yellowish green.
Yes. Yes. All right." He hangs up and complains to nobody in
particular, "My God, it's really dreadful to have an intelligent
wife."

On the far end of the lobby, on a long wall directly opposite the
coatracks, hangs a floor-to-ceiling mirror in which you can see the

rest of the lobby — the coatracks, the wall telephone, the door marked "Sitters" and another marked "Pointers," and the heavy double door leading to the street. It is only when you stand directly in front of the mirror and *don't see yourself in it* that you realize it is a painting of a mirror.

It is a joke of long standing to line up before "the ultimate in Socialist realism," as Octobrina likes to call it, on the way out of Krimm. Without a word they line up now. Mister Dancho tugs on his cuffs. Octobrina peers at her three-quarter profile and adjusts her shawl. Popov centers the knot of his tie. Elisabeta puts on a new layer of lipstick, then blots her lips on a piece of toilet paper. The Racer unbuttons the top button of his shirt and rearranges his shirt collar so that it overlaps the collar of his sport jacket.

Only the Flag Holder doesn't play the game. Instead, he stares into the mirror as if he has noticed, for the first time, the fact of his nonexistence.

2

MISTER DANCHO wants to use the back entrance to Hotel Balkan, which means going out of their way, but the Racer says nobody will bother them at this ungodly hour, so they make straight for the great revolving door with its corroded brass handles and gold-lettered "BALKAN" in English on the glass. The lettering reads " ALKA " on the panel the Racer pushes with his palms and "BAL AN" on Mister Dancho's.

The teen-age girls pounce as they step into the lobby.

"Look, Mister Dancho," they squeal, clustering around him like iron filings on a magnet.

"Oh, do us a trick," cries one, smacking away with open lips on a piece of gum.

"The thing you did on television — the thing where you cut the rope and make it whole again."

"Do the bit where you — "

"No tricks, no tricks," Dancho calls good-naturedly, pushing through the group after the Racer, who has started up the stairs toward Club Balkan.

A tall girl, bolder than the others, tugs at Dancho's blazer. "An autograph then," she demands, tilting her head coquettishly and batting false eyelashes, one of which is peeling away at the edge.

Dancho turns back. "Open your shirt," he instructs her. The girls giggle — until they see her reach for the first button.

"Oh, Maya, don't."

"Come away, Maya."

Maya unbuttons her shirt down to her waist, exposing full breasts sagging into a washed-out brassiere. Dancho uncaps a felt-tipped pen, grips her shoulder to hold her steady and scrawls "Dancho" on the swell of breast that spills over the brassiere.

The girls stare after Dancho as he walks away. From the first landing, he glances back. The tall girl is buttoning her shirt as her friends pull her toward the revolving door. "Bitch," Dancho hears one of them hiss at her. "How could you?"

Dancho catches up with the Racer inside the threshold of Club Balkan.

"You missed the fun," he tells him, but the Racer makes no answer, and the two of them stand there for a moment to get their night vision. Gradually Club Balkan emerges from the darkness — a long, narrow room, dimly lit, with a bar down one side and small round Formica tables down the other. There is no decor, just four windowless walls. The bar is packed, three and four deep in places, with Japanese members of an export exhibition currently being held in one of the hotel's banquet halls. The tables are taken up by foreign tourists and a sprinkling of Bulgarians.

Mister Dancho strains for a glimpse of Katya at the tables nearest the door. Not finding her, he starts down the room between the bar and the tables. The Racer follows. Elbows jostle them where the crowd at the bar is the thickest. Snatches of conversation drift out of the darkness.

"Couldn't sleep — someone was building Communism with goddamn jackhammers across the street — "

"Life shouldn't be an open book — it should be a poem. Open or closed, it should be a poem."

"They have them at ZUM, right next to the grocery counter with the imported mushrooms. West German. Smooth, aren't they? Here, feel — "

"Workers are shits — they can be bought off for an extra wet dream a week. Look at what happened in Paris — "

"The worst is having to listen to things you can't stand from someone with bad breath. Did you — "

" — shortcoming of governments is that they balance conflicting interests instead of determining where the rights of the matter lay."

In the twilight the Racer bumps into a journalist he knows. "*Dobăr večer*, Marko — what do you hear?"

Marko flings an arm over the Racer's shoulder and draws him aside. "My editor just decided he'd better spend his budget before the end of the year if he wanted to get more money next year, right? So he gathered us together today and asked who spoke English. The lady who raised her hand gets to go to London, England, for a

month! Who speaks French? A horse's ass is off to Paris, France!
Who speaks Spanish? Ha! I speak Spanish! I'm off to Madrid,
Spain, next week! Say" — Marko hesitates — "how's that race of
yours shaping up? I'm toying with the idea of maybe putting
some money on your boys. What do you think?"

Tacho considers the matter. "What I think is: the man who bets
on a bicycle race will never profit from his mistake."

"Funny," Marko says dryly. "Very funny."

Further on a man and a woman scrape back their chairs and start
for the door. The third man at the table looks up from his cognac.
"*Salut*," he calls, waving Mister Dancho and Tacho toward the free
places.

"*Salut, salut. Kak ste?*" Dancho says vaguely. Suddenly he recognizes the man: he is the film director known as "Poleon" after
Napoleon because of his dictatorial manner on the set. "Ah, you,
Poleon, I couldn't make you out in this cave." Dancho slides into
a seat. "Found an apartment yet?"

Poleon has divorced his wife but is still living with her because
neither one of them has been able to find an apartment. "Still
looking," he mutters sourly. "Only thing worse than living with a
wife, take it from someone who knows, is living with an ex-wife. If
you get wind of something, please god let me know. I'm going out
of my mind. It's been eight months now. I'd sell my grandmother
for an apartment."

Dancho laughs appreciatively and summons the waiter with a
wave of his hand. "Three cognacs. And none of your Pliska
three-star dry rot. It corrodes the stomach lining. Imported, you
understand?"

"How long have you been back?" Poleon asks conversationally.
He is a heavy man gone to seed, and what hair he has left falls in
long, pasted-down strands across his freckled scalp.

"Just got in," Mister Dancho replies, his eyes scanning the room
for a sign of Katya. "I played in London, England." Mustering
what enthusiasm he can, he proceeds to tell Poleon about the
embassy reception and the lapel buttons.

The waiter sets three cognacs on the table, and places a cash
register receipt face up on a small dish.

"What are you up to these days?" the Racer asks. Poleon has
had a huge success with a film entitled *I.D.* The picture won some

sort of award at the Berlin Film Festival, and actually ran for ten days in a New York art theater after the *New York Times* called the Bulgarian director "half poet, half magician." Since then Poleon has done two other films, but neither one has been released by the censors.

Poleon takes another sip of cognac and laughs dryly. "I'm in the most delicate stage of film making, which is to say I'm negotiating with your friend and mine, the censor. He has certain ideas about which camera angles or shreds of dialogue or gestures contribute to the building of Socialism. I on the other hand have certain ideas about which camera angles or shreds of dialogue or gestures contribute to the creation of an artistic entity commonly referred to as a motion picture. We project the rough cut again and again, we sip mineral water because his section chief is too cheap to authorize vodka, and we bargain. Oh how we bargain. I agree to cut a close-up of the hero's eyes and he in return agrees to leave in a particular inflection that gives to the dialogue a shade of meaning not apparent when it was passed by the scenario censor eight months ago. We've been at it every morning for three weeks now."

"What do you save the afternoons for?" Mister Dancho asks jokingly, but Poleon takes the question seriously.

"My afternoons are taken up with a different censor. We go over, scene by scene, paragraph by paragraph, line by line, word by word, syllable by syllable, the scenario for my next film. He has certain ideas about what will contribute to the building of Socialism. Et cetera. Et cetera. I once calculated I spend three fifths of my professional time with the censors and two fifths actually working at my metier." Poleon glances at his watch. "Another good hour till the trolleys start — might as well." And he signals the waiter for a refill. "Jesus, I hope to god it doesn't rain tomorrow."

Tacho laughs. "You say that as if the weather makes a difference."

"But it does, it does," Poleon insists. "You don't believe me? I can see you don't believe me. Listen. My morning censor has rheumatism. The wet weather makes him irritable. When he's irritable, he makes fewer concessions. My afternoon censor has a mistress, and the mistress has two small children who stay in and watch television when it rains. The censor can only go over there when the sun shines and the children are out playing. So when it rains, he never concedes a point. He just sits there shaking his pointed head and obliterating the offending words or sentences with thick black ink."

"The things that go into a film," Mister Dancho marvels, glancing over his shoulder toward the door. Tacho remarks:

"You should do a film on how you make a film."

"Tried that," Poleon snaps. The waiter sets a brimming cognac in front of him and he brings his head down to the glass and sips it so that it won't spill. "The project was killed at birth by the evening censor — the one who is oblivious to the exigencies of time and weather, the one" — Poleon smiles sweetly — "who deals with ideas."

Tacho snickers sympathetically. "Your new film, the one the morning censor is working on, what's it about?"

"It's a portrait of a fictional capitalist country where everyone, in one way or another, works for the police. The characters have no names, only numbers. The hero, whom I call 'Eight-eighty,' is the chief of the directorate that provides an appropriate amount of crime in order to justify the existence of the police. I call the film *Police State*."

"But that doesn't sound like something you should have problems with," Tacho observes.

Poleon snorts. "So I thought, but my morning nemesis flares his nostrils and sniffs the air and says he smells ambiguities which might place my fictional police state closer to home. I argue, with as straight a face as you'll find in the movie industry, that one has only to look around one to realize that this is absurd, but my friend the censor persists, lifting words as if they were rocks and poking around underneath for worms of treason."

Poleon laughs hoarsely and takes another sip of cognac. "Sometimes I almost feel sorry for the poor sons of bitches," he says seriously. "With what's happening these days, they don't know which way to jump."

The Racer remembers the conversation at Krimm and asks Poleon what he thinks about Czechoslovakia.

Poleon lowers his voice. "I don't have anything against the Schweiks, but I'll be goddamned if I know what they expect to gain from all this. They're just building up people's hopes with all that talk of real elections and a free press. The Russians will never put up with it, mark my words. I heard Novotny's already in Moscow organizing his comeback. Meanwhile the rest of us have to suffer." Poleon leans forward. "They're holding everything up until this thing sorts itself out. I got that straight from a make-up man who has a brother who works for the Central Committee." Tacho starts to say something, but Poleon cuts him off. "A friend of mine was supposed to have his novel in the stores this week — it was cleared two, maybe three months ago — but they've stopped distribution. When he asked why, they told him there was a shortage of cartons for shipping." Poleon leans back. "Cartons my ass. They're just afraid to put themselves on the line as long as this thing with Czechoslovakia is up in the air. I heard another story — "

Someone two tables down starts to scream. It isn't a very loud scream, but it is a scream all the same and it brings conversation to a stop. Everyone turns to see — except the Japanese, who are too discreet. A second person at the table opens her mouth to scream, but clamps it shut again without a sound.

"Try," a man coaxes.

"I can't do it," the woman groans. "I just can't do it."

"What's going on?" Mister Dancho whispers.

"Don't you know about the Scream Therapist? No, of course, you were out of the country — "

"Scream what?" Tacho demands.

"Scream Therapist." Poleon swivels around so he can get a better look at the table. "See the bald guy, the one sitting between the two women. Name's Hristo Evanov. He's Bulgarian by birth. His father was a factory owner who fled just ahead of the Russians in forty-four. Took Hristo with him to America. He's a psychiatrist now, but a special kind of psychiatrist — he practices something he calls scream therapy. He came here last week to bury his mother. Since then he's been going around trying to get everyone to scream."

"Now I've heard everything," Mister Dancho scoffs.

"No, it's really very interesting. The odd part is he hasn't been able to elicit one good ear-splitting, glass-shattering scream in all of Bulgaria. Or so he says. You've got to meet him — it'll make your night. Here" — Poleon starts to get up — "I'll ask him to join — "

The girl materializes out of thin air. One second there is nobody there, the next she is standing before the table looking from Poleon to Dancho to Tacho, and the waiter is stammering:

"Excuse the intrusion, please, but this lady asked me to point you out — eh, she insists on meeting you. I'm sorry if — "

It all happens so suddenly that Poleon, who has had quite a bit to drink, thinks she is an apparition. Sinking back into his seat, he tries to blink her away.

She won't go.

Dancho is the first to pull himself together. "Dear lady, by all means," he beams, adjusting his cuffs as he hefts himself out of his seat.

"Eh, excuse me again, please, but she doesn't want to meet *you*," the waiter interrupts apologetically. "She wants to meet *you*." He looks at the Racer.

"Me!" exclaims Tacho. He looks at Mister Dancho, plainly embarrassed and at a loss for words.

The girl takes a step toward Tacho. She is wearing embroidered Kazan felt boots, a khaki miniskirt, a thin white T-shirt through which no bra straps are visible and a bright yellow scarf tied around her neck cowboy style. She is almost as tall as the Racer, and thin, with the bone structure of a small bird. Her hair is cropped short, and dark. She is flat-chested and round-shouldered and straight-hipped and nervous, though the nervousness isn't so much in her body as in her eyes — ghetto eyes, permanently wide, ready for flight. She stares at the Racer without changing her expression, as if her facial muscles or her emotions are paralyzed, as if her appetite is dulled, as if her anger or her fear or her sexuality has lost its edge. Later, the Racer will tell her that she gave him the impression, the first time he saw her, that whatever she wanted, she could wait to get it.

Mister Dancho pokes the Racer in the ribs. "Tacho, dear boy, where have you been hiding this flower?"

"I never saw her before in my life," Tacho swears, reddening.

"Look at those eyes, will you," Dancho plunges on. "They're *enormous*. What do you take her for, Poleon? German? Swiss? Dutch perhaps?"

"I'm neither German nor Swiss nor Dutch," the girl says in flawless Russian.

Dancho's jaw sags. "My god, you don't look Russian!" he blurts out, lapsing into Russian himself.

"You don't look Bulgarian," the girl fires back.

Poleon laughs and Dancho, regaining his composure, bows from the waist. "I take that as the ultimate compliment, dear lady. You hear that, Poleon, she says I don't look Bulgarian."

Dancho offers the girl his seat and she slips into it. The waiter brings another for Dancho. The girl looks at the waiter. "Please — I think I'd like a cognac now."

Dancho covers her hand with his. "Dear lady, if you are really Russian, then our opinions on womanhood in that vast motherland of importunity, that Mecca of antireligious fervor, will have to undergo revision."

The girl slides her hand out from under his. "I am American," she informs him quietly.

For a moment nobody says anything. "American!" Dancho looks around, stunned. "Dear lady, say it isn't so?" He turns on Poleon. "She says she's *American!*"

"I have ears," snaps Poleon. Through all their minds races the same thought: things being what they are, this is not exactly the time to be seen with an American.

The girl fixes her eyes on the Racer as if she knows him, as if they have a past. "You are Abadzhiev," she observes. "You look like your photograph — the one with your hand reaching into the sky." And she half demonstrates.

"What is it you want of me?" Tacho asks.

The girl thinks about that for a moment. "I'm not sure," she says finally. Then, as if it will explain a great deal, she tells him: "My family name is Krasov."

"Krasov," Tacho repeats. It is vaguely familiar — no, he knows the name, but from where?

"The Krasov who . . ."

The girl looks at him without changing her expression.

Tacho nods slowly. "Now I . . . I'm sorry."

The waiter brings the girl's cognac. He leans close to the Racer's ear. "Please believe I had no intention — "

Tacho shakes off the apology. "It's all right," he says. He pushes the cognac toward the girl and motions with his head for her to drink. She hesitates, then lifts the glass to her lips and sips the liquid as if it is medicine. All the while her eyes are fixed on his.

There is another half scream from the next table, but nobody turns toward it this time.

"Who is Krasov?" demands Dancho.

"I'll explain later." Tacho says this in a way that leaves Dancho no room to repeat the question. To the girl, Tacho says:

"What is your given name?"

"Melanie."

The Racer tries to pronounce it, and she has to say it several times before he can produce a reasonable facsimile.

"And your patronymic?"

"Americans don't have patronymics," she informs him. "I have what is called a middle name — Daisie."

Tacho tries it out, then Dancho. "It's very melodious," concedes Mister Dancho, who comes closest to getting it right. "Melanie Daisie," and he rocks his head back and forth on his shoulders in appreciation.

Tacho catches the girl looking at him. Flustered, he asks:

"What are you? I mean, how do you describe yourself when someone asks you to describe yourself?"

"I say I'm a practicing Capricorn," the girl replies. Both Mister Dancho and Poleon explode in laughter, and she smiles for the first time — a slow smile that begins uncertainly in her cheek muscles, takes hold and spreads to her lips and to her eyes. It lingers deep in her eyes, obscuring the fright.

Tacho starts to ask her something when he becomes aware of a shifting of weight, a moving of feet, a cutting off of conversation. There is no commotion, just a self-conscious silence that spreads from person to person — and then the scraping of a dog's claws on linoleum. In the girl's eyes, fright gets the upper hand.

"The Dwarf," someone whispers, and Mister Dancho observes with careful nonchalance:

"Angel must be here."

The Hungarians come first, three pubescent girls with milk white baby's skin and crimson lips and buds of breasts visible through their filmy dresses. All three are barefoot, and the one in the middle wears a garland of poppies woven into her hair, which falls in knotted ringlets over her bony shoulders. They walk with gawkily graceful children's steps, holding hands and whispering to each other in Hungarian.

The runt of a dog comes behind them, its short legs claw-dancing across the floor like a crab's, its wrinkled rat's head straining against the leash. "Down," a voice commands, but the dog stands its ground, panting. Saliva spills from its jowls. Its unblinking fog-filled eyes stare straight ahead, seeing nothing.

The dog is stone blind.

"Down, Dog," the voice commands again. A dwarf-leg shoots out and pushes its rear feet out from under it, and the dog sinks onto the floor. The girl with the poppies in her hair drops to her knees beside the dog and, wrapping her thin arms around its neck, buries her head in the folds of skin above the collar.

The Dwarf looks down at the girl and mutters something in Hungarian. The girl looks up. He repeats the phrase. Lowering her eyes, she climbs to her feet and takes her place alongside him, slouching so as not to appear taller than he is, her arm hooked lightly through his.

Smiling at some private joke, the Dwarf glances around. The people at the nearby tables turn away under his gaze and quietly resume their conversations.

Angel Bazdéev is the most famous dwarf in the world. He is retired now, and incredibly rich by Bulgarian standards — he wears a diamond ring on his pinkie and drives around in a taxi that he hires by the year and pays for according to what is on the meter. But every Bulgarian over five, along with hundreds of thousands of Europeans, remembers him in his heyday — Bazdéev the king of clowns, with his painted angel's face and his mocking smile and his exploding fedora and his baggy trousers out of which the dog called Dog leaped on signal to snap at the toes of his oversized shoes. At one time or another, Bazdéev has played in all the great circuses on the Continent. When television came into its own in the early 1950s, he became an international star, commanding huge fees for twelve minutes of antics. In France his forty-eight-inch figure with its bulging chest and slightly out of proportion head, his broad wrinkled brow, his jet black hair, became a comic-strip character and Bazdéev still gets royalties twice a year from this. The only sour note in his career came in 1956, when he applied for a visa to perform with Barnum and Bailey in America. There was some confusion when it was discovered he had been born and raised in Hungary, but was a citizen of Bulgaria; apparently the State Department handbook made no mention of this particular type of hybrid. This had barely been ironed out (by a command decision on the "highest level") when a well-known Washington columnist accused Bazdĕev of being a card-carrying Communist (true: he fought in the Flag Holder's partisan unit during the war) who was "playing the clown to further the international Communist conspiracy," as the columnist put it.

The columnist also raised the specter of moral turpitude by revealing that Bazdĕev had once been beaten up for molesting a child in Warsaw. This was an exaggeration. What had actually happened was that a small girl broke away from her mother during a performance and wrapped her legs around Bazdĕev's as if she were a mating dog. The clown lost control of himself and had to be pried off her by a Rumanian lion tamer and two Jugoslav jugglers. Some peasants started into the ring to teach Bazdĕev common decency, but the other clowns laughed as if the whole thing had been part of the act, and the show, or what was left of it, went on. Needless to say, the columnist's rehashing of the incident resulted in the denial of his visa application — and the denial of the visa resulted in the breaking of every window in the American legation in Sofia.

Bazdĕev, who neither forgot nor forgave, was not without friends.

At home Bazdĕev had his detractors too. A woman professor accused him in print of really hating children because they were considered normal while he, although the same size, was not. (Bazdĕev bought and burned the entire press run as soon as he got wind of the letter.) And another clown, in a fit of professional jealousy, stood up at a meeting of circus Communists and asked Bazdĕev to his face whether it was true he surrounded himself with Hungarian nymphets upon whom he performed unspeakable acts in public as well as in private. There was an embarrassed silence. Bazdĕev waddled up to the stage, climbed up on a stool so he could reach the microphone and said with great dignity that the accusation was an out and out lie — he never touched them in public!

By that time Bazdĕev's sexual appetites were already a matter of legend. And except for a crank or two, the general tendency was to see in him what the Flag Holder saw in him: a nobility of spirit that was in constant state of rebellion against the role the world wanted him to play — that of a freak.

The Dwarf comes right to the point. Now, as always, there is no shaking of hands; Angel doesn't like to be touched except by his

Hungarians. "I heard the Witch of Melnik said twenty August is the end and the beginning — of what, she was not sure," the Dwarf rasps, his voice pitched high. "I organize to celebrate this end, this beginning with a wedding, and I invite all you to it." His eyes flit over the American girl — over her knees and thighs — and come to rest on the girl with the garlands in her hair. "I have intention to make honest child out of this petal of Hungarian flowerhood." Bazdéev smiles his mocking smile.

Bazdéev's "marriages" are spur-of-the-moment bacchanals that he organizes when the spirit moves him: sometimes to coincide with one of the solstices, sometimes with a national holiday, sometimes with a political event he wishes to mark and mock. Among the' cognoscenti, invitations are as valuable as exit visas.

"When is the wedding?" Mister Dancho inquires, rubbing his hands together happily.

"Tomorrow night . . . sundown . . . Paradise Lost." Paradise Lost is the name Popov has given to Bazdéev's mansion on Vitoša, the mountain that slopes up like the sides of an amphitheater south of Sofia.

The Dwarf produces a cigar and sticks it between his lips. Mister Dancho extends his empty hand and offers him a light. The Hungarian girls squeal in delight. As Angel puffs the cigar into life, clouds of blue smoke obscure his head. Poleon says:

"Some day I mean to get you roaring drunk and find out what you're trying to prove with these weddings of yours."

Angel, whose face comes up to Poleon's even though one is standing and the other is sitting, waves his hand to disperse the smoke. "But I can be telling you now. You have noticed, no, how in dreams, bizarre things are taken as normal everyday occurrences? It is my contention to demonstrate the same holds true for events who are taking place during waking hours!" Again the mocking smile.

"Do you remember your dreams?" Mister Dancho asks.

"Bits, pieces, like Popov's images, but I never being able to reconstruct the whole." Angel is suddenly afraid he has given away too much. "Why is it are you asking?"

"I was curious, that's all."

"Will you take a drink with us?" the Racer asks to smooth things over.

Angel's eyes darken and he ignores the invitation. "My taxi waiting. Can I drop any of you?"

Poleon immediately accepts and starts counting out some bills to cover his share of the check.

The Dwarf nods to the Hungarians and they lace their fingers together and skip toward the door.

"Dog," Angel orders, pulling the leash taut, "on feet — your seeing-eye Dwarf being ready."

Without a word of goodbye he starts after the Hungarians, with the blind dog Dog clawing the floor at his side.

Poleon hastily shakes hands all around and follows the trail of silence toward the door.

The American girl, who has gotten the gist of the conversation (Bulgarian and Russian being similar), is bursting with questions. "I've never seen anything like him — he's fantastic. Who is the Witch of — "

"Melnik," Tacho supplies.

"Witch of Melnik — who is that?"

"She is a famous seer," Tacho tells her. "She is old and blind and lives in a small peasant cottage outside of Melnik, near the Greek border. If you pass that way you can visit her. You smile at things you know nothing about. Some of our academicians have written books about her. The peasants come from as far away as Blagoevgrad to see her; the Greeks even try to slip across the frontier. The ones who get there line up outside her cottage before sunup, holding a piece of sugar in each palm. As the first cock crows, the Witch emerges and calls out to the people by name; people, remember, she cannot see, so she has no way of knowing who is there. She tells them whom they will marry and when to plant and what to plant and whether their children will be born with birth defects. Sometimes she says mysterious things — they're like puzzles and you have to figure them out."

"Have you seen her?"

The Racer stares at the back of his hand thoughtfully. "I was raised in Melnik, which is a half-hour's hike from the Witch's cottage. On my twelfth birthday my mother led me by the hand up the path that runs past her cottage and we waited with the peasants. I held the sugar tightly in each fist. The Witch was young then, but she looked old; the peasants say she was born old. She called out,

'The boy from Melnik, Tacho.' My mother pushed me forward until I stood right in front of the door. I was very frightened, but I looked up, looked into her eyes. They were like Angel's dog — filmy eyes, without pupils, filled with smoke. She took my sugars and smelled one and then the other and said: 'You will be a boy of motion but a man of movement.' "

"But what does it mean?" Melanie wants to know.

"I'm still trying to figure it out. I think she wanted me to know that there was a difference between the two." And the Racer adds: "She is a very great lady."

"I'd like to meet her — after all, I am a practicing Capricorn!"

Mister Dancho looks at his watch again and then glances with annoyance toward the door. Katya at last! She is standing in the entrance way, squinting into the darkness. Mister Dancho springs up.

"Pay for me and I'll settle with you later, Tacho. Dear lady, I shall count myself the poorer if our paths don't cross again," he adds in Russian to the girl. And pulling at his cuffs, he disappears.

"Where's the fire?" Melanie wonders, looking after Mister Dancho. She turns back to the Racer. "Is the Dwarf really going to marry that girl? She's only a child."

Tacho explains about the Dwarf's weddings. "Last year he had three."

"I feel sorry for the girls. Are they really Hungarian?"

Tacho nods. "They don't speak a word of Bulgarian."

"But how can they live in a country when they don't speak the language?"

"You can only live in a country when you don't speak the language," the Racer says matter-of-factly.

"That sounds like something your Witch of — "

"Melnik."

" — Melnik might say. Here" — she playfully thrusts a cube of sugar into his hand — "I'll be the Witch. I'll tell you something mysterious." She raises her chin and closes her eyes and says slowly:

"You have a . . ."

Suddenly her eyes open wide; the game is over. "You have a dark interior."

"What does that mean, dark interior?"

"Dark, as in the absence of light. You remind me of those apartments where they close the shutters during the day to keep out the
sunlight."

The Racer remembers the farmers crowding into the Melnik
market at harvest time. "The peasants say there are two kinds of
people: those who push downward into the earth, like radishes or
carrots, and those who push up, like cornstalks or sunflowers. In
Melnik, the old ones still talk about the dark and the light as they
finger seeds or a newborn baby."

"You're not angry?"

"I'm not angry."

Club Balkan is beginning to empty out; there is a steady trickle of
people toward the door. Tacho tries to catch the waiter's eye to
pay the check, but the girl says:

"When I was little, my father took me to a bike club to see a film
clip of you setting the world record." The memory releases a flood
of reminiscenses which moisten her eyes, but she shakes her head
and blinks back the tears. "You looked like a knight in armor to
me. When you threw your arm into the sky, my heart stopped. I
think I must have fallen in love with you then." She finishes what
is left of her cognac and stares into the empty glass. "Later, when
my father . . . I hated you after that."

"Is that why you came here — because you hated me?"

"I told you before, I don't know why I came here. I mean, I do
know why." She takes a deep breath and begins at the beginning.
"I work as a dance therapist in a small town in New Jersey." She
sees that New Jersey makes no sense to him. "A small town near
New York. Anyhow, about a year ago, my uncle died and left me
five thousand dollars. I wanted to do something with the money
that would be — well, something I'd remember all my life. So I
flew to Paris, bought a Deux Chevaux and started driving. I've
always wanted to see where my father was born, so I headed for
Moscow by way of Germany and Poland. I stayed there a week,
then I went south to the Black Sea. From there I went to Persia.
I stayed in Persia for a while, then I started back through Turkey.
I hated Turkey; I never imagined such poverty existed. I spent a
week in Istanbul. Then I went up to the Black Sea at Varna — "

"Varna is a tourist trap. The best part of the coast is further
south — "

"I spent three days in Tŭrnovo — "

"Popov was born in Tŭrnovo. You don't know him. It's a great town, isn't it? It was our capital during the Second Bulgarian Kingdom, when we ruled everything between the Adriatic and the Caspian."

"And here I am in Sofia."

"How long have you been traveling, all together?"

"I left New York in, let's see, in September." She counts on her fingers. "That's eleven months ago. Eleven months."

"Any Bulgarian would give his right arm to make a trip like that. But we don't have the possibility. What does it feel like, to make a trip such as the one you are making?"

She looks at him, then lowers her eyes and speaks into her glass. Her voice, full of shades, is pitched low and tense with contained fright. "I feel like a fly scurrying across a movie screen, trying desperately to make out the figures and the booming dialogue. But it is all patterns of shifting gray and black and white, no matter which direction I run."

Melanie doesn't say anything for a moment. Then she looks up. "I felt that way before my trip too."

Only a handful of people remain in Club Balkan now, and the barman switches on the overhead lights and begins collecting ashtrays and glasses from the tables. The sudden light makes the Racer feel exposed and vulnerable. He turns to a man at the next table who is counting out small change and asks him the time. When the man looks back blankly, Tacho taps his bare wrist where a watch would be if he wore one. The man, drowsy with drink, smiles a silly smile and says in English:

"Sorry, fella, but I'm not from around here."

Melanie translates his answer into Russian and the Racer shrugs. The barman calls over the time and Tacho peels off some bills and piles them on top of the cash register stubs.

"Where are you staying?" the Racer asks.

She names a hotel where foreign tourists are usually put up.

"I'll walk you over and catch a trolley in Place Lenin."

They walk side by side down the stairs, past a gallery of blown-up photographs, including one of the Racer with his hand thrust into the sky. In the lobby the night clerk looks up from his magazine to admire the bare legs of the girl. His once-over makes her ner-

vous and she runs her fingers through her hair, which is parted in
the middle, with wisps escaping from the sideburns. Quickening
her pace, she follows the Racer through the great revolving door
into the street.

The night is cool and quiet, and the two of them stand there for a
moment savoring it. The street is deserted except for a drunk weav-
ing away from Club Balkan. They turn in the opposite direction
and start up Don Dukov, then cut across Benkovski to Ruski Boulevard. A few blocks ahead they can make out the giant red star atop
the Central Committee building, and Tacho explains what it is when
she asks. The cobblestones in Place 9 September are wet, and
further along they come to a water wagon with the hoses manipu-
lated by husky women in long blue smocks.

As they walk, Melanie's soft Kazan boots make no sound, but the
Racer's shoes echo on the cobblestones. At the corner they have to
leap across a rivulet of water to reach the curb. Dimitrov's tomb,
a carbon copy of Lenin's in Red Square, looms ahead and the two
honor guards standing like statues before the door follow the girl's
legs with their eyes, not their heads. Wilting funeral wreaths with
satin inscriptions — "From the Plovdiv Komsomol" — lean against
the side of the tomb; new wreaths will be substituted before the
morning rush hour, and a lush bouquet or two from visiting digni-
taries will be laid, with full press coverage, during the day.

On Stambolski, they come to where the girl has parked her Deux
Chevaux. In Persia she paid someone to paint a map on the driver's
door, with a thin red line to indicate her route. Now, squatting
alongside the car, she travels it again for the Racer with her thumb-
nail, ticking off the cities she has seen. "Paris, Luxembourg,
Bonn, Berlin, Poznań, Warsaw, Brest Litovsk, Minsk, Smolensk,
Moscow, Kharkov, Odessa, Tbilisi . . ."

Tacho notices the windshield wipers are still on her car. In
Sofia, people with private cars lock them away in the glove compartment so they won't be stolen; at the first drop of rain, everyone
pulls over and races around trying to put them on again. Tacho
insists she lock hers away too, and she opens the car and finds her
tool kit and hands him a screwdriver. He unscrews the wipers and
stows them away in the glove compartment. "Now you're part
Bulgarian," he says.

Further along they come across two men and a woman pulling

strips of film out of a tangle of reels in a garbage can in front of a motion picture developing studio. They thread the strips between their fingers and hold them up against the light in the window of the American legation, which is across the street, to see what they have. "For Christ's sake, don't tear it," one of the men tells the women irritably. "Maybe we can sell it."

Nearby another woman sits on the curb with one shoe off, massaging her stocking foot and hiccupping. "Are you holding your breath?" the other woman calls over.

"How can I hold my breath and answer you," the woman complains, hiccupping again. Suddenly she turns on the Racer. "What are you staring at? What is he staring at, huh? Haven't you seen anyone with the hiccups before?" And she hiccups again.

Overhead, television antennae jut sideways like metal antlers from the shuttered balconies of apartment buildings.

They are not far from the girl's hotel now; Tacho can hear the first trolleys starting up. He turns to the girl and asks her the question he has been aching to ask since he found out who she is.

"Why did your father do it?"

She answers instantly, as if she has been expecting the question. "For the money. A bicycle company offered him twenty-five thousand dollars. That was only the beginning; he would have made a lot more endorsing products."

"What does that mean, endorsing products?"

"In America, well-known people go on television and say how they always use such and such a product. It's called endorsing."

"And they pay you for doing that?"

"Yes, of course. Why else would anybody do it?"

The Racer nods thoughtfully. "And did the company give you anything after . . . afterward?"

The girl smiles faintly. "They gave me a bicycle."

At the corner, Place Lenin opens before them: the Black Church on an island in the middle, the hotel off to the right and across the square, a giant statue of Lenin silhouetted against a huge billboard with a graph showing the increase in milk production expected under the next Five-Year Plan. Just around the corner, a young man leans a wooden ladder against the side of a building, climbs gingerly up and begins pasting a small poster onto the wall. As they pass, the girl notices dozens of other posters just like it. They all have black borders and badly reproduced photographs of a man or woman on them.

"Death notices," Tacho explains. "When someone dies, his relatives or friends have the right to put up twenty-five around the city. They used to put up as many as they liked, but the walls became papered with them, so now they limit you to twenty-five. He's using the ladder to put his poster as high as he can. That way it will remain longer when the workmen come by to clear the wall."

Tacho steps closer to one and points to the picture of an old man. " 'Alexander Nickilov Denev, age 52, died 16 August 1968, after a long illness; an anti-Fascist fighter and a builder of Socialism, mourned by his beloved widow, Tsola Vsilava, and numerous comrades in arms.' There's a quotation too — can you make it out?"

Melanie reads:

" 'I don't know whether, if things change, they will get better. But I know if things are to get better they must change.' There's a name after it. Lichtenberg. Who is Lichtenberg?"

"I'm a bike racer," Tacho says. "I haven't the vaguest idea."

"The fifty-two must be a mistake; he looks at least eighty in that photograph."

"He spent two years in a concentration camp."

"Oh." Then:

"Did you know him?"

"I fought in the Resistance with him. I was a boy then. I remember he was an oak of a man, but that was before he was wounded. He was an invalid the rest of his life."

"Was he important in the Resistance; was he a general or something like that?"

"He was important, yes. He was a flag holder, the one who carries the flag and leads the men in an attack."

"In America there's a tradition that when the man with the flag falls, someone else picks it up. Do you have the same here?"

"We have the same," Tacho says. "When he fell, someone else became the Flag Holder."

"Did you see it?"

"Yes."

"Oh," she says again.

At the hotel she starts up the steps, hesitates, turns, looks down at him. The moment is awkward. The seconds tick loudly away.

Dawn drains the sky over Vitoša. Not knowing what to say, the girl says the first thing that comes into her head. "Do you still race?"

He has not expected that. "I ride a lot, but I don't really race. I'm too old for that. I'm training a team for the Sofia-Athens race in three weeks. One day we do roadwork up in the mountains" — Tacho nods toward Vitoša. "The next we work on sprinting in the stadium." He almost lets the thought trail off. At the last instant he adds:

"We're sprinting tomorrow afternoon. Would you like to watch? Afterward, if you like, I'll take you to the Dwarf's wedding."

"I'd like that," she says with conviction.

"Well — " says Tacho.

"Well — " says the girl.

From somewhere nearby comes the delicate ticking of spokes. The man on the ladder hears it too and stops what he is doing to listen. The ticking grows louder. From around the corner appears a man on a unicycle. He is a mime, old and wiry and dressed in black trousers, a skintight black turtleneck and a top hat. His face is painted chalk white. He pedals briskly up to the Racer, stops his unicycle on a dime, balances for an instant as he tips his hat and bows from the waist.

"Oh, he's beautiful — " the girl exclaims.

The Mime hops off his wheel, leans it against the wall and turns, with a bow, to the man on the ladder. The man looks embarrassed. The Mime stares at him with wild, crazy eyes and bows again, insisting. The man on the ladder shrugs and grudgingly inclines his head back. The Mime bows to the girl and she smiles warmly and bows back. The Mime turns to the Racer and bows fiercely. Holding his bow, he glances up. Their eyes meet and Tacho bows back as if he is honoring the man.

Everybody is engaged now, and the Mime retreats a few paces toward the street. He draws on imaginary skintight gloves, then turns and slaps his palm onto an imaginary glass wall behind him. The girl thinks she can hear the smack of his palm against the glass. The Mime turns back, crosses his ankles, laces his fingers together behind his head and lounges against the wall he has created.

"Oh, look," the girl cries happily, and she claps her hands in delight.

Suddenly a cloud passes over the Mime's face: his brow furrows, his eyes listen. He leaps upright and darts a few steps to the right — to come up against a glass wall there. He recoils, then approaches the wall again and begins to slap his palms onto it to see how far it extends. His eyes grow panicky. His hand motions become quicker. *The wall is everywhere around him.* He feels wildly for an opening, a door, a window, a crack, but there is nothing, nothing but solid wall. Now it is pressing in on him — no room to reach out — his elbows pinned to his sides — his fingers describe the wall — his nails scratch at it. He thrusts one arm straight up as if to climb out the top and discovers a ceiling. He can't get his arm back down again — no room — the wall squeezing him. His eyes bulging in terror, one arm over his head, the other pinned to his side, he opens his mouth and screams a silent scream that makes the three people watching him wince.

Then it is over and the Mime is bowing and holding out his top hat and the Racer is rummaging in his pockets for some change. The Mime slips the money into a small leather pouch that hangs from his belt, climbs onto his unicycle and, tipping his hat, pedals off into what is left of the night.

"Who is he?" the girl asks when she can no longer hear the spokes.

But the Racer stares into the accumulating light without replying.

3

THEIR YELLOW JERSEYS whipping around their waists, their wheels almost touching, the four riders lean into the turn, soar high on the curved bank and swoop down again for the pull along the straight-away. The chain on the last bicycle jumps into the sprocket a fraction of a second late. Instantly the Racer's voice comes crack-ling over the battery-powered megaphone that the bicycle club bought from the customs inspector who stole it from a foreign yacht at Varna.

"You muffed the gear changes again, Sacho — close it up. Tony, keep your elbows in. You look like a pigeon flapping its wings. Goddamn it, Evan, how many times do I have to tell you, *don't look back*. Let the Greeks do the looking. You *pull*. And hold the goddamn wheel down on the turns. Lean on it. That's right, that's better. Now *attack* the flat, bite into it. Go. Go. Go."

The Racer stands on an old wooden table in the center of the bicycle stadium, turning round and round like a circus master putting his horses through their paces. Once each lap his eyes flit over the girl high up in the empty bleachers. Somewhere in the back of his mind it occurs to him that she doesn't sit like an American. Angel, in a rare burst of humor, once said they had invented the chair, the Americans, but Mister Dancho credited it to the Russians, claiming it came "just after the rectal thermometer and just before the flush toilet, which they are still perfecting." But even Dancho had to admit that the Americans knew how to sit better than anyone in the world. "They have a way of folding them-selves into chairs," he said, "as if they are going back to the womb. My god, I've even seen them put their feet up on coffee tables!" But not the girl in the bleachers, the Racer thinks, lapping her again with his eyes; she appears to be sitting at attention, her feet flat on the floor, her palms flat on the bench at her sides, following the four riders with small jerks of her head.

The Racer whips the megaphone up to his lips. "Jesus, Sacho, anybody with big lungs can ride a bicycle, but you've got to use your brains to win." Normally Tacho would have let it drop there. But something is irritating him, something he can't put his finger on. And so he steps out of character and flings after the retreating riders:

"If you have any, that is."

"You ride them too hard," the Flag Holder warned earlier in the day. As usual a Rodopi hung from his lower lip and great clouds of stale smoke swirled around his head.

"You don't ride them hard enough," Poleon maintained.

"They still make a lot of mistakes," the Racer explained, "and the race is three weeks off."

"They make mistakes because you make them nervous," the Flag Holder argued. "The big one, what's his name?"

"Sacho."

"Sacho. He shifts perfectly when you're not around. I saw him heading up to Visoša last week. He moved through nine gears without losing a centimeter. Then you turn up and he starts fluffing the changes."

"If you don't ride them, you won't get any work out of them," Poleon interjected. He arranged the thin strands of hair so that they fell over his bald scalp.

The Flag Holder was annoyed. "You should concentrate on getting your films past the censor, Poleon."

"I was only trying to be helpful," Poleon sulked.

It was noon — the siren atop the Central Committee building had just sounded the hour — and they were waiting for the others to join them in the Milk Bar, their midday hangout. They stood next to a chest-high table drinking black coffee. The others would go on to the Journalists' Club for lunch, but Tacho would be doing some laps and preferred to ride on an empty stomach. In the street outside, trolleys and trucks and automobiles poured past the large window of the Milk Bar in a stream that let up only when the Tomato (Dancho's nickname for the ripe cop on the traffic beat outside) let the cars on the side street have a turn.

The Milk Bar is run by an ex-soccer star named Gogo Musko, who is still living off the winning point he scored against the Russians in the world cup quarterfinals five years before. Because of Gogo, the bar is something of a hangout for soccer players. The long wall that runs at right angles to the bar is lined with pegs, and hanging from each one is a jockstrap, put there, with appropriate fanfare, by well-known players as they retire. (Gogo's jock — manufactured in America, a gift from Dancho — hangs from peg number one.) The only other things on the walls are two travel posters from Scandinavia and a photograph of Tacho crossing the finish line in the Milan – San Remo race in 1952. Again his right hand is thrust high in triumph.

Mister Dancho squeezes through the crowd at the door and salutes Gogo with a wave. He stops in the corner to weigh himself on the pay scale. (It was broken when Gogo took over the Milk Bar and therefore not listed on the books as "income producing." With a sure instinct for private enterprise, Gogo jury-rigged a spring and started pocketing the ten stodinki pieces that accumulated in the coin box. In a good week they add up to twenty leva, half again as much as his salary.) The needle on the scale quivers and settles, and Dancho groans.

"I put on two kilos in London, England," he complains, shouldering in next to the Flag Holder. "Hello, Poleon. Greetings, Tacho my boy. God, you can really eat there. What's this I hear about Dreschko? Octobrina woke me at the crack of dawn" — Mister Dancho smirks — "well, at ten, to tell me you saw him last night? It's not possible; he's supposed to have bought it in Siberia."

"That's what I thought too," the Flag Holder agrees. They both look at Tacho.

"I'm telling you, I saw him last night. There aren't two men in the world who look like that. Wasn't Dreschko in the circus before the war?"

"Hey, Angel" — Mister Dancho has just spotted the Dwarf coming through the door, along with his dog and half a dozen of his Hungarians — "Angel, you remember someone named Dreschko who worked in the circus before the war?"

Bazdéev waves the Hungarians over to the counter, where they start pointing out the eclairs they want. "Dreschko? Dreschko? Sure thing, there was someone Dreschko who rode the unicycle —"

"You see!" the Racer exclaims.

"Put together good act for himself," the Dwarf recalls. "How come you asking?"

"Tacho here thinks he saw him last night doing a mime's act in Place Lenin!"

"No, no, not possible," the Dwarf says flatly. "He turned political. Was in Spain. You remember, Lev? Then with Dimitrov in Moscow. Then disappeared. Dead, sure thing."

"He's not dead," the Racer insists. "I tell you I saw him last night. He must have been in the camps all these years" — the Racer is piecing the story together in his mind — "maybe in a cell, maybe solitary. That's what it was, and he was telling us about it." And he describes the Mime's act with the wall.

"Jesus," whistles Dancho. "If it's really him —"

"I asking around," the Dwarf is still dubious. "I find us this Mime, then we seeing."

"Jesus," Dancho says again. "Do you think it's possible?"

"Anything is possible," observes the Flag Holder. In his lifetime, more than one person has disappeared into nowhere, or turned up out of nowhere. "If it is Dreschko, I'll have to revise his entry in my book."

Two well-known soccer players stroll in and start flirting with Bazdéev's Hungarians, whose mouths are all chocolaty from the eclairs. The Dwarf's eyes narrow as he watches to see how the girls will react. At first they pay no attention. Then a thin arm reaches out and a single finger hooks itself over the belt of one of the athletes. Bazdéev roars a word in Hungarian — so suddenly that the dog, Dog, sprawling at his feet, heaves himself slowly off the ground in fear. The thin arm shoots back and the two soccer players, looking around nonchalantly in every direction except Bazdéev's, go their way.

Tacho walks over to the corner table, where the American girl is being quizzed by Octobrina's brother, Velin, a translator who is in the midst of preparing Steinbeck's *Of Mice and Men* for publication in Bulgaria. Melanie is wearing blue jeans with flowers embroidered down the legs like vines, Indian sandals, a white T-shirt and a man's felt fedora with a rose stuck in the band.

"This is fun," Melanie says in Russian, looking up as the Racer approaches. "I like your friend," she whispers, indicating the Flag Holder with her chin.

The Racer accepts the statement as if it is a gift.

"She's a big help," Velin interjects in Bulgarian. He turns back to Melanie and they continue in English. "Here's another one that confuses me. George undid his 'bindle.'" Velin taps the point of his pencil on the word in the book open between them. "What means *bindle?*"

"Bindle is bundle. It's probably his sleeping sack. I had an uncle who used to pack his bindle to go camping."

Velin scribbles something in the margin and draws an arrow from what he has written to the word, which is circled. "How about this one. The grain team is short two 'bunkers.'"

Melanie screws up her face. "I can't help you with that one — no."

"How about: George says, 'What the hell's he got on his shoulder?' But he doesn't have anything on his shoulder. I don't understand."

Melanie leans over and reads the paragraph. The Racer sees Velin steal a look at her breasts, which are visible through her shirt. "Ah, that one's easy," Melanie declares, looking up. Velin's eyes flash back to hers. "We have an expression in English, 'To have a chip on your shoulder,' meaning to be hostile. When he says, 'What does he have on his shoulder?' he's really asking, does he have a chip on his shoulder? D'ya see?"

"Chip?" inquires the translator, thoroughly confused now. "What is this chip?"

Tacho saunters back and helps Popov carry his cake and coffee to the table.

"How was your morning, Atanas?" the Flag Holder asks.

Popov reaches into his pocket to turn up his hearing aid. "What did you say?"

"I said, how was your morning?"

"Ah, my morning. Sssssssss. Mediocre. Yes, yes, mediocre. Wait" — he pulls his ledger from his pocket — "I'll show you. Sssssssss. One Maxwell House coffee tin, empty, without a lid. One Russian iron without electrical cord." Popov shakes his head to emphasize the poor quality of his list. "One Polish mousetrap without a spring. A model of a zygodactyl; actually, that isn't too awful. An empty can of East German hair spray. I suppose my best is a crumpled portrait of Jaurès haranguing a crowd

in France — you can tell it's in France because there is a 'Café' sign
in the background." Popov perks up. "They say Jaurès always
spoke in the future tense. Did you know that? Sssssssss."

"I prefer the past imperfect," remarks the Racer.

"I only feel at home in the present ridiculous," snaps Mister
Dancho.

"Not to worry," the Racer murmurs cynically, "these days everything is conjugated in the present ridiculous."

"Let me see," Popov continues, "hardly anything else worth
mentioning. A petrified peach pit. A buckle for a woman's bath-
robe. Bits and pieces. Bits and pieces. Sssssssss."

"Do you remember last night Dreschko's name came up in conversation," the Flag Holder reminds Popov. "Tacho thinks he saw
him at — " The rest is lost in a fit of coughing.

"The poet Dreschko? But he killed himself — "

"No, no, not the one who was the poet; his older brother, the one
who was in Spain."

"I thought you said he died in Siberia."

"Tacho thinks he saw him last night," Mister Dancho explains
patiently.

"Oh." Popov's interest runs out like the string on a kite. He
nods and turns down his battery. "Coffee," he mutters, shaking his
head. He stirs some sugar into his cup absent-mindedly. "Maxwell House coffee. Sssssssss."

Mister Dancho leans closer to the Racer. "That American bird's
pretty enough to make my watch stop. On the thin side, maybe,
but" — he sizes her up with his hands and nods appreciatively.
"Did you get any last night?"

"Quit it, Dancho."

"Touchy bastard, aren't you. Come on, you can tell Uncle
Dancho. My lips are sealed. It won't go any further." He lowers
his voice to a whisper. "Take it from someone who knows, the
best part about the kissing is the telling."

"I told you to knock it off."

Dancho shrugs and sips his coffee. After a while he thinks to
ask the Racer who Krasov was.

"Krasov," Tacho says, "was one of the six poor sons of bitches
who've been killed trying to break my record."

"Ah, now I see — " Dancho looks at the girl, who is engrossed
in conversation with the translator.

"It was nineteen fifty-two or -three. He rode behind a Cadillac across a salt flat in America. It was never established whether his wheel hit a pebble, or the rim just collapsed. The front wheel went out from under him at one hundred eighty-six kilometers an hour."

Mister Dancho grimaces. "I'll never understand how you brought yourself to do it. What was in your head?"

The Racer smiles mysteriously. "I was trying to combine motion with movement — "

"Don't give me that motion-movement crap again. What really made you climb on a bicycle and try to ride two hundred kilometers an hour? Christ, I wouldn't go that fast in a car!"

"Tell you what, Dancho, I'd rather talk about the kissing and the telling."

"Slippery bastard," Dancho laughs.

"Here comes Octobrina and the Rabbit," the Flag Holder announces.

Octobrina goes off to the counter for a coffee, but the Rabbit comes straight over. She looks drawn. "Oh, Lev." She puts a hand on the Flag Holder's arm. "Lev, one of our paratrooper brigades has been flown into the Ukraine near the Czech border. Georgi's with them, Lev."

There is a long silence.

"You're sure of this?" the Flag Holder asks finally.

The Rabbit nods grimly. "I heard it from a major who was complaining about not being allowed to go with them. He says the lucky ones who get to go would find promotions waiting for them when they return."

"Georgi's a smart boy," Mister Dancho assures the Flag Holder. "He'll stay out of trouble."

"He's entitled to some action," Poleon puts in. "Like father, like son."

The Flag Holder turns on Poleon coldly. "I didn't put down revolutions. I made them."

"It can't be happening," Tacho murmurs. "It's a contradiction of everything we believe in."

Popov, who has tuned into the conversation, intones:

" 'The dialectic is the science of creative contradictions.' Ssssssss."

"That's easy," Mister Dancho says glumly. "Lenin."

Disappointed, Popov turns down his battery again.

Elisabeta says, "I saw a transcript of what went on in Moscow yesterday. It is being prepared for Central Committee distribution. Our leaders were met by Suslov. Brezhnev didn't even bother to show up. The Minister was there, by the way. He asked if our side was being consulted or informed. Suslov said: 'You are being consulted about decisions that have already been taken.' "

The expression on the Flag Holder's face doesn't change and Elisabeta turns on him angrily. "You know what I can't stand about you? What I can't stand is that every time I tell you some juicy item, you act as if you've heard it already."

"You will begin to understand me when you realize that I have heard it already."

The Rabbit presses her forehead against his shoulder. "Oh, Lev, I'm sorry. I didn't mean that. I'm — I'm jumpy. The Ministry is wild with rumors. They say that Soviet tank columns are on the Czech frontier ready to link up with Russian paratroopers already inside the country. They say the Czechs are secretly mobilizing, that they have caches of Western arms which are being distributed to the workers. They say roadblocks and barricades are going up all over Prague. Oh, Lev, there's going to be a war."

"Maybe the Schweiks will fight after all," ventures Mister Dancho.

"Schweiks don't fight," Octobrina declares, placing her coffee on the table. "They survive."

"If you're so sure they won't fight, why are you all worried about Georgi?" Poleon demands stubbornly. He smirks and looks around, thinking he has scored on the Flag Holder.

For an instant — just an instant — the Flag Holder's bitterest enemy, spontaneity, gets the upper hand. Words spill from his lips. "It's a bluff. The Russians won't dare . . . I tell you, it's got to be a bluff." Then the moment passes and he is in full control again. "No man can accept being on the side, even through force of circumstances, of the oppressor."

"I agree with Lev," Tacho argues. "The Russian will never —"

A middle-aged man carrying a violin case under one arm limps into the Milk Bar, and all conversation fades away. Nobody looks at the man, but the silence wraps itself around him like an accusation. His step slackens; he would turn and run if he could, but having started, he has to continue as if nothing has happened.

"Coffee, please," he tells Gogo, and he tries to put the thirty stodinki onto the glass counter without making a sound.

"Black?" Gogo asks loudly.

"Cream," the man replies.

"I didn't get you?"

"I said cream."

"No cream," Gogo announces.

"Black then," the man says. He hesitates. "Why do you ask if I want cream if you have none?"

Gogo slides the coffee cup across the counter, spilling most of it in the saucer as he does. "The instructions under which I operate require me to offer my customers a choice of black or cream. They make no reference to the possibility that I lack one or the other. So I offer."

A few of the athletes at the far end of the Milk Bar guffaw at this.

"You think you are funny," the man with the violin case whines, turning on them.

"What's bothering you, comrade?" Mister Dancho taunts. "Our constitution gives us the right to laugh when we please. Even in the presence of informants for the militia. So go write up a report. Time: twelve twenty-three. Place: Milk Bar on Rakovski Boulevard. What's your number here, Gogo? The magician Dancho was heard to laugh at an unspecified joke."

"You'll regret — " the man with the violin case blurts.

"Ah, fuck off," one of the soccer players groans. They all burst out laughing.

The man with the violin case turns beet red and starts stuttering. Outside someone leans on a car horn. Everyone in the Milk Bar turns toward the sound. Traffic has stopped and pedestrians are converging on the small raised island where the traffic policeman stands.

"It's the Tomato," one of the soccer players yells. "Come on."

Within seconds, the athletes have spilled through the door and joined the crowd. From the street someone calls back:

"Hey, Angel, it's your taxi fellow — "

"Kovel," roars Bazdéev. "Come quick. This being good."

In the middle of the intersection, a bald, fat taxi driver has squared off against the Tomato. They stand toe to toe, shouting into each other's faces.

"Where can I park then?" Kovel demands.

"You can park on your hat," the Tomato yells back. "I answer that question a hundred times a day."

"If you only answer it a hundred times you're not earning your salary." Kovel surveys the crowd for support. There are catcalls and whistles and an occasional "Give 'im hell" from the back of the crowd.

The Tomato seems to realize he is in a fight he can't win. He lowers his voice and backs away, obviously willing to forget the whole thing. "You don't pay my salary," he says sullenly.

Kovel appeals directly to the audience. "I don't pay his salary?" He pauses before delivering the coup de grâce. "I pay it, and" — he points to an old lady in the front rank — "grandma here pays it, and" — pointing to a black-robed priest whose beard is bobbing in agreement — "grandpa here pays it, and" — picking people at random — "he does and he does and he does." There is some angry muttering from the crowd.

"Hand over your license — I'm punching it for illegal parking," the Tomato orders in his most official police voice.

Kovel pulls out instead a paper and pencil. "Go ahead and punch it; me, I'll ask your general how is it I can park on my hat. How are you called?"

"I am not required to give you my name," the Tomato says sullenly. "If you want to identify me, use my number."

There is applause from the crowd as Kovel peers at the Tomato's shield and starts to write down his number. "Bravo, Kovel," someone with a voice remarkably like Dancho's yells.

Melanie comes running up behind the Racer. "What's happening?" she asks, straining on tiptoes to catch a glimpse of the action.

"Nothing unusual," Tacho tells her, "just two of our citizens demonstrating that mutual belligerence is the human condition."

The Racer's voice — grainier, less distinct, like an enlarged photograph — peals through the megaphone. "All right, ten minutes."

There are whoops of delight from the four riders. Their tight formation splinters and a few moments later all four are sprawling on a grassy patch off the track. Tacho walks over and hands around a water bottle.

"Don't swallow — just rinse and spit," he reminds them.

"Rinse and spit," the rider named Tony says good-naturedly. "I hear it in my dreams."

"How'd we look?" the big rider named Sacho demands. His breathing is only slightly affected by the hundred or so laps he has done.

"Like four women taking a Sunday stroll," the Racer teases.

"Ah, come on — "

"You've got to be kidding — "

"How did we look, coach, really?" Sacho asks again.

"Not bad," Tacho concedes. He squats alongside them. "You're fast enough to win, but so are the Greeks. The race will go to the smartest. You've got to *think* your way to the finish line. If the sun is behind you, watch their shadows and drift to cut them off. If the road is wet, brake lightly a hundred fifty meters before you corner to burn the water off your rims. Jump when your opponents least expect it: at the most grueling part of a climb, for instance. Or go flat out when you're behind them and sprint past them on their blind side. And for god's sake don't look back. Every time you look back, it costs you."

The Racer squints into the sunlight; the girl is still there.

"What do you say, five fast laps and you can call it an afternoon," the Racer tells them. Suddenly he knows he will sprint with them today, and he adds:

"Let's see if you can keep up with an old man."

"You gonna pace us, coach?" Evan asks.

"I'm not going to pace you; I'm going to beat the pants off you," he informs them.

They start out five abreast on the flat. The Racer slips his left foot into the toe clip, reaches down to tug the strap tight, then dips his right toe into the other clip.

"All right," Tacho calls. He lifts himself off the saddle and stands on the right pedal.

"Go."

He jumps on the pedal and the bike leaps forward. By the first bank they are strung out in a line, with big Sacho first, Tony second and the Racer clinging to Tony's rear wheel. The other two have lost a bike length on the impromptu start.

The first two laps are relatively easy and the Racer holds his position without straining. By the third lap, though, he starts to feel the tightness in his leg muscles. He pushes the tightness into a corner of his brain reserved for pain and concentrates on holding his own. On the fourth lap Sacho glances back, sees the Racer is still with them and forces the pace. Tony fluffs the gear change trying to keep up with him and the Racer slips past him into second position, hugging Sacho's rear wheel.

As they lean into the last turn the numbness begins to spread across Tacho's knees; he knows from experience they will swell during the night. On the turn Sacho rides high and whoops and swoops down for the final flat. The Racer fights his front wheel and comes out of the turn high up on the bank. Sacho steals a look behind — over his *left* shoulder — thinks the Racer is no longer behind him and whoops again. The glance costs him and Tacho pulls even with him now, Sacho on the low edge of the track next to the grass, the Racer high above him on the bank. On the final sprint, Tacho turns his front wheel slightly left — he will be riding for the finish line going *downhill*. By the time Sacho realizes what has happened, the Racer is half a wheel length ahead and accelerating.

High on the bleachers, the girl exhales slowly. She has the impression it is her first breath in minutes. When she stands up, she discovers that her body has a stiffness that comes from holding yourself ready for an accident.

4

THE HUNGARIAN NYMPHETS tug shyly at Mister Dancho's tuxedo jacket and giggle in Magyar — "Please, do us some tricks" — but he is determined to finish the story.

"So the man on the bicycle rides up and leans his bike against the Central Committee building, you picture it?" Dancho shakes off the Hungarians and hisses "Sssssssssscat" as if he is chasing alley cats, and everyone smiles. In a corner of the room a cork pops and champagne sloshes onto the floor. A woman leaps back, laughing hysterically. Waving his hand to dispel the cigarette smoke, Mister Dancho goes on:

"So the militiaman comes up to him and tells him" — Dancho tries to imitate the Tomato here — "'You can't park your bike there. A high Soviet delegation is due to arrive any second.' So what does the man on the bicycle say?"

Dancho twists around and calls across the room:

"Dear child, could you turn that *down?*" Then back to his audience. "He says: 'That's all right, *I'll chain it up!*' "

The dozen or so guests around Mister Dancho roar and Dancho, who wanted to be a standup comic long before he wanted to be a magician, laughs happily with them. Only the Fat Lady, sitting with the Dwarf's circus friends, looks blank.

"He'll *chain* the bike," the Lion Tamer explains, "so the Russians won't *steal* it!"

"Of course," shrieks the Fat Lady, "steal it," and she slaps the Juggler so hard he falls over the chair he is lounging against, spilling champagne on Poleon's ex-wife.

"Now see what you've done!" she cries shrilly. "Oh my god. Salt, somebody. Where's salt? Somebody know where some salt is? Oh my god!"

Rolling the long stem of a glass half full of champagne between his fingers, Poleon stares though half-closed eyes at his ex-wife without moving a muscle. "I should have Lot's luck," he mumbles.

One of the Dwarf's Hungarians slips a new Beatles record onto the phonograph and scratches the needle across the grooves until she reaches a band she likes. "Liv-ing is easy with eyes closed . . . with eyes closed . . . with eyes closed . . . with eyes closed . . . with eyes closed . . . with eyes closed . . . with eyes closed."

"Can't somebody fix that?" Tacho complains irritably. His knees are swollen and his calf still aches from a muscle cramp that brought tears to his eyes during dinner at Krimm.

The Rabbit goes over and edges the needle onto the next groove. The Hungarian, swaying dreamily in the embrace of one of her girl friends, sings along with the record. "Stror-perry fee-ulds fur-ever."

Someone hands Poleon's ex-wife a saltcellar and she covers the champagne stain with a layer of salt.

"That's only good for wine, dearie," the Fat Lady tells her.

"Come on, Dancho, make the stain disappear," the Fire Eater challenges.

Mister Dancho takes Poleon's ex-wife by the wrists and helps her step onto the chair so that everybody can see her. She once was a great beauty and is aging well, so she enjoys the limelight. Dancho takes the fabric of her long skirt in his fingers and studies the stain intently. Finally he shakes his head. "Too difficult," he says. He turns away, leaving her stranded on the chair.

"Losing your touch, huh, Dancho?" scoffs Poleon.

"My watch!" shrieks Poleon's ex-wife from atop her perch. "I've lost my watch."

"You probably gave it to Poleon to carry," Dancho plays innocent. He dips into Poleon's breast pocket and extracts — a photograph of Alexander Dubcek. The crowd roars. Dancho produces a pocket scissors and makes an elaborate show of cutting the photograph in half. Then he carefully folds the two halves, passes his palm over the paper and, holding on to a corner, shakes the poster free. It is back in one piece again. For good measure, Dancho extracts the missing watch from the folds of Octobrina's shawl.

"Ah, Dancho — "

"You son of a gun — "

Laughing, Dancho starts up the stairs. Octobrina calls after him: "What are you two cooking up this time?"

"Patience, dear lady," Dancho replies over his shoulder.

Dancho is the life of any party he attends, and with him gone, even temporarily, the mix seems to curdle. Most of the circus people edge toward the bar to refill their champagne glasses. Four or five of the younger couples move into what was originally the dining room, which is littered with 45 r.p.m. discs and comic books, and start dancing to a Frank Sinatra record. Octobrina settles on a banquette in the bay window with the Rabbit, Poleon's ex-wife and the Fat Lady. The Rabbit says something and Poleon's ex-wife shakes her head no and says:

"I see people on the street talking to themselves all the time. What I try to figure out is whether they're rehashing conversations behind them or rehearsing conversations ahead of them."

"They're trying to figure out who they are, dearie," the Fat Lady declares. "Everybody's always trying to figure out who they are."

"They're trying to organize their relationships," says the Rabbit.

Octobrina sighs. "My mother and I had a perfectly wonderful mother-daughter relationship, only I was the mother!" She means it as a joke, but a certain amount of resentment seeps through in her tone.

The Fat Lady laughs until the rolls of fat around her waist quiver. The Rabbit laughs too and says that in her experience reverse parent-child relationships are common among artistic and academic types.

"I can't stomach academic types," observes Poleon's ex-wife. "They're always going around muttering about how someone is not very *sharp*. They're always *judging*."

Atanas Popov wanders over and Octobrina pats the cushion next to her, offering him a seat. Popov is dressed in a prewar cutaway; he deftly tucks the tails behind him as he settles onto the banquette. Octobrina smiles warmly and asks him if his afternoon has been productive.

"Not bad for August," Popov concedes modestly, producing his pocket ledger. He slips his pince-nez onto his misshapen nose and starts reading. "Let me see. Sssssssss. One brass birdcage without a bottom. One clay swan without a left wing. Half a love letter, written in the month of June, nineteen forty-four, torn vertically; from the half I have it seems clear that the lover is proposing something, though what it is I cannot say."

"Maybe the lover was halfhearted," the Fat Lady quips. "Maybe the letter was sent that way."

Both Octobrina and the Rabbit silence her with angry looks.

"One cameo brooch without a clasp. One *Book of Innocents*, in Latin, containing the biographies of Innocent Roman Numeral One, Two, Three, Four, Five, Six, Eight, Eleven, Twelve and Thirteen." Popov's eyes, but not his head, come up. "The last Innocent, Roman Numeral Thirteen, died in seventeen twenty-four. I doubt very much whether anyone would have the nerve to use that name again. Sssssssss. Ah, here's a small gem. One porcelain praying mantis. One leather-covered travel clock, broken, with smaller faces on the back to tell the time in different cities. The small faces are labeled 'St. Petersburg,' 'Smyrna' and 'Constantinople.' One Prague street sign, 'Král Vinchrady Praha 12,' with a typewritten note glued to the back which says, according to a comrade of mine who reads Czech, that the street sign was removed the day the Hitlerites invaded Prague, March fifteenth, nineteen thirty-nine, to prevent them from finding people they wanted to arrest." Popov looks up. "Perhaps our Czech friends will have occasion to remove the street signs again."

"It won't surprise me," Octobrina declares vehemently.

"Bite your tongue," the Rabbit snaps.

"Let me see, where was I? Sssssssss. Yes, yes. One miniature plastic rainbow with a small painted pot of gold at the end; did you know that the ancient Hebrews took the rainbow as a pledge from god there would be no more great floods? Genesis nine, thirteen. I wrote a poem about the need for floods once, but I don't remember it. Sssssssss. One lock, with a key that doesn't fit, attached to it with a wire. One meter of soiled English white lace — "

"The Racer can't stand white lace," Octobrina recalls. "That's why I always wear black shawls."

"Do you know why?" Popov asks.

"As a matter of fact, I don't think I do."

"During the war, Lev led an attack against a German short-wave radio station. The station was protected by a tank parked in a field of snow. The tank was camouflaged with white lace stolen from a lace factory in the nearby town."

"Were you there?" the Rabbit asks.

"No, I wasn't, but Mister Dancho was. I heard the story from

Mister Dancho. They crept close to the tank and fired a rocket into it at pointblank range. For a moment it looked as if the lace was exploding; it billowed up like a parachute before it disappeared in flames. Needless to say, the soldiers in the tank never emerged."

"I never heard that story before," Octobrina confesses. "Thank you for telling it to me, Atanas. Is there anything else?"

"Anything else?"

"On your list?"

"My list? Oh, yes, yes, my list. My last but not least is: one quill pen with the quill point replaced by a ball-point refill cartridge. That's my last but not least. Sssssssss."

"It's a lovely list," Octobrina assures him. "Perfectly lovely."

There is a burst of laughter from the dining room. A crowd is forming around Valentine Barbovich, the opera singer, who is just back from Rome.

"Who is your favorite composer?" a woman in a long gown asks him.

"Mozart."

She makes a face. "But everyone loves Mozart."

"I love him for the right reasons," Valyo replies evenly.

He leans back on the couch, his chin jutting at an imperial angle, his arms and legs flung possessively wide. Seeing him in this position, Octobrina once told him to his face that he reminded her of a country that covered more than its share of a continent. Valyo took it well. He chuckled and smoothed down his hair, which was combed forward in the style of a Roman senator, and stroked his "twin phallus" (Octobrina's phrase) — the solid silver tuning fork that Toscanini had given him after his New York debut.

"But it is not at all true," Valyo tells someone else, his lyrical voice wafting to the far corners of the house. "I *adore* mezzo-sopranos, even the ones that don't sing well. They have the two physical qualities which one most admires in women: long necks and large breasts."

"How were the mezzos at La Scala?" a man shouts.

Valyo taps his tuning fork against his knee (without apparent muscular reaction) and cocks his ear to it. "Four-forty — what a comfort in this world of ours to have a standard that never changes. La Scala? There was nothing at La Scala this season except music, friend. And the music has lost its edge; this is the price one pays for being a professional. Pieces that once reduced me to tears no longer move me. Only performances move me, and, then, usually only my own. La Scala, I tell you in all humility, was redeemed by my rendering of Verdi."

"He's delicious," Melanie whispers in the Racer's ear. They are standing together on the fringe of the crowd. "He looks more like a defrocked priest than an opera singer."

"He almost became a priest once," Tacho whispers back. "But he decided he couldn't give up women." Tacho raises himself on tiptoes. "Tell again about your audition at La Scala, Valyo," he calls. "There are some here who have never heard the story." And to the girl he whispers:

"Listen carefully."

"Our Racer wants to hear about my audition at La Scala. Good god, one hardly remembers, it was so long ago. Dawn of history, practically." Someone hands Valyo a glass of champagne and he sips it zestfully. "I was young then, of course; what they call a babe in the woods." Valyo chuckles to himself. "They had never seen a Bulgarian before; god only knows if they even knew where Bulgaria was. When I said I had trained at the Sofia conservatory, one of them actually laughed. I stood on the edge of that stage and looked out at the maestro. He was wearing a black cape and sitting in the last row, off to one side, quite alone. And I called out to him that there was only one thing on trial in the hall: his ability to recognize a great talent when he heard one. When I finished singing, the old man came forward slowly. He tapped his cane on the floor and nodded and told me he had passed."

"Did you get all of that?" Tacho asks the American girl.

She nods enthusiastically. "He's quite a character, your Valentine Barbovich."

"Try Valyo," someone shouts.

"Yes, Valyo can do it if anyone can," a woman adds, pushing a man out of the crowd. It is the Scream Therapist, the one who was at the table next to Poleon's the night before.

Valyo leans forward. "Do what?"

"Scream," the Scream Therapist explains. "I'm taking a kind of survey: I'm trying to see if I can get anybody in Sofia to emit that peculiar sound commonly referred to as a scream."

"But scream for what?" Valyo inquires, puzzled.

"Well, actually, for love. I subscribe to the theory that it is the need for love, and not sexuality, that is supressed in children; that when the child is screaming, he or she (as the case may be) is screaming for love, if you follow my meaning. I'm trying to get adults to duplicate this scream. Would you, eh, care to try? I warn you, so far nobody in Sofia has been able to, eh, to scream."

Valyo is clearly disconcerted. "But surely it is easy — "

"Not so easy as you think," the Scream Therapist asserts. "For you it will be especially difficult. You've spent your life learning to control your vocal chords, and I am asking you to free yourself of control. Go ahead. Try. All you have to do is open your mouth and *scream!*"

Valyo looks around uncertainly. All right. Give me room." Motioning everyone back with his hands, he fills his lungs, opens his mouth so that his soft, pink uvula is plainly visible and — closes his mouth again. "This is ridiculous," Valyo decides. "Of course I can scream if I want to, but this makes no sense." Valyo shrugs and laughs, and a few people, out of politeness, laugh with him.

"How about you?" the Scream Therapist demands, looking directly at the Flag Holder, who is sitting quietly on a stool in front of the bar. A full glass of cognac, untouched, stands before him. A cigarette dangles from his lips. He looks gray, preoccupied, angry almost; his friends, sensing his mood, have steered clear of him at the party, and with good reason. For the Flag Holder has detected, on his way to the Dwarf's house on Vitosa, a certain uneasiness in Sofia: people talking quietly in knots, all the lights burning after working hours in the Ministry of Defense, twice as many militiamen as usual on the streets. "What's the matter with you?" the Rabbit whispered early in the evening, and when Lev didn't answer she turned irritably to Octobrina and told her so that he could hear:

"He has a low threshold of pleasure; he can't take too much without feeling guilty."

Now the Flag Holder looks back at the Scream Therapist and shakes his head once.

The Scream Therapist doesn't ask him again.

"I'd like to try," volunteers Poleon's ex-wife. She thrusts through the crowd until she stands facing the Scream Therapist. "What's the prize? What do I get if I do it?" she laughs, playing to the audience.

Poleon leans against the bar next to the Flag Holder. "If anybody can do it, she can," he snickers. "She's had a lot of practice."

"The trick is to think of someone you hate," the Scream Therapist advises Poleon's ex-wife.

"Oh, that part's easy," she calls over her shoulder. The crowd applauds in delight.

"Close your eyes and imagine that the person you hate the most in the world is in this room now."

"I don't have to imagine," she throws at the crowd, giggling wildly.

"You feel anger and resentment welling up inside you. Now open your mouth and scream and expel the anger. Go ahead, scream."

Poleon's ex-wife shuts her eyes and takes a deep breath. Her breaths come faster. Her mouth contorts in anger. Her nostrils flare. Suddenly her facial muscles sag. She starts to say something, then shakes her head. "I need a drink," she mutters, moving off toward the bar.

"Would anybody else like to try?" the Scream Therapist demands.

"Could you do it?" Melanie asks the Racer. "Scream, I mean?"

"I suppose so," Tacho replies.

"Go ahead, try. I dare you!"

Tacho laughs off the dare. "Let's get some air." He takes a firm grip on her arm and leads her into the garden.

"This place is enormous," Melanie gasps. "How did the Dwarf get a whole house to himself? I thought you were limited to so many square meters a person?"

"You forget he has fifteen Hungarians living with him. He had himself declared their legal guardian. All of them together are entitled to this much living space." Tacho looks up at the house. "Angel says it was built after the turn of the century for a mistress of our King Ferdinand. Did you notice the inscription over the wrought-iron gate when we came up the path? 'Free your mind — move your ass.' Angel swears Ferdinand had it put there, but a lot of people think Angel did it himself. Ferdinand fled the country after the First World War, and his mistress disappeared soon after. The house was used by the Ministry of Foreign Affairs during the summers for a while; Sofia gets quite hot this time of the year, but Vitoša stays cool. Sometime in the nineteen thirties — does all this interest you?"

"Yes, please."

"Sometime in the nineteen thirties it became a house of prostitution; Angel says it was run by the Foreign Ministry for foreign diplomats, but I think he's inventing that; it was probably private enterprise. At any rate, when the Communists came to power in nineteen forty-four, we expropriated the building and divided it into apartments, which were sold at low prices to retired workers. When Angel began making a great deal of money, which was in the early nineteen fifties, he started buying up the apartments one by one. Each time he bought an apartment he brought in another Hungarian and had himself declared her guardian. When they grow taller than he is, usually when they're thirteen or fourteen, he sends them back to Hungary and brings in a substitute."

"But your government isn't fooled by all this?"

"What can the government do? Angel is known all over Europe!"

"Still, there has to be a limit to what he can get away with."

"Of course there's a limit. It's just that the Dwarf hasn't reached it yet." The Racer laughs out loud. "None of us has."

Tacho leads the girl around to the front of the house. "Look — you can see all of Sofia from here." The front lawn slopes away toward the city. "There's the TV tower; see the blinking red light? And you can just make out the gold dome of the Alexander Nevsky — see there?"

They stand for a time in the cool, dark shadow of the crest of Vitoša, the soft damp earth underfoot, Sofia spread out at their feet. The city seems like a model in the window of a department store. Streetlights dance, the headlights of cars flow through the thoroughfares, but no sound of traffic reaches their ears.

A burst of laughter comes from the house behind them, and someone turns up the volume of the phonograph again. Half a dozen figures spill onto the lawn and begin dancing wildly. A few of them take off their shirts, but it is too dark to see if they are men or women.

"Come," Tacho says, and he leads the way to an octagonal white structure on the rim of the property.

"Angel's gazebo," the Racer explains. "This is where he spends

most of his time in the summer. Here" — Tacho snaps on an overhead bulb, throwing latticework shadows onto the grass around the
gazebo.

"Oh, it's a child's room!"

"No, it's the Dwarf's. And the Hungarians — don't forget they
are children. Everything is scaled down to size. Look how low the
light switch is."

Wide-eyed, Melanie takes in the gazebo from the threshold. It
is filled with children's things: dwarf chairs and tables, potted Japanese dwarf trees, a beautiful painted rocking horse, even a doll's house
filled with miniature chairs and tables. On one latticework wall of
the gazebo hangs a framed color photograph showing the Dwarf,
in full clown regalia, standing before a bleacher packed with laughing children. His back is to the camera, but he is looking over his
shoulder directly into the lens, smiling as if he knows something
that everyone else can only guess at.

The Racer settles onto the floor with his back to the wall and his
knees drawn up to his chin; his knees feel better when they are flexed.
Melanie tries out the rocking horse. "Cow-boy," Tacho says in
English, and Melanie laughs at his pronunciation. She wanders
around the room fingering the toys strewn about, and finally sinks
down next to Tacho.

"It's funny," she says. "My father never wanted to be a bike racer.
He wanted to have money, and racing was the only way he could think
of to get it. What about you? Did you always want to race?"

Tacho leans his head back against the wall. "There was only
one paved street in Melnik when I was a child. I spent most of my
time riding up and down it on an old bicycle my father got for me.
For a long time I thought he stole it, but then I found out he paid for
it by guiding pilgrims up into the mountains to a monastery on his
days off."

"But did you always want to race?"

Tacho kneads his knees with his fingertips. "As far back as I can
remember, I wanted to be a bicycle racer. But I wanted the racing
to be something more. I wanted to get someplace."

"But you are someplace — "

"No. Wherever I am, I have the feeling I'm passing through.
Atanas says the present is a small village through which we are
passing on the way from what was to what can be. I don't know.
I'd like to *be* someplace, instead of in transit."

The girl leans over to touch his hand. He takes her hand in his and holds it and looks at it, as if he is making up his mind about something. Then he looks up and reaches awkwardly for her breast and twists around to kiss her. She stiffens at his touch; she tries not to pull away, but she can't help herself.

Tacho leaps to his feet.

"Please — " Her voice is softer than a whisper. "I'm not used . . . you must understand . . . it's not that I don't want . . . please." She holds her breath and says, "I'm sorry."

Melanie sits still after the Racer leaves, listening to the crickets, listening to her pulse, trying to sort the thoughts from the feelings, trying to place them in separate piles and assign some weight to them. After a while she gives it up and starts to think about leaving Bulgaria.

There is the rustle of steps coming toward the gazebo; for an instant Melanie thinks that Tacho has changed his mind, has understood, has come back. But it is the Rabbit who walks in. She settles herself sidesaddle on the rocking horse and regards the American girl.

"Did Tacho send you?" Melanie asks.

Elisabeta smiles. "He told me you were here, yes." She studies Melanie and sees the contrast between the passivity of her face and the intensity of the fear in her eyes. "He likes you, you know," she tells her suddenly. When Melanie doesn't respond, she says again: "Tacho, he likes you. He could have the pick of Sofia. He is very famous."

The American girl says nothing. "Do you understand my Russian?" Elisabeta asks. "I speak it with difficulty."

"I understand you very well."

"Then how is it you don't answer to me?"

"I don't answer because you didn't ask a question."

The Rabbit runs her thumb under the bra strap on her shoulder. "I envy you — not having a brassiere. I don't have the nerve." Then:

"The Flag Holder is very famous too. More famous than the Racer. You have seen his photograph? There, a question for you."

Despite herself Melanie smiles. "You can hardly be in Sofia and miss it."

"Yes, that is so. It is also in the textbooks of our schoolchildren. It is also displayed on huge banners on nine September, which is the anniversary of our liberation. The man on Lev's left in the photo-

graph is the Second Secretary of our Party. The man on his right
is our Prime Minister." Elisabeta pauses, as if gathering herself
for a leap. "Did the Racer tell you that he and I were lovers once?"

Melanie's expression doesn't change. "No," she says evenly.
"Isn't it awkward for you, the two of them being so close?"

"It is no problem for me, loving at various times the two of them.
They are opposite sides of the same coin." She hesitates. "Did
you know that Tacho was married once? There, another question!"

"He hasn't told me much about his personal life."

"I will tell you then. It came about soon after he set the record of
two hundred kilometers an hour. He was young and beautiful and
all the people were in love with him. We are a small inconsequential country, and Tacho gave us the gift of feeling important. He
married our most beautiful actress. She was older than he was, a
queen and a crazy lady. A few months after the marriage she took
off her clothes and walked into the Black Sea. The fishermen on the
beach saw her write in the sand before she swam for the horizon.
But the tide came in before someone with the ability to read could
be brought to the beach. And so Tacho lost the message too."

The story creates a bond between them; they meet in the no man's
land between the listening and the telling. And so the silence that
follows is not at all awkward.

After a while the Rabbit suddenly smiles. "From now, perhaps
you will answer my questions without my having to ask them."

Melanie nods gravely. "I'll try."

There is a commotion at the back door of the house. "They're
starting," a woman shouts in an excited voice.

"I'm coming," a man calls back, and another woman begs, "Button this for me, will you?"

"Hurry up or we shall miss the fun," Elisabeta urges. Together
they run across the grass and crowd into the large front room on the
main floor, the Rabbit alongside the Flag Holder, Melanie alongside the Racer. Their shoulders touch and he looks down at her and
she slips her arm through his.

The overhead lights dim. Talk dies down as if before the opening
curtain of a play. There is the amplified sound of wind blowing
through a tunnel; someone is blowing the dust off the phonograph
needle. Then the solemn notes of "The Wedding March" fill the
house. An array of spotlights bathes the long flight of steps leading
from the first floor in cruel white light. The houselights go off

completely and a mildly pornographic film is projected, from behind, onto the movie screen that has been set up near the bay windows. The film shows the Dwarf's Hungarians, naked from the waist up, fondling each other. They keep giggling and looking at the camera out of the corner of their eyes.

"Good camera work," Poleon mutters, but he is drowned out by a chorus of "Shhhhhhhhhs."

Popov starts down the stairs. On his arm is the Dwarf's "bride." She is dressed in white voile, through which her gangly legs and a sparse patch of pubic hair and her nipples are visible. Her face is heavily rouged; that plus the high-heeled shoes make her look like a little girl dressed up in her mother's clothes. When Popov and the girl reach the movie screen, they turn and, using the screen as a backdrop, face the audience.

Behind them a title card, the old-fashioned kind used in silent films, flashes on the screen. It says:

"We live in a fool's paradise."

The music fades. There is a scraping sound at the top of the stairs. Then something steps off into the white light. First the feet, and then the body of a puppet come into view; it is the spitting image of Mister Dancho. Behind it, manipulating the strings of the puppet, comes the Dwarf. He is dressed in white leotards which emphasize the deformities of his body — his bulging chest, his broad hunched shoulders, his foreshortened torso. A bright red sash circles his waist. His face is grotesquely made up with false eyelashes and blue eyeshadow and rouge. As he slowly descends, all the time working the puppet down the steps ahead of him, it becomes apparent that he has black strings attached to him. And behind him comes Mister Dancho, holding high the crossbar to which the strings from the Dwarf are attached, working Bazdéev down the steps as if he were a puppet too.

The audience bursts into applause. "Bravo, bravo, bravissimo," cries Valyo.

They are halfway down the long flight of stairs — the puppet of Mister Dancho, the Dwarf and Mister Dancho — when a figure leaps out of the darkness onto the landing on the ground floor. He is dressed in black and wears chalk white pancake make-up on his face. For a moment everyone assumes he is part of the Dwarf's act.

The trio on the stairs freezes.

"It's him again," the American girl whispers.

Tacho turns to the Flag Holder. "Now you will believe me. Do you recognize him?"

"I'm — I'm not sure."

The Mime's eyes demand silence. He pivots on his heel and bows deeply to the three figures on the stairs above him. The puppet of Dancho, and then the Dwarf, and then Dancho bow back. Then the Mime turns toward the audience and takes it in with a deep bow. Some of the people in the front row bow back. The Mime looks around angrily and bows again, insisting. This time everyone responds. As the Mime takes a single step forward and begins his performance, the only sound in the room comes from the projector throwing its pornographic pictures onto the screen.

With his hands the Mime creates pieces of cloth billowing out of the sky. Vehicles of some sort are climbing over mountains. Planes are landing at an airport. There is a sense of urgency and organization to what he is describing. The pieces of cloth, the vehicles, the men from the planes are converging now, have come together, have become like a wave in the ocean. Others watch its progress from the side with fright, with amazement, with a sense of betrayal, with a feeling that this is the end and the beginning of recorded history. Some of the younger ones in the path of the wave argue with it, pry up bricks from the pavement and throw them at it, put their bodies in its path. But they are swept away. Nothing can slow it. There is a great surge of people into the streets. There is shock, panic, dispair, a sense of having lost something. Two or three men have their wrists handcuffed behind their backs and are led away, far away. A small boy pasting posters on a wall crumples to the ground. The body is covered with a jacket and loaded into an ambulance. Someone places a bouquet of flowers on the spot where he fell. Flags come down and others are hauled up. Clocks stop. People weep. Night comes, but not calm.

The Mime assumes his impassive face, signaling the end of his performance, and bows.

And then he is gone.

The Dwarf's guests look at each other uncomfortably. The same thought occurs to everyone.

"What he is describing — " The Racer begins, and the Flag Holder finishes the sentence:

" — is happening now."

The puppet of Mister Dancho collapses with its head on its chest, and the Dwarf, black strings dangling from his hands and elbows and knees and head, climbs back up the stairs. He returns almost immediately with a large short-wave radio, which he places on the landing. People turn their backs on the pornographic film and huddle around the radio. The dial skids across a band of static and words and notes and comes to rest on a male voice speaking Russian with an American accent. Occasionally the voice fades, but it always comes back again.

". . . reports that occupation troops approaching the radio station are firing tracer bullets and live ammunition. They are a few dozen meters from the building now. A barricade has been erected facing Wenceslas Square. Several hundred people are trying to stop the advancing tanks with their bodies. The radio building has been hit by dozens of shots and is being buzzed by aircraft of the Antonov type. Czechoslovak Radio asks the people to try and engage the troops in conversation — it is our only weapon, they say. Now the broadcasts of Czechoslovak Radio are coming to an end. The national anthem is being played. A voice announces over the air that the staff is remaining in the studio and will continue broadcasting the news as long as possible. But the speaker warns: when you hear voices on the radio you are not familiar with, do not believe them!"

The overhead lights come on. Some of the guests are already leaving.

"Goddamn Bolsheviks," Mister Dancho exclaims disgustedly. "They're a bunch of gangsters."

"Let's get out of here," Poleon whispers, pulling his ex-wife toward the door.

"But my coat — "

"Forget your coat, damnit."

"For god's sake, turn that thing off," the Racer snaps. The pornographic movie is still playing. The Dwarf says something in Hungarian and the girl who was to have been his "bride" ducks behind the screen and pulls the plug out of the wall.

Octobrina sinks onto the landing. "I told you hope was a luxury," she says bitterly. She buries her face in her hands, sobbing softly.

"They are what the Romans called *lacrimae rerum*," Popov remarks. Almost shyly, he explains:

"That means, tears of events."

The dozen or so people left in the room gather around the Flag Holder.

"Oh, Lev," the Rabbit gasps, near to tears too.

"There is only one thing to do," Valyo declares. "The Czechs must defend their integrity like the pupil of one's eye."

"How could they do it?" the Racer wants to know. "How could they betray us like this?"

The Flag Holder's hands are shaking as he speaks. "Our condition — one of utter subservience to corrupt ideas — is a judgment on us. What we must understand from all this is: *We*, by our inactivity, are the invaders of the human spirit."

The Rabbit settles down next to Octobrina and takes her hand. "A group of students once asked Dubček, 'What are the guarantees that the old days will not be back?' And he told them, 'You are the guarantee. There is only one path' " — Elisabeta's voice breaks — " 'and that is forward.' "

Lev Mendeleyev looks into the faces of his friends. "He is more of a Flag Holder to his people than I am to mine." After a while, he adds:

"For us too there is only one path."

5

THEY SKIP the Milk Bar the next day and meet instead in the Jewish Centre on Patrice Lumumba. Taking care to straggle in casually and separately (their conspiratorial juices are already flowing) they file past the English language sign just inside the main door ("Welcome to the Juish Centre — donations in any currency are thankful"), past an original "Dreyfus is Innocent" poster (a gift from Dancho), past the black marble Star of David about the size of a spread-eagled man with the eternal flame in the middle that has a habit of going out at the height of memorial services. One flight up they make their way through the Memorial Museum, a collection of photographs and paintings and etchings and maps glued on to plywood panels stretched between floor-to-ceiling metal poles. The display, which looks at first glance like a labyrinth of scaffolding, is meticulously organized. You come in one door to be confronted by a four-color map that shows where in Europe the concentration camps were. (Like sprinkles on ice cream cones, they were everywhere.) You follow the red footprints painted on the floor (children often ignore the walls and leap playfully from footprint to footprint) and wind up, eighty-eight footprints later, facing a tall, narrow photograph of a chimney with smoke coming out of it. At which point, as the Flag Holder put it, "You know everything there is to know about concentration camps — and nothing."

As the Director of the Centre and the editor of Sofia's only Jewish newspaper (a monthly, with a circulation of 5000), Lev Mendeleyev had a hand in setting up the Memorial Museum. He also survived seven months in Auschwitz. So when he spoke about concentration camps (which was rarely), it was with a certain amount of authority. "We are the custodians of terror," he once told a group of American Jews who stopped off in Sofia on their way back from Israel, "terror lodged like a splinter in our memory; terror recollected in tranquillity; terror alphabetized, systematized, catalogued, sorted, arranged chronologically, indexed, numbered and codified. And not comprehended."

The visitors, who felt more at home with abstractions such as "six million" than the Flag Holder, left for Yugoslavia a day earlier than their schedule called for.

Now the members of the October Circle gather in the large, bare room behind the Memorial Museum that serves the Director as an office. The two Jewish volunteers who put in a few hours a week "rolling psychological bandages" (Octobrina's phrase) have been sent home for the day. Great flakes of paint are peeling away from the high ceiling. Three of the four windows in the room are wide open; the fourth, which is right above the ventilator for the only toilet in the building, has been nailed shut. Trolleys run back and forth beneath the window; the soft friction of their wheels cause the panes of glass to vibrate, as if from a distant earthquake. A small electric fan placed atop the bookcase with glass doors lifts loose papers with currents of warm air. The Flag Holder sits on a wooden desk chair, his jacket off, his tie loosened, his shirt sticking to his back, staring intently at the Cyrillic keyboard of his ancient Remington.

"I saw the Minister in front of the State Bank this morning," he remarks. He pauses to light another Rodopi, and pulls on the new one. "His bodyguard was holding open the door of his limousine, but he stopped to chat anyhow. He talked about the weather. He talked about the German tourists flocking to the Black Sea. He talked about your Sofia-Athens bicycle race, Tacho; apparently he's been assigned the chore of turning up at the frontier for the crossing ceremony. He mentioned the death of Alexander Denev, our former Flag Holder; he said he had just approved a pension for his widow. He asked about the Centre. He asked about my newspaper. He asked when I was taking a vacation and where. Not a word about Czechoslovakia."

"Maybe he hasn't heard about it yet," sneers Mister Dancho. That brings a grim laugh.

"What's more likely," Octobrina quips, "he hasn't worked out what the Party line is yet." She puffs mischievously on her cigarette holder.

"All political parties have the same line," the Racer reminds her. " 'You've never had it so good, and the best is yet to come.' "

"Suspect every Party line," declares the Flag Holder. And he adds almost reluctantly, in a voice that seems to come from the crusted lips of a man suddenly grown old:

"Watch out for vanguards that propose to make revolution on someone else's behalf."

Popov hasn't heard a word, but the rest of them lower their eyes to the floor and the Racer, talking to the floor, says the obvious:

"We were the vanguard that made revolution on someone else's behalf."

"We joined the Party when the joining of the Party *created* the Party," Octobrina appeals earnestly. "Surely that . . ." The thought trails off into silence, and the silence (broken only by a softly exhaled "Sssssssss" from Popov, so light and inaudible it seems to sail around the room on the current from the fan) puts them on new ground, and the newness of it makes them edgy. Dancho scrapes his chair around so that it faces the fan and opens his collar button to expose his neck to its breeze.

"It's all a crock of — " Dancho cuts himself off and turns sheepishly to Octobrina. "Dear lady, excuse my gutter language."

"But you didn't say anything," Octobrina assures him.

"He never says anything," Valyo remarks.

Dancho wrenches around. "What do you mean by that?"

"Calm down, friend," the Racer pleads. "He was only joking."

"I was only joking," echoes Valyo.

Dancho returns to the breeze.

Popov sits forward in his chair. "How about this one: 'Can I be only a witness to history?' " He peers out over his pince-nez, waiting to see if anyone can identify the quote.

"It sounds like Count Tolstoy," Octobrina says absently.

"Lenin, before he rode that sealed railroad car across Germany to join the revolutionaries," Valyo guesses.

"Our one only Georgi Dimitrov, when he being in trial for putting fire to that Nazi Reichstag," says the Dwarf. An automobile horn sounds and the dog, Dog, lifts his sightless eyes to listen.

"You're way off," Mister Dancho maintains. "It smells Western. Freud maybe. Or Nietzsche. Or Spinoza or Kant or Aquinas — someone like that."

"No, no," Popov announces happily. "It is the Frenchman Camus."

"I was closest," alleges Dancho.

"How did you decide that?" Valyo challenges.

Dancho looks as if he is about to jump down his throat again, then shrugs and lets it drop. To the Dwarf, he says:

"What about the Mime last night? Is he the one you knew from the circus — what's his name again?"

"Dreschko," the Flag Holder supplies.

"Is he this Dreschko?" Dancho inquires.

"Not thinking so," Angel shakes his head. "Fat Lady she says she remembering Dreschko very good, and the Mime from last night he too short for him. She says he being Mime who committed to be in insane asylum about eight, maybe ten years ago. Name of Drumev, she says."

"That's not what I heard," Octobrina breaks in. "Poleon's going around telling everyone the Mime is the crazy half brother of that general who defected a few years ago — "

"Bonev?" the Racer asks.

"That's the one: Bonev. Poleon says he went to school with Bonev and met the half brother once. The family kept him locked in the attic until the housing authority expropriated it. Then they sent him away to work on a collective farm in the South."

Tacho is shaking his head. "I'd bet my life on it — it's Dreschko."

"Fat Lady, she got a good memory," Angel argues. "For sure it's that crazy Drumev fellow."

"Poleon seemed quite certain," Octobrina offers, baffled.

The Racer stands up to unstick his trousers from the chair, and then sits down again. "You're sure the Rabbit knows to come here?"

"She knows," the Flag Holder says.

There are footfalls in the Memorial Museum next door; someone is following the eighty-eight red footprints. "Ah, at last," sighs Octobrina. The Rabbit hurries into the room.

"You won't believe how many militiamen there are in Sofia," she says breathlessly. "I swear there is one on every corner."

"But how is that possible," Dancho jokes grimly. "We haven't taken any decision yet."

"In a police state," the Dwarf says, "police know what you going do before you know what you going do."

"Poleon's just done a film entitled *Police State*," Dancho remembers. "The censors are dining on it now."

"Something about Poleon rubs me the wrong way," the Flag Holder confesses. To the Rabbit, he says:

"Tell us what you've heard."

The Rabbit settles into a chair and wipes the perspiration from her forehead. Octobrina pulls a delicate accordion fan from her pocketbook and hands it to Elisabeta. The Rabbit flips it open and begins fanning herself.

"There was fighting around the radio station last night," she reports, "but nothing that looks like organized resistance."

"Where is the Czech army?" the Racer asks.

"In their pubs probably," sneers Dancho.

The Rabbit shakes her head. "The army's been confined to barracks."

"On whose orders?" The Flag Holder leans forward. "The Russians?"

"Apparently the Czechs," replies the Rabbit. "Their military people issued orders saying that resistance would be futile. They claim there are half a million soldiers involved in the invasion, mostly Russian, but with units from the German Democratic Republic, Poland, Hungary and" — she flashes a look at Lev — "our paratroopers. The whole thing was planned down to the last detail. They took the airport at Prague first, and then started bringing in troop transports at the rate of one a minute for hours. The Soviet military attaché here is very pleased with himself. He was boasting that nobody ever credited the Russians with an air-lift capability. He said they surrounded most of the government and Party buildings before the Czechs knew they were even in the country."

"Bully for the bastards," Dancho groans. The Racer observes: "It doesn't look much like a spur-of-the-moment affair, does it? Which means that all the time they were talking to the Czechs — at Cierna nad Tisou, at Bratislava — they knew they were going in."

The Rabbit hands the fan back to Octobrina with a damp smile.

"Dubček's been taken to Moscow," she continues. "Nobody knows anything on him for sure, but our people assume he'll be tried for treason and shot as soon as things quiet down. Czech Radio says — "

"I thought Russians they occupied Radio — " the Dwarf interrupts.

"They did," Elisabeta explains, "but Dubček's people must have hidden transmitters around the country, because the reformers are still broadcasting bulletins. The Russians are flying in jamming equipment, but that will take a day or so to set up. Anyhow, Czech Radio has called a general strike for noon tomorrow. And they've warned everyone to remove all street and house number signs to make it more difficult for the Russians to find people they want to arrest."

The Flag Holder and the Racer exchanged looks. "So it is starting," Tacho comments.

Valyo asks whether the Russians have been able to field a collaborationist government.

"That's the strange part," the Rabbit says. "The Russians haven't formed one yet. It's apparently the only flaw in the operation. The Russians must have a collaborationist government to support their story about being invited in. I saw some mimeographed material this morning for distribution to regional Party leaders. It comes straight from the Soviet Embassy by the feel of it. The paper makes the case that Moscow has the moral right to intervene anywhere in the Socialist Commonwealth to prevent counterrevolution — "

"Counter — that's a laugh," snorts Dancho.

"And they claim that a counterrevolutionary situation existed in Czechoslovakia."

"But how can they say that?" cries Octobrina. "It wasn't at all like Hungary. There were no hostilities — "

"They've taken care of that small inconsistency," the Rabbit replies. "They've invented what they call a 'new phenomenon of history.' Are you ready for this? It's called 'peaceful counterrevolution!' "

"Peaceful counterrevolution!" echoes Mister Dancho, dumfounded.

"Peaceful counterrevolution," Elisabeta repeats. "That's going to be their ticket for this trip. The line hasn't been authorized for mass consumption yet, but it will probably be used as soon as the political situation in Prague is straightened out."

"My god," moans Valyo.

"Say what you want about them," Mister Dancho observes. "They're creative bastards."

The Dwarf shakes his head and mutters some dark phrases in Hungarian.

"It is just not possible for anyone to be that cynical," declares Octobrina.

"What about the Americans?" asks the Racer. "Is there any word on their reactions?"

Mister Dancho shakes his head in despair. "You still think the Americans will save the day, don't you?"

The Rabbit turns to Tacho:

"One of the men I work with says he heard from his brother-in-law, who is over at the Ministry of Defense, who got it from a Russian major general, who said he saw a limited distribution memo which said that the Americans had quietly let the Russians know that they would make appropriate noises but take no action in the event of a military move against Czechoslovakia."

Another trolley goes by and the window rattles slightly in its pane. "The central question," the Flag Holder asserts quietly, "is what are *we* going to do."

Valyo jumps up. "We must consider seriously the possibility of making some sort of protest."

"And end up in jail for our troubles," Octobrina cries in alarm. She flicks her cigarette ash nervously and it floats around in the breeze from the fan.

The Racer says:

"You forget we have our photographs — "

"Then it is agreed we must do something?" Valyo persists.

His feet dangling from the chair, the Dwarf smiles his mocking smile and nods slowly.

"But what will we do?" demands the Rabbit.

"There is no possibility of your taking part in this," the Flag Holder announces matter-of-factly. When Elisabeta starts to protest, he cuts her off sharply. "It is out of the question. You have no photograph to protect you. You are vulnerable. We are not."

Octobrina smiles at Elisabeta. "The very least they'll do is take away your job. And then we will lose our source of information."

"We will have to resort to the newspapers to find out what is happening," jokes Dancho.

Popov coughs nervously. "I could try to write a poem," he offers. "Something obscure enough to get past the censors. It is easier, you know, to get poetry past them than prose. In poetry, you can hide what you want to say between the words." He looks around shyly.

"That's very generous of you, Atanas, and very brave too," Octobrina says. "We all know what it would mean for you to write poetry again. But I think we had something more — " She looks around for help.

"Immediate," Dancho prompts.

"More immediate in mind," Octobrina continues.

"Something in the nature of a protest letter perhaps," Valyo suggests.

"But to whom sending it?" demands the Dwarf.

The Rabbit reminds them that the Russian dissidents always send their letters to the *New York Times*.

The Racer begins pacing back and forth in front of the open window. "They send their letters to *somebody*, with a *copy* to the *New York Times*," he notes.

"How about the Minister?" Valyo ventures. "We could send it to him. 'We, the undersigned' — that sort of thing." He glances around hopefully.

"I have it," Dancho interrupts excitedly. "What about boycotting the nine September parade. My god, what could be more appropriate: protest against the Soviet liberation of Czechoslovakia by boycotting the parade marking the twenty-fourth anniversary of the Soviet liberation of Bulgaria!"

"But that's almost three weeks from now," the Racer reminds him. "In three weeks everyone may have forgotten about Czechoslovakia."

"If we're going to send a letter," Octobrina insists, on a wavelength of her own, "we might as well go all the way and send it to the United Nations."

"Or Soviet Politburo," the Dwarf throws in. "Or Brezhnev."

"We should consider other possibilities," the Racer suggests from the window.

"Like for instance?" asks Dancho.

"I don't know, for god's sake. We could all refuse to pay our dues, or quit the Party altogether. That would shake them up."

The Flag Holder rests his hands on the keyboard of the Remington and stares for a moment at his fingertips. "Look, friends," he says, "we must begin by facing reality. And the reality that we must face first is that we have no access to the press or to the people. Even the articles in my little newspaper must have a Central Committee stamp on them before the Lamplighter will set them in type. No, friends, there is only one way that we can protest."

The Flag Holder bends his head and sucks another Rodopi into life. "We must give them theater."

6

WITH EACH STEP Popov's left shoe squeaks like an unoiled hinge.
(The squeak doesn't appear to bother him, which means he has
turned off his hearing aid.) Mister Dancho, gallant to a fault, carries
Octobrina's placard for her. (His lids droop; he has spent most of
the night with Katya, and he is very tired.) Octobrina holds a long-
stemmed rose with pale red petals. (She once wept at television
clips of young Americans thrusting roses into rifle barrels; it struck
her as a poetic gesture, and she had in mind to do the same thing if
it came to that.) The Flag Holder, walking with the Racer, flicks
the butt of a Rodopi onto the pavement. (He sees a "Littering is
Against the Law" sign, scoops up the butt and deposits it in his
trouser cuff.) Valyo (toying nervously with his tuning fork) and
the Dwarf (with his blind dog, Dog, farting loudly into the early
morning stillness) come last.

"If he was on roller skates," Valyo whispers disgustedly, "he'd
be self-propelled."

"When you into becoming his age, you farting all the goddamn
time too," the Dwarf replies evenly.

Valyo snickers loudly. "I'm already farting all the goddamn
time."

"Shhhhh," hisses Mister Dancho, glancing angrily over his
shoulder.

"How old is he anyway?" Valyo whispers, indicating Dog with
his placard.

"Hundred thirty-three dog years." The Dwarf urges the dog on
with his foot and mutters:

"All years are dog years."

"Shhhhhhhhh," Dancho hisses again.

Octobrina taps him on the shoulder with her rose. "Why are
you whispering?"

"I'm whispering," Dancho whispers, "because" — he leans

close to Octobrina's ear, as if he is about to let her in on a state secret — "because it has been my experience that women will believe anything you tell them *as long as you whisper!*"

"What a rat you are, Dancho!" cries Octobrina.

They are making their way along Stambolski, and have just passed the Deux Chevaux with the route traced on the driver's door. Octobrina feels more comfortable with Dancho talking, so she taps him on the shoulder again with her rose. "'What do you do about mosquitoes this time of year?"

"I kill them," Mister Dancho whispers.

When he doesn't say anything more, Octobrina offers:

"I try to kill them, but they always get away."

"The trick," whispers Dancho, "is to approach them in such a way so as not to throw a shadow across them. If they see a shadow, they jump."

"What about stockinged feet?"

"Stockinged feet help, of course," concedes Dancho. "I hold my breath too."

"What do you prefer in the way of a weapon?" Octobrina inquires.

"The Party theoretical journal. It's long, but not overly flexible when folded. The only drawback is it leaves ink smudges on the wall. But then you are obliged to wipe the blood off anyhow, so the ink smudges are not much of a problem."

"What's this about the Party theoretical journal?" Valyo whispers from behind them. "Did they print something about Czechoslovakia?"

"Dancho uses it to kill mosquitoes," Octobrina explains.

Somewhere along the way Popov has tuned into the conversation. "How can you talk about mosquitoes at a time like this?" he demands. He looks down at his left shoe with disgust. "Why didn't somebody tell me?"

They turn the corner of the National Archeological Museum. The cobblestones underfoot are spotlessly clean and bone dry; the water wagons have long since passed this way. Dimitrov's tomb, sooted white marble hulking in the grayness of the early morning, looms ahead.

"Whatever happens," the Flag Holder instructs them, "stay together. Remember, friends, we have Octobrina with us."

Their footfalls (and the squeaks from Popov's shoe) echoing on the cobblestones, they make their way into the center of the square and take up positions in a circle, facing outward. Dog farts and sinks onto the ground next to the Dwarf's legs.

"My god, but it's quiet," Dancho whispers after a while. His voice is huskier than usual. Valyo makes a soft, wheezing sound. Popov runs a finger under his starched collar; his shoe squeaks as he shifts his weight. The Flag Holder clears his throat. The Racer runs his tongue over his parched lips.

There is whispering from the soldiers riveted at attention on either side of the iron door leading into the tomb. A few minutes later there is a crablike scurrying in the park behind the tomb. Fifteen minutes later a door slams in the National Art Gallery, across the square. A walkie-talkie blares for an instant and then goes dead. A light comes on in the Central Committee building further on down Ruski Boulevard, and then another, and another. Then shades are drawn, blotting out the light. For a long time there is no sound at all. Then comes the clatter of hobnailed boots running in lock step across the cobblestones near the National Archeological Museum. Popov pivots in that direction; his shoe squeaks again. On the other side of the square, trucks come roaring up Ruski Boulevard and squeal to a stop in front of the People's Army Center. There is a scraping sound, as if furniture is being unloaded onto the street. It is growing lighter now, and there are more trucks, and more furniture being unloaded in front of the Central Committee Building, just out of view from the square.

"Look there," the Racer whispers. "There — near the side of the tomb."

"I don't make out anything," Octobrina says nervously.

"What time is it?" whispers Dancho.

"You don't have to whisper," snaps Valyo. "They know we're here."

"Roof," shouts the Dwarf, and he points with his placard. There are half a dozen men in army uniforms on the roof of the Central Committee building studying the small circle of people in the square through binoculars. "Make them into seeing slogans," cries the Dwarf. He curses in Hungarian at the men on the roof and thrusts his placard up in their direction. Octobrina takes a deep breath to control the pounding in her chest and holds hers aloft too with both hands. The slogans are printed on the back of blown-up photographs of themselves, and they spin the placards around so the eyes behind the binoculars can see both sides. ("Let's think of some catchy slogans," Dancho suggested when they were preparing the placards the previous afternoon. "Everyone arms himself with slogans and assaults the intelligence," the Racer complained. "Let us say instead what we feel, even if the sentences are not short and catchy." But the Flag Holder disagreed. "We only have time for slogans," he said, so slogans it was.)

The sun edges over the rooftops and into the eyes of the Dwarf and Octobrina.

"But where are the people who go to work at this hour?" cries Octobrina. She calms down, and gesturing toward the windows facing the square, says:

"I have a feeling they are eyes."

"This is the first demonstration in history to be observed by only two," quips Dancho, and he calls to the soldiers guarding the door of the tomb, a hundred or so paces away:

"Ho, comrades, and a good morning to the both of you."

The soldiers, staring into each other's eyes, never move a muscle.

"I'd hate to be in their shoes," observes Valyo.

"They must be exhausted," agrees Octobrina.

"That's not what Valyo means," the Racer says. "He means they'll probably be transferred to some outpost on the Greek border to keep them quiet."

The Flag Holder takes a few dozen steps in the direction of the Central Committee building and listens and walks back to his place in the circle. "They've sealed off the square," he announces. "They've closed the streets with barricades. They've quarantined us."

"How will people know about our demonstration then?" demands Octobrina. She lowers her placard heavily to the ground.

"That's just the point," the Racer remarks bitterly.

"They not owning balls for making arrestations," sneers the Dwarf. He shouts something obscene in Hungarian toward the Central Committee building.

"Listen," Dancho declares, "we can hold out here as long as they can. Let's not lose heart. They'll have to keep the square closed all day. People will begin to ask questions." He looks around for encouragement.

"Here, no one asks questions," the Racer says. He lowers his placard to the cobblestones too.

"We should have brought some water," moans Valyo. "My throat is dry."

The sun is high now, and hot. Octobrina looks faint and Valyo slips an arm under her elbow to support her. Dancho takes her placard.

They wait a while longer, but still no one comes to arrest them or to observe them. Even the men on top of the Central Committee building have disappeared. At midmorning, one of the two soldiers in front of the tomb faints — his rifle clatters to the pavement — but the second soldier makes no move to help him.

It is almost noon when the Flag Holder lowers his placard to the ground.

"What the hell," murmurs Dancho.

"Win some, lose some," shrugs Valyo.

The Flag Holder fumbles for a Rodopi, and Dancho produces a light from out of nowhere. The Flag Holder exhales, and the tension seems to drain out of his body with the smoke. "We must learn," he says, "to protest in a way that does not convey to them the impression they have forever to set things straight." He looks at Tacho, and then at the others. "Change comes only to those who are crazy for change."

7

OCTOBRINA CLAIMS it is his imagination, but Mister Dancho isn't convinced. It is nothing he can put his finger on, he admits, but . . .

"For instance," demands Octobrina, and Valyo agrees:

"Give us an example."

"For instance," Dancho says, and he raises his eyes and studies the ceiling and remembers that his portrait-painter friend, Punch, *turned away* when he, Dancho, sauntered into Krimm. That for starters. And the crowd at Punch's table seemed to avoid his eye. The television actor Rodzianko shook hands warmly enough, but he turned back to his companion, who happened to be a beautiful woman, without introducing her to Dancho.

"He's afraid of the competition," Octobrina concludes.

"Maybe," Mister Dancho says not very convincingly. "But what about Poleon?"

"What about Poleon?" Octobrina bites.

Even Poleon seemed — well, *strange*, Dancho says. He was half out of his seat, slopping champagne into tall-stemmed glasses as Dancho passed. "We're celebrating," Poleon cried. "They've promised me an *apartment* — one with a balcony up near Boyana. Not far from the Dwarf's. They'll be able to roll me downhill after his weddings."

"I'll miss the sex," Poleon's ex-wife giggled. Everyone at the table laughed at that — too loudly, it occurred to Dancho now as he goes over the scene. Poleon's ex-wife downed what was left of her champagne and thrust out her glass for a refill. "Oh, we've had good sex, Poleon and I, since the divorce" — she hiccupped — "we just don't get around to it all that often."

Poleon leaned toward Mister Dancho. "My morning censor says they're going to release my film too. Can you believe it?" He lowered his voice. "They need a favor from me, it's plain as the nose on your face. They haven't said what it is yet — probably want me to put someone's mistress into my next film." Poleon laughed wildly. "Well, I'll do it — I'll do anything to get that film released. Not to mention *an apartment!*"

"He sounds his usual self," Octobrina comments when she hears the story.

"You don't understand," Mister Dancho insists, trying to pass it off as a joke. *"He didn't offer me any champagne!"*

Mister Dancho perks up when the Racer arrives with the American girl. He lets his eyes drift over her bare midriff, which is brown and firm, and starts telling Rumanian jokes. Even the Flag Holder, who is in one of his deeper depressions, can't help laughing at one of them. Later Dancho runs through some of his repertoire of tricks. On an inspiration, he asks Valyo for his tie.

"Be careful with it," Valyo cautions him. "it's a Turnbull and Asser."

Mister Dancho takes out his pocket scissors and makes a great show of snipping the tie into three pieces. Valyo looks mildly worried. Dancho pulls the tie through his fingers and *voilà* — it is still in three pieces! Valyo is furious.

"Next time use your own tie," he grumbles. "You owe me forty leva fifty."

Valyo leaves soon after.

The Flag Holder asks whether a tie really costs forty leva fifty in England. When Mister Dancho explains that it can cost anywhere between fifty stodinki and fifty leva, Lev just shakes his head. "Forty leva for a tie!"

Popov hauls out his pocket ledger and turns up his hearing aid. "Let me see. Sssssssss. One earring made from fingernail clippings linked together with tiny gold rings. One glass paperweight, chipped, with a tarantula inside. Did you know there was a time when people believed that tarantism came from the bite of a tarantula? But then people will believe anything, won't they? Sssssssss. One wooden leg with a hinged knee; it looks like the leg from a life-sized puppet. One . . ."

Popov's voice trails on and on, and Mister Dancho no longer hears it. Carefully avoiding Octobrina's eye — he is sure she would give him a dark look for interrupting Popov — he slips quietly out of the inner sanctum. A few people in the main dining room nod, but nobody invites him for a nightcap. In the lobby, Dancho straightens his tie in the painting of the mirror out of force of habit. From behind the coatracks comes a muffled cackling, as if someone is laughing with a hand clamped over her mouth, but when he spins around the woman who checks coats in the winter has her head buried in a magazine.

At Club Balkan, Mister Dancho spots Katya in the hotel lobby; she looks right through him as if he doesn't exist. He is about to say something sarcastic when her husband, the Minister, puffing on a cigar and heavy with the importance of being just back from Moscow, takes her elbow and guides her up the stairs toward the club.

Mister Dancho hesitates. He doesn't want to give her the opportunity to look through him again. On an impulse, he turns and leaves.

The night is cool for August, the streets are empty and Dancho savors the walk home. He has a four-room apartment on the second floor of a building in what was Embassy Row before the war. Dancho bought it for two hundred thousand leva, about ten years before, from the widow of a prewar minister of agriculture. He is wondering what has happened to the widow as he unlocks the front door and absent-mindedly flicks on the hall lights.

A cold fright slices through to the bone.

The hall carpet has been rolled up. The drawers in the small hallway bureau have been pulled out and the contents have been spilled in a corner. The two antique light fixtures dangle from the wall by their electrical cords.

The living room is in the same condition. The drawers in the teak desk are stacked in a corner, their contents scattered on the floor. Feathers seep from slits in the sofa. The Persian carpet has been rolled up and some floor boards have been pried loose. Dozens of phonograph records have been pulled from their jackets and flung in another corner. His priceless pewter collection has been swept from the shelf onto the floor. The large painting Octobrina gave him for his forty-fifth birthday, two years before, has been cut from its frame and draped across the back of the sofa. The hi-fi speakers Dancho brought back from West Germany the year before have been dismantled. And the puppet of Mister Dancho, which the Dwarf gave him the night of the wedding, has been stripped down to bare wood and dismembered; amid all the disorder, it looks grotesque.

A middle-aged man with a hammer and sickle pin in the lapel of his sport jacket sits on the windowsill kicking his heels impatiently against the wall; Mister Dancho can see from the scuff marks that he has been there quite some time. A thin young man dressed in workman's overalls, and a woman wearing an apron over her housedress, stand stiffly on one side of the room with downcast eyes; Dancho takes them for the obligatory "civilian" witnesses required at every arrest. Another man, younger than the one on the windowsill, with a round baby face, leans casually against the door jamb next to a large framed photograph of Dancho as a young man taking a curtain call. An "X" has been drawn in red across Dancho's head.

Baby Face smiles and flicks his cigarette ash on the floor.

"That's an Aubusson you're standing on. Be a good fellow and use an ashtray."

Baby Face sucks again on his cigarette, then lets it fall to the floor where he grinds it into the rug with his heel. Two more men come into the room behind Dancho.

"You are Anton Antoňov Dancho," Baby Face declares. He says it as if there is something wrong, or funny, or obscene about the name.

Mister Dancho nods grimly. He has not been called by his first name and patronymic in twenty years, and they sound strange to his ears.

"You are to come with us," Baby Face instructs him crisply. He permits himself to smile slightly and tilts his head to watch Dancho's reaction. "It goes without saying, you are under arrest."

"It goes without saying," Mister Dancho repeats dryly. He forces himself to smile back at Baby Face. "Is it for this morning?" Dancho wonders if they are arresting the others too.

"We know nothing about this morning," Baby Face says. "But there are other irregularities for which you must answer."

He pokes with the toe of his shoe at a small pile on the floor. Mister Dancho can make out his ribbon of Czech flags, some Dubček posters, a thick wad of American dollar bills and another of British pounds.

Baby Face casually picks up a schoolchild's notebook and opens it at random. " 'The degeneration of the revolution in Russia calls into question not only the Stalinist phase, but also the Leninist model,' " he reads tonelessly. He looks up. "Who wrote that?"

"That notebook's ten years — me, I wrote that."

" 'The state lottery gives the people the one thing that the system has failed miserably to supply: something to look forward to the next day.' " Baby Face looks up. "Who wrote that?"

"I wrote that."

" 'Communism seeks the common good. But who is to decide what is the common good? The Communist Party? Its version of common goodness bears a strong resemblance to self-interest.' " Once again Baby Face raises his eyes. "Who wrote that?"

"I wrote — " Mister Dancho begins, but Baby Face is already reading the next item.

" 'Socialism and Capitalism have this in common: They have abandoned the pursuit of excellence.' Who wrote that?"

"I wrote — " Mister Dancho confesses loudly, but again Baby Face doesn't pause.

" 'Marxism no longer knows anything.' " Baby Face looks at Dancho.

"Sartre wrote that," Mister Dancho replies pleasantly. "Do you know who Sartre is? Perhaps you've come across the name in other material you've confiscated."

Baby Face smiles and steps toward Mister Dancho and slaps him hard across the face. Then he grabs his lapels and pulls him close and hisses:

"You must learn not to fool around with the wives of ministers."

Stunned, Mister Dancho backs away and looks at the witnesses, trying to catch their eye, but they both continue to stare at their shoes. The man on the windowsill starts throwing the things on the floor into one of Dancho's leather suitcases. Baby Face tosses in the notebook and the other man clicks the locks shut. One of the men behind Dancho steps in front of him with an open pair of handcuffs. Dancho looks at them as if he doesn't understand their function, then offers his wrists. The man snaps them on with a practiced motion.

"All right, let's go," Baby Face orders. He thrusts another cigarette between his lips and pats his pockets for his lighter. Mister Dancho produces a lighted match from thin air.

"How very elegant," sneers Baby Face. He bends toward the match.

Mister Dancho raises his manacled wrists, but his hands are shaking so much that the flame goes out.

8

THE TELEVISION ACTOR Rodzianko used some of his precious Max Factor (a gift from Mister Dancho!) for the occasion. But no photographers have turned up and he is annoyed now at having wasted it.

"Could you speak up, please," the Prosecutor commands.

"Sure, sure," Rodzianko replies quickly. He twists in the witness box toward the three judges. Directly behind them is a floor-to-ceiling portrait of Lenin arriving at the Finland Station. The geography of the courtroom is such that a witness is made to feel as if he is speaking directly to Comrade Lenin.

"Like I was saying, he stops by my table over at Krimm, see — "

"The 'he' in question being the defendant, Dancho," the Prosecutor interrupts. He points his finger at Mister Dancho, who is lounging, a guard on either side of him, in the defendant's box. Dancho is wearing a blue blazer and light gray slacks, and is adjusting his cuffs.

Without glancing at Dancho, Rodzianko nods. "Dancho, right." When he makes no move to continue, the Prosecutor prompts:

"You were up to where he stopped by your table at Krimm."

"So he stops by my table over at Krimm, right, and he leans close to me so no one will hear, see, and he gives me a tip on the Paris, France, stock market."

"That's a lie, of course," Mister Dancho points out coolly. The Lady Judge wags her finger at him, and he laughs and closes his mouth.

"And after he gave you the tip on the stock market?" the Prosecutor demands.

"After" — Rodzianko looks lost — "he says . . ."

Rodzianko's voice fades. The three judges lean forward to hear better, and the Prosecutor coos:

"Could I trouble you to talk more distinctly, Witness Rodzianko."

"Louder. Right." Rodzianko takes a deep breath. "After he gives me the tip on the Paris, France, stock market, he tells me he's going to cable his broker in the morning. Naturally, this surprises me, right, because I know what everyone knows, which is that speculating like this is strictly illegal. So I ask him how he can cable his broker without getting into trouble. And he says he is going to *cable him in code.*"

"Shame, shame," cries Octobrina from her bench in the back of the courtroom. The Racer, sitting next to her, whispers in her ear and she sinks back.

Dancho's Defense Attorney, a polite old man with thick-lensed spectacles, approaches Rodzianko and peers up into his face. "Have you known Mister Dancho a long time, Witness Rodzianko?"

Rodzianko plays to the audience. "Everyone in Bulgaria's known Mister Dancho a long time." Some in the court start to laugh, but the Lady Judge looks sharply in their direction, and they stop instantly.

"Have you known Mister Dancho to joke a lot; put people on — I believe that's what you call it these days. Have you known him to do that sort of thing?" the Defense Attorney inquires.

"Sure," Rodzianko concedes. "He's a very funny man."

The Defense Attorney tilts his head and in an almost apologetic tone puts another question. "Did it ever occur to you that his remark about sending a cable in code was a joke?"

Rodzianko hesitates. He looks at the judges, who stare back at him, and then at the Prosecutor, who is busy shuffling notes. The overhead fan that hangs from the ornate ceiling stirs the warm air in the courtroom. Sunlight splashes the sill. "No," Rodzianko murmurs. "It never occurred to me."

Mister Dancho snorts loudly and one of his guards puts a hand on his shoulder.

Punch, Dancho's portrait-painter friend who has switched to landscapes, takes the stand next. He closes his eyes and tells the judges that Mister Dancho tried to commission a portrait of the Czechoslovak revisionist Dubček. His eyes still shut, he goes on to describe how Dancho produced small Czechoslovak flags from the bosom of an actress.

"And what was the *tone* with which he produced these flags?" the Prosecutor asks.

"Mister Dancho is a magician," the Defense Attorney objects.

"He has been producing odd things from odd places for twenty years. How is it that one of his performances can be described as having a tone?"

The three judges whisper among themselves. Then the Lady Judge, who is also the chief judge, says:

"The witness is directed to respond to the question."

The portrait painter steals a look at Mister Dancho. Dancho smiles at him and nods. The portrait painter clamps his eyes shut again. "He produced the Czechoslovak flags in a way that indicated his support for the counterrevolution taking place in that country."

"Czechoslovakia is a Socialist ally," Mister Dancho calls. He can't keep from sneering. "How is it you can make a crime out of producing the flag of a Socialist ally?"

The next witness never takes his eyes off Mister Dancho from the moment he enters the courtroom. "Now it's my turn," he mutters as he limps past the box containing the accused.

"Who is it?" Octobrina whispers to the Racer.

"It's the Police Informer Dancho ridiculed in the Milk Bar. He was carrying a violin case then, remember?"

"State your name and occupation," the Prosecutor orders.

The witness identifies himself as a violinist with the Sofia Philharmonic.

"Were you in the Milk Bar on Rakovski Boulevard on or about — " The Prosecutor names a day and an hour.

"I most certainly was."

"Can you tell the court why?"

"Yes, yes, of course I can tell you why. I was asked to drop by on my way home by my block captain. Apparently there has been a good deal of illegal gambling going on there, and the block captain asked me, as a loyal Party member, if I could — "

"Did you encounter the accused during the course of your visit there?"

"I most certainly did. I have done reporting for the Party on a number of occasions. Apparently that . . . that . . . that *magician* knew about my contribution." The witness leaps to his feet. "He held me up to public ridicule. He made me the butt of his humor. He incited them against me — "

"That will be all — "

"He ridiculed me for my loyalty to the Party — "

"Thank you," the Lady Judge says. "You can step down — "

"He s-s-s-s-tarted to l-l-l-l-laugh — "

The old waiter Stuka shuffles toward the witness box after the Police Informer has been helped from the courtroom. He starts to say something to Dancho as he passes.

"It's all right, old man," Mister Dancho tells him gently. "I understand."

"The accused will refrain from speaking to the witness," the Lady Judge warns.

"How long have you been a waiter in the restaurant Krimm?" the Prosecutor begins.

Stuka glances at Mister Dancho. "Twenty-seven years, sir."

"You know the accused Dancho?" Again the Prosecutor points theatrically toward the defendant.

"Mister Dancho is a great man," Stuka insists.

"No doubt. No doubt. Now, on a great number of occasions, Mister Dancho has made you the object of one of his — how shall we call them — *tricks*. Can you describe that for us?"

Stuka clenches his lips shut.

"Perhaps he hasn't heard the question," the Lady Judge coaxes.

The Prosecutor moves closer to Stuka. "I asked you to describe for us the so-called tricks that Mister Dancho was always pulling on you."

Still nothing from Stuka. Finally Dancho tells him quietly: "Go ahead and tell them, old man. It's all right."

Stuka looks at Mister Dancho, who nods encouragingly again. "Mister Dancho would put his hand in one of my jacket pockets and pull out money . . ." Stuka's voice trails off.

"Pull out a thick wad of bills — is that not correct?"

" — pull out a thick wad of bills, yes."

"And he would pretend he discovered the money in your pocket?"

"And he would pretend he discovered the money in my pocket, yes, that it was my tip money."

"What kind of bills were they?"

Again Stuka peers at Dancho. Again Dancho nods. "United States of America money. Great Britain money. There were others I didn't recognize."

"But they weren't our own Bulgarian leva?"

"No, sir."

The Lady Judge has a question. "Were you aware, when the accused pulled these bills out of your pocket, that possession of foreign currency is a violation of Article Twenty-eight, subletter B of the Revised Penal Code?"

"Article Twenty-eight . . ." Stuka looks around in confusion.

"Were you aware that possession of foreign currency is against the law?" the Prosecutor explains patiently.

"If you say so," Stuka replies.

"That will be all," the Prosecutor says. When Stuka makes no move to leave, he repeats:

"You can go now."

The three judges order a midmorning recess. When the trial resumes, the clerk calls the name of the next witness. "Maya Drakanova." Mister Dancho looks blank; he can't place the name. A tall girl with her hair tied up in pigtails, and wearing clothes that emphasize her youthfulness, makes her way to the witness box.

"Who is she?" Octobrina whispers to the Racer.

"I never saw her before in my life," he replies. He looks pointedly at Dancho, but Dancho only shrugs.

"You are Maya Drakanova?" the Prosecutor asks.

The girl nods shyly.

"What is your age?"

She answers in a low voice, barely glancing up at the Prosecutor. "Sixteen come next month, your honor."

"Do you know the accused, Mister Dancho?"

The girl turns angrily toward Dancho. "I'll say I know him. He's the one what made indecent advances at me."

There is a murmur from the audience. The Lady Judge lets it go on for a few seconds, then gavels for silence.

"It was this way," the girl explains without being prompted. "Me and my girl friends was hanging around the lobby of the Balkan like we sometimes do to get autographs, which is our hobby — autographs, I mean — and Mister Dancho here, he walks in. I seen him on TV, and right off I asked him for his autograph."

Mister Dancho remembers her now and rolls his eyes skyward.

"And did he give it to you, this autograph?"

"I'll say he did! He *unbuttoned* my shirt down to here" — the murmur from the audience rises to a growl — "and wrote his name on my chest with his *pen*."

"Pervert," someone in the courtroom calls.

"I never been so humiliated in my whole entire *life* as when he done this thing to me." Maya has her claws out now, and the illusion that she is an innocent child is rapidly vanishing. "I mean, I jus' hope — "

"You can step down," the Prosecutor interrupts, but she plunges on:

" — you do something to him so he learns real good he can't go 'round *humiliating* innocent people like they was *animals* or something. I mean, who the *hell*" — her voice turns shrill — "*who the hell does he think he is anyhow?*"

"She appears to be aging at the rate of a month a word," Mister Dancho observes dryly.

"Next witness," the Prosecutor calls, and the clerk reads out the name of the film director Poleon.

"Poleon!" The Racer starts out of his seat. "That spineless son of a bitch."

For the first time in the trial, Mister Dancho's eyes harden. His mouth twists into a grim smile. His knuckles whiten on the handrail around the prisoner's box.

Looking neither right nor left, Poleon makes his way to the witness box. He is all business.

"You are" — the Prosecutor calls Poleon by his real name.

"Yes, yes. My friends call me Poleon."

"If you still have any left after today," Mister Dancho jeers. The Lady Judge gavels for silence.

"The witness was present at a party at the home of the circus performer Angel Bazdéev on the night that allied soldiers responded to the request for assistance in Czechoslovakia?"

Poleon nods once. Without waiting for the Prosecutor to prompt him, he plunges right into his testimony. "Early in the evening in question, I heard the accused Dancho recount a slanderous anti-Soviet joke. The joke went like this. The streets around our Central Committee building are blocked off in preparation for a visit by a delegation from the Soviet Politburo. Somehow a Bulgarian citizen manages to maneuver his bicycle past the barriers. As he leans his bike against the Central Committee building, a soldier tells him: 'You can't do that — a high Soviet delegation is due any minute.' The Bulgarian replies: 'That's all right, I'll chain it up.' "

Nobody in the courtroom smiles — except Mister Dancho, who bursts out:

"You can't even tell it well, you bastard."

"One more such outburst," the Lady Judge admonishes Dancho, "and you will be removed from this courtroom."

"That same evening," Poleon continues, "Mister Dancho reached into the breast pocket of my dinner jacket and pulled out a photograph of the Czechoslovak revisionist Dubček."

"Is this the photograph in question?" the Prosecutor demands, picking up a small poster from the table piled high with notebooks taken from Dancho's apartment.

"Yes it is," Poleon agrees. "He pulled it from my pocket and waved it around, and it was clear, to me at least, from the way he gloated over the picture that he supported the counterrevolutionary activities of this Dubček fellow. Shortly afterward, when word of the allied intervention in Czechoslovakia spread, I heard Mister Dancho slander the Soviet leadership."

"Do you recall his exact words?" growls the Lady Judge.

"As it happens, I do. He said they were a 'bunch of gangsters.' "

There are gasps from the spectators, almost all of whom have been selected for their loyalty to the Party.

The Prosecutor turns toward the audience and throws the next question over his shoulder:

"He called the Soviet leadership a group of gangsters?"

"A *bunch* of gangsters," Poleon corrects him.

"Group, bunch, what's the difference. He called them gangsters," the Prosecutor insists.

"Gangsters, that's correct," Poleon says.

As Poleon passes the defendant's box on his way from the courtroom, he looks at Dancho. "Please understand, there was nothing personal," he says under his breath.

"Go hide in your new apartment," Mister Dancho sneers, and he looks away in disgust.

Dancho's attorney puts the defense's case succinctly. He argues that the charges against Mister Dancho — producing rolls of foreign currency or Czech flags or Dubček posters — are the result of a misunderstanding. Oh, the defense is willing to concede that the "tricks" — for that is what these are, just the stock in trade of an entertainer — were in poor taste. But should a man be punished for his poor taste? Especially a man like Mister Dancho, who fought heroically in the Resistance, who has since contributed a great deal toward the building of Socialism, who has in fact been one of Bulgaria's leading ambassadors for almost a decade. Should not these inconsequential "missteps" be put on the scale and weighed against the positive aspects of his life? One can see, Dancho's attorney sums up, that the Prosecutor is only doing his duty in pressing charges against Mister Dancho. Vigilance, after all, is everyone's business; witness the recent events in one of the neighboring Socialist states which shall remain nameless. But hasn't the court already achieved its purpose by drawing attention to these "missteps"?

"I thank you." The attorney bows and backs toward his seat.

The judges are out for forty minutes. When they file back into the room, Mister Dancho is instructed to rise and face the bench. The Lady Judge stands and reads tonelessly from a piece of paper:

"In consequence of the evidence presented this day, we the judges find you not guilty of corrupting the morals of a minor. We find you guilty of slander of a Socialist ally, which is to say, anti-Soviet agitation: slander of government policy, which is to say, counterrevolutionary activity: violation of currency regulations, which is to say, criminal activity. We hereby declare you to be a Socially Dangerous Element, and sentence you to a term of five years in prison at hard labor."

"*A fiver!*" cries Mister Dancho. The blood drains from his face, and his knees buckle beneath him. The guards, experienced in such matters, catch him under his armpits, one on each side, and hold him up.

Octobrina leaps to her feet as he is being led from the courtroom. "*Zaklyuchenny,*" she cries — for some reason it is the Russian word for prisoner, not the Bulgarian, that springs to her lips. Mister Dancho winces, and reaches toward her with his empty hand. With a twist of the wrist, he produces out of thin air a small brown paper flower. Inclining his head gallantly, arranging his facial expression into what in happier times passed for a smile, he flicks it into her outstretched hands.

9

It is a measure of their mood that Popov never once turns down his hearing aid.

"If trouble comes," he asks, squinting through his pince-nez and running two fingers under his starched collar, "can the Minister be far behind? Sssssssss."

They are seated around the table at Krimm, taking bets on when the Minister will show up. Octobrina thinks he will be discreet: he'll wait a day or two, she predicts, and then make small talk for half an hour before he comes to the point. The Dwarf is sure he'll send a deputy to do his dirty work. But the Flag Holder, who knew the Minister long before he ever dreamed of becoming a minister, agrees with Popov: he will turn up in person that night, he says, and he will come straight to the point. The point being Mister Dancho.

In the event, the Flag Holder knows his man.

"About Dancho," the Minister begins as he settles into the first vacant seat he comes to; it is, of course, Mister Dancho's.

"How is he getting on," the Racer inquires, "in that hotel of yours?"

"He is in high spirits," the Minister reports. "They tell me he's fabricating paper flowers out of toilet paper to toss at people — as he did to you, dear Octobrina. His jailers, who are nothing if not conventional, want to put a stop to it. Their handbooks warn that flowers in whatever shape or form are subversive. But I instructed them to let Dancho have his fun. Was there a message in Dancho's flower? I ask you, you have my solemn word on it, out of nothing more than curiosity."

Octobrina remembers the Minister's curiosity from the war; his soft-skinned peasant boot kicking *curiously* at the corpses of some German officers who preferred suicide to capture by the Communist partisans. "As a matter of fact, there was a message," she acknowledges. Her usually musical voice is almost metallic. She plucks Dancho's toilet paper flower from her handbag and twirls it in her long, wrinkled fingers. Then she peels back a single petal and reads:

" 'A Communist is someone who, when he smells roses, looks around for the coffin.' "

She looks up and smiles sweetly. "By that standard, even you could pass for a Communist."

"When I smell flowers," the Minister retorts evenly, "I sneeze. I have hay fever."

"Workingmen of the world unite," snaps Octobrina, "you have nothing to lose but your allergies."

Stuka approaches with a menu, but the Minister ignores him and he backs out of the room. The Minister looks around the table. They are all, in a sense, old friends. In the famous photograph, in which he can be seen marching alongside the Flag Holder, the Minister's eyes are darting off to one side, proud and flashing; now they appear dull and steady, the eyes (according to Octobrina, who specializes in eyes) of a professional poker player.

"About Dancho," the Minister says agan. This time nobody interrupts. "I put it to you frankly: what are we to do with him? He's been terribly naughty, but I'm ready to concede that the judges were a bit eager on this one. Five years" — the Minister runs the tip of his forefinger over his lips, which are chapped — "five years is a long time to put Dancho on ice, wouldn't you agree?"

When nobody says anything — there is almost a conspiracy to manufacture strained silences — the Minister leans forward and runs his fingers over his lips again. In another context, it could be a sensuous gesture. "Come now, let's not beat about the bush. Dancho's appeal sits on my desk even as we speak here. No matter what you think of me, I *am* a Communist, and being a Communist implies a certain — how to phrase it — *solicitude* for mankind — "

"People who have difficulty relating on a one-to-one basis usually compensate for this by exhibiting a solicitude for mankind," Octobrina lectures him.

The Minister reddens at the neck. "The trouble is," he tells them, "your idea of Communism is not my idea of Communism."

"Your idea of Communism, Comrade Minister, is not Communism," the Flag Holder retorts, looking him in the eye.

The Minister is not accustomed to being baited. He leans forward, flushed now, and speaks sharply:

"And what is it, in your opinion, about my idea of Communism that is not Communistic?"

The Flag Holder smiles thinly. "There does not exist, within your scheme of things, the clash of ideas necessary for practice to make perfect."

"If you're speaking about the bourgeois notion of a clash of ideas — "

"I'm speaking about the Marxist notion of thesis versus antithesis — "

"But my dear Lev, surely we must have done something right. We are, after all, members of that small group" — he gestures vaguely to the photograph above the Flag Holder's head — "who have succeeded in making a revolution."

"Taking power, or for that matter staying in power, does not make a revolution *successful*," the Flag Holder says.

"What does, then?"

"To call a revolution successful, it must make some lasting contribution to human dignity." And he adds:

"This was something you knew before you became a minister."

The Minister has a sense that the exchange has gone as far as it ought to, so he cuts off the conversation with a wave of his hand.

"About Dancho," he begins a third time. "Let me be unmistakably clear about it; his arrest and trial were intended as a warning to all of you in this room. I tell you as a friend, there were some who felt that your escapade of the other morning demanded a bolder response. The Soviet Ambassador, who is normally the soul of mildness, was beside himself when he heard of the affair. But there were others, myself among them, who argued that a bolder response was precisely what you were looking for, indeed, what you had calculated on. And so it was decided not to play into your hands, to warn you instead with a rap on the knuckles — "

"You dare to call a five-year prison sentence a rap on the knuckles!" Octobrina explodes.

"My dear Octobrina, when you consider the rumors that have reached my ears" — the Minister pauses for effect — "you must surely take Dancho's arrest as a rap on the knuckles." He massages his lips thoughtfully. "No, no, no, someone has to tell you. You have made the error of thinking that this unfortunate business in Czechoslovakia is an area in which you can play your usual games with us. I am here to correct this misconception."

The Minister appears to be growing bored with the conversation. "If you were going to make waves, you should have done so years ago when we collectivized agriculture, or when we expropriated the private sector."

"Those were things we agreed with," Tacho says coldly. "You forget, Comrade Minister, that we are not dissidents — we are Communists."

The Minister looks at Tacho, amused. To everyone, he says: "I require your word that you will not repeat the escapade of the other morning. Give it to me and Dancho will be free to return to his silly tricks and his silly women and his silly friends. But be clear about it: *No more manifestations.*"

Tapping his foot impatiently, the Minister turns to the Flag Holder. The others look toward him too. The Flag Holder sucks on the butt of a Rodopi for what seems like an eternity. Then he nods to himself as if he has just explained something to himself, and looks up. He is about to speak when the Rabbit pushes through the curtain into the room.

"Oh, Lev," she cries. She takes a deep breath — she has obviously been running. "Georgi's back."

10

THE DWARF'S taxi driver, a fat man known only by his last name, Kovel, has had a difficult day. He spent the morning tracking down a tourist who was rumored to have a supply of German sparkplugs. En route he double-parked near the flower market for the time it takes to run into a *tabac* for a package of Rodopies, and returned to find a dent in the right rear fender of his two-year-old Fiat.

"It was a lady XX what done it," a vendor shouted — an "XX" on the license plate indicated that the car was owned by a foreigner.

"Which XX, for god's sake?" Kovel demanded, but the Vendor merely shrugged and muttered:

"I didn't see nothing."

When Kovel finally found him, the tourist had a box of *East* German plugs, hardly worth a trip around the corner, much less across town. In disgust, Kovel went back to his apartment, only to have his wife dispatch him across town again to the hard currency store; she had heard on the grapevine that it had just received a shipment of electric hair curlers from Italy and she wanted to give a set to their daughter for her birthday. (Kovel bought two sets and sold the second, at a profit, to the wife of the man who shared the kitchen of their apartment.)

After lunch Kovel moonlighted around the tourist hotels for a while before checking in with the Dwarf, who instructed him to put one of the Hungarians on the Budapest train. Kovel's wife went with him hoping to find some peasants at the station with fruits and vegetables fresh from the countryside. All the way to the station she kept peering over her shoulder at the Hungarian girl, who was tall for her age, in the back seat.

"She's the same age as our Ekaterina," the wife whispered to Kovel. "God knows what goes on up there."

"Everyone knows what goes on up there," Kovel responded.

"And you don't have to whisper — none of them speaks a word of Bulgarian."

Kovel glanced at the girl in his wide-angle rearview mirror (French manufacture: a gift from Mister Dancho). The Hungarian girl was huddled in a corner of the seat, clutching a synthetic leopard-skin coat and an embroidered cloth carryall with a bread and sausage jutting out of it. Obviously on the verge of tears, she reached down to scratch her behind, then absently lifted her thin fingers to her nose. At the station, the girl became hysterical. A crowd gathered and a militiaman pushed through to see what was happening.

"What's this?" the militiaman challenged officiously.

"My niece," Kovel explained, talking quickly and shepherding the girl and her belongings toward the waiting train. "She's crying because she's sad to leave us, that's all."

In the late afternoon, just when he was supposed to take the Dwarf into the city, Kovel discovered that the Fiat had a flat tire. When he turned up at the Dwarf's house on Vitoša twenty minutes late, Bazdéev was furious.

"Plenty goddamn taxi drivers around if you not wanting job," he warned. But he calmed down quickly and passed Kovel a packet of hashish which he wanted him to deliver to an actor who lived on the outskirts of Sofia, along the highway that ran toward Plovdiv and the Turkish border. Kovel ate at his brother-in-law's on the way back into the city, then parked, as usual, in front of Krimm to wait for the Dwarf.

He is slumped in the front seat, sound asleep, when the Dwarf, the Racer, the Flag Holder and his lady friend, Elisabeta, come out of the restaurant on the run.

"Driving fast, Kovel. Army hospital in — " The Dwarf names a village about twenty kilometers outside of Sofia.

They drive for a long while in silence, with Kovel flinging his passengers from side to side as he corners without braking. On Ruski Boulevard, workers are already erecting wooden bleachers on either side of Dimitrov's tomb for the pass-in-review the following day, September 9, marking the twenty-fourth anniversary of the liberation of Bulgaria by the Red Army. A militiaman directing traffic motions Kovel to give way to a truck carrying wreaths for the tomb. The Dwarf, sitting next to Kovel, taps him sharply on the shoulder and he accelerates instead. Through his rearview mirror he sees the militiaman peer angrily at his license plate as he reaches for his notebook. The Flag Holder is in the rearview mirror too, puffing on a Rodopi, staring out the window lost in thought.

Suddenly the Flag Holder turns to the girl. "How did you find out about it?"

"Someone telephoned me in the Ministry on an interoffice line," she recounts. "He didn't give his name, and I didn't recognize his voice. He said he knew you and honored you. He said he thought you should know that your son was back, was in the Army Hospital. Then he clicked off."

They are off the cobblestones now and on to the smooth paved surface of the suburban roads. Small clusters of wooden shacks, each one with two or three chickens pecking around the front door, fly past the window. Then a factory with a giant hammer and sickle over the arched entranceway.

"How bad is he?" the Flag Holder asks.

"Is someone sick?" Kovel whispers to the Dwarf.

"Just you driving," Bazdéev shoots back.

"I don't know," Elisabeta tells the Flag Holder. "I called the hospital to make sure he was there. The girl who answered said they only give information to relatives. I told her I was his sister. She let the phone dangle for a few minutes — I could hear it tapping against the wall — and came back and said he has no sister. That's how I know he's there. I mean, they wouldn't have the dossier of someone who isn't there, would they?"

They turn into a narrow lane lined with trees, the trunks of which have been whitewashed, and suddenly they are in front of the hospital, a gray building full of angular shadows.

The nurse on duty in the lobby looks up from her magazine suspiciously when they troop through the door.

"I have come to see Georgi Dimitrovich Mendeleyev," the Flag Holder announces. "I am his father."

He tells the same thing, in he same tone, to the night intern, and then again to the army doctor with the cropped mustache who identifies himself as the duty officer.

"How is it you know he is here?" the doctor inquires.

The Flag Holder snaps his head from side to side, shaking off the question the way a dog shakes off water. "The boy — where is he?"

The doctor hesitates, looks at the telephone on the desk, then back at the Flag Holder. Then he jerks his head in a "follow me" gesture and starts briskly down the corridor. The footfalls from the group follow him through the dimly lit hallway. The doctor stops with his back against the door marked "Unit 9."

"You should know what it is that is wrong with him," he tells the Flag Holder softly.

The Flag Holder nods imperceptibly.

"The boy will recover, but you should know that he has been — "
The doctor hesitates. Then, in a barely audible voice he finishes the sentence:

"He has been mutilated."

Elisabeta turns away and covers her face with her hands. After a moment the Flag Holder asks:

"How mutilated? Mutilated how?"

The Racer starts to say something, but the Flag Holder repeats the question. His voice is flat, deliberate.

"Mutilated how?"

The army doctor glances at the Rabbit. "Perhaps it would be better if she — "

"Mutilated how?"

The doctor shrugs and tells him, in cold clinical terms, what has been done to the boy Georgi.

"Oh my god my god my god my god," the Racer whispers hoarsely. He puts his hand and head against the wall to steady himself.

The Flag Holder shuts his eyes and fills his lungs with air and lets it out again slowly, unevenly. When he has controlled himself, he pushes past the doctor into the room. The Racer and the doctor follow him. The Dwarf and Elisabeta stay behind in the corridor.

The Flag Holder calls his son's name.

"Georgi."

The boy, propped up in bed, turns his head in the direction of the voice.

"How is it with you, Papa?"

The Flag Holder touches the boy on the part of the arm not covered in bandages.

"How is it with you?"

"I'm fine, really," the boy assures him. The bandages over his face muffle his voice, which sounds extraordinarily nasal. "Oh, I'm missing bits and pieces, so they tell me. But it's nothing compared to what they did to the others — "

The boy's voice breaks. He strains forward. "The little cunts," he cries. His words have a liquid sound, as if they are rising like bubbles in a pond and popping wetly when they reach the surface. He collapses back into his pillow, sobbing softly. After a while mucus seeps onto the starched pillow case from between the folds of the bandage covering his nose.

11

THE GIRL'S HAND darts to the Racer's arm in alarm.

"There — do you hear it?" she whispers.

The Racer stops talking and listens.

"Hear what?"

"There — *there*. Can't you hear it?"

They are sitting at the kitchen table in the Dwarf's house on Vitoša, snacking on lukewarm coffee and stale pastry. The girl squeezes his arm again and Tacho hears it this time: a faint but utterly unmistakable sucking in of air. The room, the house, the hillside *seem to be breathing*.

"Oh, go look" the girl pleads, her eyes full of fear.

Tacho scrambles to his feet and disappears into the house. Soon the breathing stops. He returns a moment later.

"Kovel fell asleep on the couch. Some of Angel's Hungarians taped his breathing. They were playing it back over the hi-fi speakers."

"I thought the house was breathing." The girl shudders. "It gave me the creeps," she says in English, and then she smiles nervously and translates it into Russian as best she can. "It frightened me."

"Georgi's breathing sounded strange too," Tacho remembers. "It came in great gasps through the gauze that covered his mouth. With each breath, the gauze was sucked in and out like a diaphragm. I thought I would faint from the smell — "

"You were up to where they — "

"Where they flew him into the Ukraine, yes. Georgi said they thought it was a training exercise until the Russians issued live ammunition. He said a Soviet colonel mustered them at dawn and read them a letter from some Czech workers requesting military assistance against the counterrevolutionary forces loose in their country. That's how it began." The Racer sips his coffee. "He had a wild night crossing the Carpathians on those Russian trucks . . ."

The Racer talks on quietly, listening all the while to the echo of Georgi's voice in his brain — muffled by bandages, at times hysterical, at times serene.

". . . we had a wild night crossing the Carpathians on those Russian trucks. The loose canvas cracked like a whip against the sides. The night was cool, cold even — when we stopped to pee, vapor rose from the piss. God, but it was a great long wild ride. The villages we went through were shuttered and dark and dead, except for one where there was a man with an official ribbon diagonally across his chest, and a woman and two children, standing at an intersection waving small Russian flags. They must have thought we were Russians, you see. We waved back and went on, stopping only to pee and, once, to eat, and every now and again to cut telephone wires.

"The first roadblocks were outside Banská Bystrica. Someone had pulled a wagon full of logs across the road and broken the wooden wheels with an ax so that the cart sank onto its axles. We found Russians and Polish soldiers in Banská Bystrica when we got there, guarding the Party building and the post office, and there were some tanks parked in a hayfield outside of town. I remember seeing this farmer cutting the hay between the parked tanks.

"We lost Sasha just outside Banská Bystrica. Shots rang out. The trucks screeched to a stop. We all jumped out and took cover in a drainage ditch along the side of the road. There was some yelling and more shooting up front. When we moved on, they were carrying Sasha back into town on a litter. His hand had fallen over the side of the litter and swayed as they carried him. There were also two dead Czechs, sprawled in pools of thick red ooze. Why did they do it, Papa? Why did they invite us in and then shoot at us?

"You wouldn't have recognized Bratislava. I was there a year ago when I went camping with . . . whom did I go camping with, Papa? I sent you a picture postcard, remember, of the cow wearing a man's hat. The Russians had taken over the city by the time we got there. They frisked the Czechs before they let them into public buildings. There was one young soldier who would blush like crazy when he frisked the women. Their jeeps were whizzing around the city, always with two soldiers in front and two civilians in back. The sides of the jeeps, and the sides of the tanks parked in the lot across from the railroad station, were plastered with spattered eggs and tomatoes, and slogans in whitewash. The slogans said things like: 'Ivan Ivanovich, go home.' I don't understand why they invited us in. I don't understand it.

"Our boys camped in a soccer stadium on the edge of the city. We kept the stadium lights on at night and patrolled the entrances. It was hard to fall alseep with the lights in our eyes like that, but after a few nights we got used to it. We shaved in the public toilets under the bleachers. The old woman who cleaned up after us asked us in Russian why we had come. She thought we were Russians too. Everyone thought we were Russians. We told her we had been invited in. She asked who had invited us in, but I couldn't remember the names on the letter the colonel read us.

"There was a workers' canteen nearby and we got permission to go there, as long as we went in a group and kept our weapons with us. We drank Czech beer at one end of the bar. The workers who were there looked the other way. A young boy, he couldn't have been more than fourteen or fifteen, came over to us and asked us in Russian, 'What right do you have here, in our country, in our canteen?' One among us started to tell him about the invitation, but he interrupted. 'We, the Czechs, don't want you Russians here. Go now.' Our boys told him we weren't Russian but Bulgarian, but he didn't seem to understand. His legs were shaking as he walked away.

"We took to going to the canteen every evening for beer, but the Czechs never spoke to us. Not once did they speak to us. Then one night we found three girls there. They weren't like the others; they were laughing and seemed interested in us. We talked to them for a while, and bought them beers, which they drank. One of them whispered they would meet us in the woods across the stream from the soccer stadium. Vasily said it was foolish to go, but we went anyhow — Dimitri, Vasily and me. We shaved carefully and showered and snuck past the sentry, who winked and turned the other way, and made our way to the woods, never thinking, never believing the girls would show up.

"They were there all right, along with twenty boys. We tried to run. Vasily almost got across the stream, calling all the while for help, screaming for help. They stripped us naked in front of the girls, who were laughing still, but it was a nervous kind of laughter. I thought that would be the end of it. But then they tied us to trees and pulled out razor blades and started in on Vasily. Some of the Czechs turned away, and one of the girls vomited. I must have fainted, but they got water from the stream and threw some on me and started in on me. I tried to tell them I wasn't Russian, Papa, but I had to tell them I wasn't in Russian because they didn't speak Bulgarian, so they didn't believe me. Vasily's dead, you know — in the hospital, he saw himself in a mirror and slashed his wrists. I don't know what happened to Dimitri. Do you know what happened to Dimitri?"

". . .he asked us whether we knew what had happened to his friend Dimitri," the Racer remembers. "Lev told him no, he didn't know. All the time he was talking, the boy Georgi was holding on to Lev's hand, gripping it, clinging to it as if he were drowning and it would keep him afloat."

There is a peel of girlish laughter from somewhere upstairs, then a barked command from Bazdéev, then a door slams and a radio comes on.

"How did the Flag Holder react to all this?" the girl asks the Racer.

"That's the point," the Racer replies. "He didn't. He listened carefully, the way he listens carefully to everybody, but he didn't react. Georgi must have sensed this — maybe he felt it through Lev's hand. Because he said something — "

The Racer bends his head again, straining for the echo of Georgi's voice. "He said that his father often told him about the war, about how he had been tortured. But Georgi said he had the impression that for his father, memory was devoid of emotion. While for him, memory was emotion. This must have released a floor of memories, because Georgi started talking about his childhood. He remembered the story about how Lev got the SS doctor who had done medical experiments on women to perform an appendectomy on Georgi. I remember it too. Lev got him out of prison and put a pistol to his head and cocked it and held it there through the operation. Later, when we examined the boy, we could barely find the scar. Georgi also remembered how his father had talked his way out of the concentration camp — "

"How on earth did he do that?"

"It was in the last days of the war. They could hear the sound of Russian artillery in the distance, rolling closer like a thunderstorm. The guards had begun shooting batches of prisoners and bulldozing their corpses into a trench. Lev told the assistant commandant that he would personally save him from the Communists if he opened the gate and let the prisoners escape. The assistant commandant asked, 'How can I know you mean what you say?' Lev looked him in the eyes and said, 'You have my word.' He is very imposing, you know for yourself, so the assistant commandant grasped at the straw and opened the gates."

"And did he save him?"

The Racer whispers the answer. "He handed him over to the prisoners, and they mutilated him."

"The boy Georgi, does he know the end of the story too?"

The Racer nods. "Georgi accused his father of having been brutal. It's odd, but I never thought of the Flag Holder as brutal. If I thought about it at all, I would have associated him with gentleness. But Georgi suddenly let go of his father's hand and touched the bandages on his face with his fingertips, which were swollen. And he said, he said" — again Tacho listens for the words, the tone — "he said, 'Violence is the opiate of the people.'"

The girl reaches across the table and covers Tacho's hand with her own. Tacho sees that her eyes are wet. A telephone rings somewhere inside the house. For a long time no one picks it up. Then Bazdéev shouts down from upstairs, and the phone stops ringing. Tacho looks at his watch. It is almost seven-thirty.

Tacho goes to the window and pushes open the shutters. "Look, it's light out already."

There is a commotion in the living room; the Dwarf is waking Kovel. The Hungarians are running barefoot through the bedrooms upstairs. The front door slams. Kovel can be heard starting up his taxi. Bazdéev sticks his dwarf head through the doorway leading to the kitchen.

"The Rabbit is telephoned," he announced huskily. "She is crazy with fright. The Flag Holder has disappeared."

12

THE RABBIT flings open the door of the apartment before the Racer's finger can jab at the buzzer. She stands there looking almost feverish, her eyes red and puffy, desperately glad to see them. With a rush of words, they all start to talk at once. Tears spurt into the Rabbit's eyes. Melanie puts her arm around her and guides her into the bathroom. When they come out, the Rabbit's face is glistening wet from the cold water that has been splashed on it.

"I'm sorry," she says, sinking into a corner of the couch. "I'm sorry."

The Racer takes her hand. "It's all right, Elisabeta, but for god's sake, tell us what happened?"

She sucks on her lower lip, gathering her thoughts. "Kovel dropped us here around midnight," she remembers, controlling herself, measuring out her words. "We came straight up. Lev didn't say very much, and I didn't ask him anything — I could see he didn't want to talk. I worked for a while on the bedroom wallpaper, then I got into bed and waited. About two or three, I don't really remember the time, I came in here. He was at his desk" — she glances over, a filmy look in her eyes — "at his desk, writing in his notebook. There was a glass of . . . cognac in front of him, and — "

The Rabbit starts to sob again. Melanie offers her a handkerchief. She blows her nose noisily and resumes her story, twisting the handkerchief in her fingers. "The glass of cognac — it was *half empty*. Lev saw me looking at the glass and told me to go to sleep, not to worry and go to sleep is what he told me. I asked him to let me stay, but he wouldn't let me, so I went back into the bedroom. I tried to keep awake, but I must have dozed, because the next thing I knew it was light out. That's when I saw that he was gone. The cognac bottle was empty. Oh, Tacho, he hasn't taken a

drink in two years!" The Rabbit shudders, chilled to the bone by
what she is thinking. "I'm frightened out of my mind. This whole
Czech business, and now Georgi." She looks unblinkingly at
Tacho and speaks quietly, as if speaking quietly will convince him
of what she is about to say. "He's going to do something desper-
ate, you know."

The Racer takes it all in, nodding, squeezing her hand as she
finishes. He stands up and walks over to the window. Directly
below the Flag Holder's apartment is an old prewar house that has
been turned into a children's day-care center. Boys and girls in
blue smocks are crawling through a length of pipe cemented to the
ground, or racing wildly around the shrubbery. The teacher sits on
the steps, her head angled up toward the sun, her eyes closed. The
boxlike prefabricated balconies of the apartments on the other side
of the school are full of crates of fruit, drying clothes, motorcycles,
tools, tarpaulins, strings of green peppers. On one balcony a
woman in curlers leans over the railing talking animatedly to a
neighbor. Beyond the apartment looms Vitoša. High up, where
the houses stop and the woods begin, the leaves are already yellow.

His mind made up, Tacho takes the Dwarf into the foyer and
speaks to him in a low voice. "Angel, get Kovel to check his hang-
outs — the Milk Bar, Club Balkan, the Jewish Centre. There's
always the chance he just went to work early. Maybe Kovel
should check out the hospital too. And get some of your circus
friends to start looking for him. You'd better alert Valyo and
Octobrina and Atanas. Use the phone in the bedroom."

Tacho sends the Rabbit and the American girl into the kitchen to
heat up some coffee. With the room to himself, he sits down at the
Flag Holder's desk. He pushes away a saucer overflowing with
ashes and cigarette butts. On one side of the desk is an ordinary
kitchen tumbler with some yellowish liquid on the bottom. The
Racer lifts it to his nose — cognac. He sees the glass has left a ring
on the table. Next to the ring are two silver-framed photographs:
one is of Georgi the day he earned his paratrooper wings; the second,
a group shot taken in front of the Rila Monastery during the war,
shows the Racer, Mister Dancho, Valyo, Popov and the Dwarf
(standing on a box), all looking very young, their arms flung over
each other's shoulders. On the other side of the desk, sandwiched
between two leaden bookends, is a loose-leaf notebook — the Flag

Holder's Nonperson manuscript. Tacho thumbs through it until
he comes to the last page that has writing on it. What he sees
numbs him; for a moment he thinks he is going to be sick.

NONPERSON no. 228
Lev Mendeleyev, known as the Flag Holder. A partisan in the period of
the Great Patriotic War, he ran afoul of the regime he helped establish
over the question of the intervention in the internal affairs of Czechoslovakia, which he bitterly opposed.

The rest of the page is blank, but the Racer's eye catches the im-
print of sentences, as if someone has been writing on a piece of paper
that rested on the page. On a hunch, the Racer looks in the waste-
basket. It smells from cigarette ashes, though there are none in it
now. His hand rummages — empty Rodopi boxes, old magazines,
blank medical forms, a crumpled piece of paper. Tacho retrieves
the paper and flattens it on the desk. It contains a series of short
scribbled notes.

It isn't Communist Power, but Communist Virtue, that will spread Com-
munism across the globe. But can the Minister be made to see this?
If I live to be a hundred, I'll never get accustomed to seeing girls who
aren't partisans wearing pants. But then, if I go through with it, I shall
never live to be a hundred.
One last effort. Communists are men of conscience. Must appeal to
that conscience. If I fail, those who come after me will know there are no
Communists here, and no conscience to appeal to.
Do I have the detachment to do it?
Do I have the detachment to do it?
Do I have

The writing ends in midsentence. On the bottom, in a tiny handwriting, is what appears to be a list. It says:

lighter
jerry can
September 9

They are having coffee when Kovel phones in. "Nothing.
Couldn't find hide nor hair of him nowhere. But Gogo says he
seen him going past when he opened the Milk Bar, maybe around

seven. Says he was carrying a plastic shopping sack and a roll of papers under his arm — "

"Does he have any idea what was in the sack?" the Racer demands.

"I didn't ask him nothing like that, but how could he know what was in a sack?"

"Goddamn it, ask him."

Melanie puts her arm around the Racer's waist. "Take it easy," she pleads.

Kovel is back in a second. "Geez, he don't have no idea what's in the sack, like I said. You want I should keep looking?"

"Keep looking, yes," the Racer tells him more calmly.

When the phone rings again, the Dwarf answers it. He listens for a moment, grunts and passes it to the Racer. "Popov," he says.

"Atanas, you find anything?" the Racer asks.

"Friend of mine who works the predawn shift on Hristo Botev thinks he saw him coming out of a shop around six, six-thirty maybe."

"What kind of shop?"

"No idea," Popov informs him.

"All right, keep looking," Tacho replies. He hangs up and turns to the Dwarf, puzzled. "Atanas has someone who saw Lev coming out of a shop around six. Up on Hristo Botev."

"What would he be doing in a shop at that hour?" Melanie asks.

"There's a man on Hristo Botev who prints the newsletter for the Centre," the Rabbit recalls. "I went there with him once. It's right next to the cinema."

"Sure," exclaims the Dwarf. "That's our Lamplighter." The Lamplighter was the wartime code name for the man who printed the underground newspaper for the Communist partisans. And *lighter* was the first word on the Flag Holder's crumpled list.

"Come on," the Racer tells the Dwarf. He waves the women back when they try to follow him. "We'll call when we know something."

The Racer peers through the glass door of the Lamplighter's shop, then opens it. A bell jingles. The Lamplighter, sturdy, bald, squinting through wire-rimmed glasses, appears from a back room. He is chuckling and looks as if he expects them.

"Hey, don't blame me," he says. "It was his idea, not mine."

"What idea was his idea?" the Racer asks sharply.

"Why, the notices, of course — " Suddenly it dawns on the
Lamplighter that something is very wrong. "What's going on?
He said it was a joke. He said — "
They find the first death notice high on the wall a block from the
Lamplighter's shop. It is taped up between a poster for a band
concert and another announcing a series of discussions on "Stimu-
lating the Agrarian Sector of the Economy." They crowd around,
the Racer, the Dwarf and the Lamplighter.
"Oh, dear god," moans Tacho.
"Jesus Mary," mumbles the Dwarf, and he crosses himself for
the first time in a quarter of a century.
The paper on the wall shows a grainy black-bordered photograph of the Flag Holder leading his partisans into Sofia. Under
the photograph, it says:

LEV MENDELEYEV
Known as the Flag Holder
Died, by his own hand, Sept. 9, 1968, at the age of 54, in protest against
the violent suppression of Socialism in Czechoslovakia.
"Violence is the opiate of the people."

They find the second death notice on the corner of Uzundžovska
and Vitoša, and a third two blocks up on Vitoša in the direction of
Place Lenin.
The Fat Lady and the Tattooed Man pull alongside in Kovel's
taxi. "Have you seen them?" the Fat Lady yells shrilly.
"We must find him," the Racer calls back, and he waves the taxi
away. It roars off down Vitoša. A large crowd is gathering on the
next corner, where Vitoša joins Ruski Boulevard.
"The parade is starting," cries the Lamplighter, breathless from
trying to keep up with the Racer. "They won't let us cross Ruski."
"Parade!" explodes the Dwarf.
"Of course," the Racer mutters to himself. "The nine September
parade," To the others, he yells:
"Dimitrov's tomb. We must get to Dimitrov's tomb."
They are running now, the Racer well ahead, the Lamplighter
and the Dwarf trailing. Octobrina and Popov wave frantically
from across the street, and Popov points to something on a wall. A
trolley passes between them. When it is clear, they are still waving

and still yelling. The Juggler rounds a corner on the run, almost knocking the Racer down. He grabs at the Racer's jacket and starts to shout something at him, but Tacho breaks free and charges into the crowd at the entrance to Ruski. A line of militiamen, drawn up shoulder to shoulder, blocks the way. Without a pass it is impossible to enter, one of the militiamen says politely. The Racer cranes, then jumps to see down Ruski. The bleachers are full; the pass-in-review is just getting under way. He hears a drum roll, a clattering of rifle butts hitting the pavement, then the notes of the national anthem. The Racer tries to talk his way past the militiamen. One of them shakes his head stonily. The Racer moves through the milling crowd and tries to push past a militia-man behind someone with a pass. He is shoved back roughly. A whistle blows. Three policemen start toward him. Tacho backs away from the line of militiamen, then catches sight of the Mime, in white face and top hat, standing before the revolving door of the Hotel Balkan, beckoning to him. Tacho bolts up the steps toward the Mime. When he reaches him, the Mime bows slightly, quickly, turns and pushes through the revolving door with the "BAL AN" stenciled in gold letters on the glass and leads the way through a maze of passageways behind the kitchen into a back alley filled with garbage cans. Here the Mime points and bows again. Tacho nods his thanks and dashes down the alley into the ruins of the Sveti Georgi Church, an archeological dig that has been closed to the public for years. At the far end of the dig he crawls through a low arch and emerges behind one of the wooden bleachers across the square from Dimitrov's tomb.

Stepping around the side of the bleachers, Tacho takes in the entire square. It is filled with workers from a steel complex in the south of the country, marching forty abreast. Dozens of red banners stream over their heads. A brass band coming down Ruski behind the workers plays the Internationale. From the reviewing stand atop the white marble tomb, the country's Communist Party Chief, puffy-faced and cordial, peers out, waving jovially. A teen-age girl with pigtails detaches herself from the line of marchers and runs up the steps on the side of the tomb to hand a huge bouquet of roses to the Party Leader. He cradles the flowers in one arm and pats the girl on the head. Flash bulbs pop. A television camera dollies in.

The crowd cheers wildly. The Party Chief acknowledges the cheers and passes the bouquet to the Minister, who stands just behind him.

The factory workers move on. The brass army band steps out, the footfalls of the soldiers marking the rhythm of the music. Suddenly, in the space between the steelworkers and the army band, the Flag Holder appears — from where, the Racer will never know. He is simply and suddenly there, facing the Party leaders atop the tomb, sinking to his knees in the path of the brass band, pulling a can from a plastic sack and emptying its contents on his clothes. The Minister leans over the reviewing stand, his knuckles white on the railing, his face muscles twisting into an expression of disgust, and shouts a command. Two soldiers with machine pistols at the ready start toward the kneeling figure. The Racer, knowing what is going to happen before he can *think* about what is going to happen, lurches toward the Flag Holder. Some men in civilian clothes grab him. He tries to pull away, turns to argue with them, presses shut his eyes and opens his mouth until it feels as if the skin at the corners will tear and screams a scream that pierces the music of the brass band.

"NOOOOOOOOOOOOOOOOOOOOOOOOOOOOOOOOO."

And again:

"NOOOOOOOOOOOOOOOOOOOOOOOOOOOOOOOOO."

The Racer struggles to open his eyes; for a terrible instant he can't locate the muscles that do the work. When he gets them open, he sees a ball of flame that has the sickening outline of a kneeling man, his arms flung wide. There is a silence so absolute it feels as if the earth has stopped rotating. The flames lick like a tongue at the kneeling man, who settles toward the ground as if he were *melting.* The civilians holding the Racer grimace but never take their eyes off the fire. One of the guards frozen at attention in front of the door of the tomb vomits over his dress uniform. The figure in the middle of the square slumps forward on what must have been its head and shoulders. Far away a whistle blows, then another. Policemen shout orders. The huge crowd stirs, but the only motion is a gentle pressing in toward the focal point.

The Milk Bar is relatively empty for this time of the day. Gogo is cleaning grounds out of the espresso machine. Poleon studies a

petition taped to the front of the espresso machine, requesting
clemency for Mister Dancho. He is trying to decide which better
serves his interests — to sign it, or report its existence to the block
captain, who is the sister of his uncle's wife and can be counted on
to give him credit. Poleon's ex-wife is picking food out of her
teeth with one of her long fingernails, and nodding at the Scream
Therapist, who is talking about the problem of sex in crowded
apartments. In the distance, a brass band can be heard playing the
Internationale.

"Women tend to freeze up if they think their cotenants can hear
them," the Scream Therapist is saying. "Men, on the other hand,
seem to care less who is listening. I know someone who tape-
recorded his neighbors making love and played it at a party — "

The distant music trails off and the Scream Therapist perks up
the way a dog does when he hears a whistle pitched too high for
human ears.

"Did you hear it?" he whispers.

A distant scream pierces the Milk Bar. Both Gogo and Poleon
turn toward it.

"Now that," the Scream Therapist announces, "is the first healthy
person I've heard in this country!"

13

EVERYONE is unfailingly polite: the starched duty officer who escorts him up the marble stairs, the thin aide with protruding eyes who ushers him into the formal room, the Minister himself who rises when he hears the soft footfalls on the thick carpet.

"Ah, I was expecting you. Can I offer you a coffee" — the Racer shakes his head — "tea then, or something stronger, a vodka, a whiskey perhaps?"

Again the Racer refuses, and the Minister dismisses the aide with the back of his hand and sits down.

"About the Flag Holder: naturally there can be no question of a state funeral."

The Racer shifts uncomfortably in his chair, aware of the black armband on the sleeve of his jacket. From the outer office comes the sound of a typewriter.

"Naturally," he says, and he is struck by the oddness, the inappropriateness, of the word. Nothing that has happened has been *natural.*

"You are authorized to bury him privately in" — the Minister lowers his eyes, but not his head, to the single sheet of paper before him and names an obscure cemetery in a workers' district of Sofia. He glances at his male secretary, who inclines his head; he has noted the order in the notebook open on his lap.

A functionary comes in and lays a dossier on the small gilt-edged antique table that serves the Minister as a desk. A prewar telephone is on one side, a porcelain inkwell on the other. The Minister sits with his back to an open window. The curtains are drawn, and billow inward every now and then when a breeze catches them. The Minister plucks the pen from the porcelain inkwell and scratches his initials in the upper-right-hand corner of the dossier. The functionary withdraws the dossier and leaves without taking notice of the Racer, who sits on an antique chair across the table from the Minister.

"Above all," the Minister is saying, "the cortege must be — how to phrase it? — it must be *discreet*. Surely you catch my meaning?"

"What are you trying to hide? Thousands of people saw the suicide — "

"There was a suicide, no one disputes the point," the Minister agrees quickly. He waves absently with his hand toward the secretary, who closes his notebook and retreats to the far corner of the room, out of earshot.

"But who, I put it to you, committed suicide? Ah, I can see the question startles you. Surely you've heard the rumors?"

"Rumors?"

"Rumors, yes. One has it that the deceased was a retired engineer whose wife just died of cancer. There are others who say the man was one" — the Minister scans the paper for a name — "Korbaj, a Serbian who escaped last week from an insane asylum in Plovdiv. I myself was a stone's throw from the victim, you will remember. Now I grant you there was a resemblance to the Flag Holder, but one can never be absolutely sure — "

"And the death of the Flag Holder — "

"Ah, yes, there is the death of the Flag Holder to account for. I must tell you that my people have already heard rumors concerning this too: that he got roaring drunk and cut his wrists after visiting his son, Georgi, who was mutilated by the Czech revisionists; that he shot himself in the mouth after he discovered he had terminal lung cancer — I might add that the name of a prominent doctor is associated with this story; that he gassed himself in the kitchen of his apartment when he caught his mistress in flagrante delicto with his best friend and her former lover, the bicycle racer Abadzhiev; that he choked on a chicken bone in Krimm — there are two waiters there who swear they saw him being carried out on a stretcher; that he died peacefully in his sleep of a coronary. It goes without saying, my people are passing on the rumors as they hear them. Within a few days, take it from someone with experience in such matters, nobody will know for certain what happened."

"The Flag Holder immolated himself in protest against the suppression of Socialism in Czechoslovakia."

"How very interesting you should mention that; it coincides al-

most exactly with one of the rumors in circulation. But I tell you
frankly, nobody puts much stock in it. It is simply not like him.
Oh, he liked to play his games with us now and then, but a death
such as you describe would have been out of character." The Minister scrapes back his chair — for an instant he seems to step outside the role of Minister. "I am not without feelings," he says
quietly. "I knew him a long time. I was there, I actually saw him
pick up the flag. I only regret . . ."

"What is it you regret?"

The Minister looks up; he is every inch the Minister again. "I
regret that somewhere along the way he stopped being one of us."

"Somewhere along the way you stopped being one of him."

The Minister's face tightens into a smile. "That's the kind of
thing he would have said. Are you thinking of playing his role?"

The telephone rings softly. The Minister lifts the receiver and
listens, his eyes glued to the Racer's; he seems to be seeing him in a
new light.

"Tell him I'm on my way," he says, "and have the car brought
around to my private entrance." He places the receiver back on its
cradle.

The Minister rises; the interview is terminated. Tacho rises also,
and the two men regard each other across the vast gulf of the small
table.

"It seems to me," Tacho declares, "that whatever you think of
him, you must give a man his death — "

"Where national security is concerned, we give nothing."

The Racer starts to leave, then turns back. "It is very difficult for
me to think about what he did. But when I can make myself think
about it, what I think is this: He . . . burned himself to death . . .
so the world would know there was one person in the Communist
world who detested with every fiber of his body the suppression of
progressive forces in Czechoslovakia."

"If that was his reason," the Minister replies—they are both
speaking very quietly — "more's the pity, for the world will never
know about it."

"There is no way you can keep it in."

"On the contrary, there is no way it can get out."

The Racer spots them as he descends the marble staircase of the
Central Committee building. One, in green socks, is reading the

sports page of *Narodna Mladej* under a giant photograph of the Flag Holder leading the way into Sofia. The second, wearing a trench coat, is chatting with the duty officer at the check-in desk. The Racer tosses his visitor's pass on the desk — he has a fleeting impression that the duty officer no longer regards him politely — and pushes through the door into the street. When he stops for the traffic light at the corner, Green Socks and Trench Coat are a dozen paces behind him.

The Racer swings aboard a trolley heading down Ignatiev toward the stadium, and hands two stodinki to the ticket taker. The old man deposits the coins in his worn leather pouch, pulls a ticket off the roll, punches it and hands it to Tacho. Green Socks and Trench Coat climb up behind the Racer and flash laminated identification cards at the old man, who hardly glances at them as he punches their tickets. The trolley jerks into motion.

" 'Bout time they switched to buses," the man next to the Racer mutters conversationally, and he is insulted when Tacho makes no answer.

At the stadium, Tacho pauses before the entrance to the locker room. His racers are changing into their sweat suits.

"Eight days," Tacho reminds them quietly, meaning there are only eight days until the big race. The racers usually respond with yelps and shouts. Today they are strangely silent, embarrassed almost.

At his office door, Tacho inserts his key in the lock. It takes a moment for him to realize that it doesn't fit. He looks at the key. It is the right one. He tries again and turns away, puzzled. Green Socks is lounging at the far end of the tunnel that leads to the stadium. Tacho looks back at the lock. It gleams against the gray of the door. *A new lock!* The four riders file past the Racer, wheeling their ticking racing bicycles toward Green Socks and the stadium.

"We want you to know how sorry we are," Tony murmurs as they pass. The others mutter agreement.

Thinking they mean the Flag Holder, Tacho nods his thanks. On a hunch, he asks:

"Sorry about what?"

"About you being suspended as coach and all," replies Boris. "The Federation people came around this morning and kind of told us."

"We're gonna win," vows Evan. "We're gonna win, and we're gonna let everyone know it was you that made us win. Isn't that right, you guys?" The others nod in agreement.

"Sure you are," Tacho tells them. "Sure you are."

His eyes narrow with the first faint inkling of a crazy, wild dangerous idea.

The idea is still percolating when Tacho stops by the funeral parlor on his way back to the Flag Holder's apartment. The chore is a painful one, but he must make sure all the arrangements are in order. The parlor occupies the ground floor and basement of a rundown, prewar house in a part of the city that used to be, but no longer is, fashionable. It is bracketed on one side by an appliance store full of Russian refrigerators and Polish gas heaters, on the other by a pastry shop with large peasant baskets full of loaves in the window.

The director of the funeral parlor, an extremely tall man by the name of Ivkov, wrings his hands as he talks to the Racer. He reminds Tacho of a doctor scrubbing up for an operation, and he wonders vaguely whether it is an occupational gesture or a tick.

"I'm very sorry to have to tell you this," Ivkov is saying, washing away on his hands, "but our hearse is hors de combat." He laughs nervously. "We have taken it upon ourselves to substitute an open pickup truck — draped for the occasion in black, to be sure, to be sure," he adds quickly when he sees the expression on Tacho's face.

"And the coffin?"

"The coffin has been attended to, but I'm desperately afraid the only thing available on such short notice is a simple pine box." Again he laughs nervously. Tacho notices the black curtain at the far end of the room sway slightly — or is it his imagination? "You understand that nothing in the way of" — the director picks at his words as if they are morsels of distasteful food — "cosmetics is possible."

"I understand." Tacho stares at the curtain; it sways again, but there is no draft.

"I should tell you too, there is a problem with the funeral band," Ivkov continues. "It has been requisitioned" — Ivkov clears his throat — "by the Commissariat of Public Parks to give a concert to old people."

"Has that ever happened before?" Tacho inquires.

"It is very common, yes," the director answers without conviction.

Abruptly Tacho turns to leave. Ivkov leaps ahead to open the door for him. "Concerning the note," he says. He coughs discreetly and hands Tacho an itemized bill. Tacho glances at it — the total comes to one hundred forty-five leva — and hands it back. "The Dwarf will settle with you."

Ivkov actually bows. "We are at your disposition," he says.

Tacho departs without closing the door behind him. He is afraid the closing of it will become an expression of his emotion, and it will come off its hinges.

The Racer intends to pack the Flag Holder's personal effects in a carton and take them back to his apartment, but the door to the Jewish Centre is locked. A handwritten note taped to the inside of the glass so that it can be read on the outside says:

"Closed for repairs."

As Tacho turns away, he almost bumps into the Scream Therapist. "I remember you," the Scream Therapist insists. "You were at the Dwarf's wedding." He looks toward the door of the Jewish Centre.

"It's closed," Tacho tells him. "For repairs. There's a note in the window."

"Damn," the Scream Therapist says. "Say, I don't mean to be crude or anything, but you wouldn't happen to know the disposition of the Flag Holder's apartment." He lowers his voice. "I've pretty much decided to stay in Bulgaria, and I'm going to need a roof over my head. I'd be willing to pay a pretty penny if I could get the inside track on it. Say, where are you going. *Hey, come back.*"

Valyo, the Dwarf and Popov are in the living room of the Flag Holder's apartment when the Racer arrives — Valyo and Popov on the worn sofa, Bazdéev pacing back and forth in front of them with giant dwarf steps. Kovel is drinking beer at the kitchen table, reading in the Party newspaper about the new coach for Stambolijski, his favorite soccer team. Octobrina and the American girl are in the bedroom with the Rabbit. Tacho looks in for a moment. Melanie smiles sadly at him, and the Rabbit jumps from the bed to grab his hand.

"Tell me, you, how could he do this thing to me?" she pleads.

"Tell me, for I am begging the answer. How is it he could do this thing to me?"

The Rabbit shivers and sinks into his arms, drained of energy, and he helps her back to the bed.

"He used to say he was a man without a mirror image or a shadow," the Rabbit says. "You were there, Tacho. Tell me — did he cast a shadow when he . . ." She sobs, but the sobs are tearless, as if her ducts have gone dry.

"Take comfort, Elisabeta, he cast a shadow the length of the square — " The Racer is unable to say more.

"Take comfort," Octobrina tells her. Her voice is soft but strong; secret strengths are flowing through her like underground streams. "It was a thing ripe with hope — "

Elisabeta hardly hears her. "How is it he could do this thing to me?" she asks again. "The whole thing is beyond comprehension — "

Back in the living room, Tacho talks to the Dwarf near the window. Down the street he can see Green Socks and Trench Coat lounging against the window of a garden supply store. Over their heads, in giant red letters, appear the words "Chemical" and "Fertilizer."

"There are problems," Tacho says. He points out Green Socks and Trench Coat, and explains about the band and the hearse. The Dwarf nods his large head.

"I am organizing all," he frowns. "*Kovel. Dog.*" He starts for the door.

The Racer watches from the window as the Dwarf lifts Dog into Kovel's taxi and climbs in behind him. As he turns back into the room, he remembers the Minister, cocksure, saying:

"There is no way it can get out."

He must talk to the American girl.

"But I want to attend the funeral," Melanie insists.

"This is just not possible," Tacho tells her. "You must understand that everything here has changed." He takes her by the shoulders. "Melanie, you must do as I tell you."

She nods reluctantly. "Is it sure you'll come?"

"If I don't it's because I'm arrested," he promises. "Now you must remember everything I have told you."

"I remember."

"Good. When you get there, take a guide and ask many questions about the history and the architecture. Make notes of what he tells you. They must think you are a student."

"What if they have seen us together? What if they won't let me leave Sofia?"

"They have only just begun following me," Tacho assures her. "They cannot know about you yet. Just walk out of the building as if you lived here. As long as you are not with one of us, they will leave you alone."

"What will you do about Mister Dancho?"

"Yes, what can we do about our dear Dancho?" Octobrina echoes, joining the conversation.

"About Dancho," Tacho admits heavily, "there is nothing that can be done."

14

THEY START from the rear door into a strangely quiet, strangely deserted street, at the hour specified in the funeral permit — 7:00 A.M. Two militiamen take up the point position, as if this is to be a military patrol through enemy-occupied terrain, and as one of them passes the Racer he whispers:

"Please understand, we are only following orders."

"Everyone is always following orders," Tacho retorts, and smiling in a way that is new to him he steps off holding aloft the placard the Flag Holder carried at the demonstration nobody saw. On one side is the famous photograph that every schoolchild in the country recognizes from his history book. On the other is a hand-lettered slogan which reads:

Cover the whole world with asphalt. Sooner or later a blade of grass will break through.

Behind Tacho comes the circus band (on loan to the Dwarf as a "personal favor") in embroidered jackets with black armbands and high plumed hats. The kettle drummer sets a funereal rhythm — boom, boom, boom, boom — with elegant flourishes of his drumsticks. The hearse (which the Dwarf "organized" from a nearby village) comes next: an ancient black-and-gilt vehicle dating back to the Turkish Yoke, with a glass compartment for the coffin, drawn by two high-stepping spotted circus geldings with braided manes and white plumes dancing from their nodding heads. High on the buckboard seat, holding the reins nonchalantly in his outstretched hands and eyeing with supreme indifference the shuttered windows and the closed doors that line the route, sits the peasant who came with the hearse.

Elisabeta walks directly behind the hearse, mesmerized by the coffin which jounces as the wagon wheels bump over the cobble-stones. On one side of her is Valyo Barbovich, wearing a silk scarf to protect his throat from the chill; on the other, in morning clothes, is Atanas Popov, his left shoe squeaking with each step. Close behind them comes Octobrina, lost in the folds of a great black shawl. The Dwarf in full clown regalia, struts at her side — he is once again Bazdéev the King of Clowns, confronting the empty streets with his painted angel's face and his mocking smile and his wild eyes — "the eyes," Octobrina once said, "of an animal trapped inside a body it finds odious." The blind dog, Dog, sulks at his feet, jerked forward, when he lags, with a leash made of a string of sausages.

Skipping along behind, two abreast, arms linked, come the Hun-garians, wearing single layers of flowered chiffon through which their pink limbs can be clearly seen. Kovel, looking as if he wanted to be anywhere but where he was, the Fat Lady, the Tattooed Man and the Juggler bring up the rear.

For the first two blocks, everyone makes an effort to ignore the obvious. Finally Valyo explodes. "Somebody's gone to a great deal of trouble for this funeral," he cries bitterly, and Octobrina, behind him, remarks:

"In a perverse way, it's really a sign of respect."

But the emptiness of the street seems to taunt them, and the Dwarf, more sensitive to such things than the others, thrusts out his de-formed chest, curses in Hungarian and barks at the circus band:

"Louder, louder, so they will know who is it we bury."

Kettle drum thumping, horses prancing, the cortege follows the militiamen through the back streets in the general direction of the cemetery. As they turn into Pavlovic, a shutter somewhere above them squeals on its hinges and then slams shut, and the petals from a dozen roses rain down on the hearse. Octobrina gathers up a few handfuls and tucks them into a fold of her shawl. Half a block further along a bouquet of wild thyme falls at Elisabeta's feet, and then a Soviet army medal from the Great Patriotic War, with a note pinned to the ribbon that says:

"We will never forget him, never!"

Popov scoops up the thyme and the medal and opens the glass door of the hearse and places them on the pine coffin.

On Pavlovic, across from a vegetable market normally crowded

with shoppers at this hour of the morning, the old waiter Stuka
steps from a doorway that smells of urine and lifts his cap at the
cortege. He is wearing a single campaign ribbon on his chest from
a war few people remember. The militiamen eye him angrily, and
a woman shouts to him from the darkness of the hallway:

"Grandpa, come in — they will mark your name."

But the old man stands his ground, his cap raised above his
head in salute. "Excuse me," he fumbles in a husky voice as the
Racer draws abreast. "Excuse me for Mister Dancho."

"Go in, old man," Tacho urges and the woman, hearing that,
darts out and pulls Stuka back into the hallway.

The cortege reaches the corner where Pavlovic turns into Petro-
han. Here the pavement ends and the road becomes ˈ ʌtted dirt,
and the houses, single-story rundown frame boxes, are set back from
the road to allow for a garden in front. The cemetery is just beyond, and as they draw near, the huge iron gates swing open,
though nobody can be seen pulling them. As the Racer passes
through the gate, a figure springs from behind a tombstone. In-
stinctively, the Racer thrusts the placard out as if to ward off an
attacker, and one of the horses neighs and paws the ground with
his front feet.

It is the Mime, barely breathing, his head lowered as if he is about
to charge. The white pancake make-up on his face is streaked
with tears and he bows to the ancient hearse and falls into step
behind the Fat Lady.

The militiamen lead the cortege past rows and rows of head-
stones to the far corner of the cemetery, where the first field joins it.
The Minister's male secretary is standing near a rectangular hole
which seems to yaw open, a pile of dirt on one side, two worn
leather straps across it.

"But there is no stone," Elisabeta whispers urgently.

"And no one to help us," adds Valyo.

The Racer calls to the Minister's male secretary:

"Are there to be no gravediggers to help us?"

The secretary, whose steel-rimmed eyeglasses have turned to
silver in the sun, only shrugs and motions with his jaw as if to say:
"Get on with it."

Tacho, Valyo, the Juggler and the Tattooed Man pull the pine
coffin from the hearse and lower it to the ground. Octobrina puts

her arms around the Rabbit's waist and hugs her tightly. Four members of the band lay down their instruments and take hold of the ends of the leather straps. The coffin is laid over the gaping hole on the straps and lowered into the grave. The straps are pulled free. The Racer, pale, trembling, walks to the edge of the hole and tosses in a handful of dirt. The sound of it falling on the wood strikes him as an obscenity.

"My friends — "

Tacho lowers his head and brings his hand to his eyes. Valyo reaches forward and touches his shoulder.

"My friends," Tacho begins again, his voice reduced to a whisper. "I . . . I have no words." He shakes his head and steps back from the edge of the grave.

Octobrina takes his place and looks for a long moment at the coffin. She blinks back tears. "Another still life," she cries and flings open her shawl, scattering rose petals onto the coffin. She almost manages a smile and returns to her place alongside the Rabbit, who sinks to her knees and fills each hand with dirt and moans dully:

"Lev, oh Lev, oh my Lev, my Lev."

The Mime appears suddenly at the head of the grave. He crouches and from the dirt creates, as a sculptor would, an imaginary candle. It is dark and he feels around the earth for an imaginary match. Finding it, he lights the candle and holds it high and slowly looks around. Then he lowers the candle and moistens his fingertips and presses the wick between them, and the people gathered around the grave can almost hear the hiss as the flame is extinguished.

The Dwarf strides forward and tosses onto the coffin the flowers and bouquets and medals that Popov gathered along the way. Then, tilting his great head, he hurls curse after curse at the sky in Hungarian.

The Hungarian girls, hanging back, start to blush and giggle.

Popov runs a finger under his collar to soothe the red welt on his neck as he steps to the edge of the grave. He reaches into his pocket to turn up his hearing aid.

"It was my intention — " He falters. "I had hoped — "

He adjusts his pince-nez and removes his ledger from his pocket. "Sssssssss. One mother-of-pearl lorgnette handle. One ostrich plume. One stuffed humming bird without its tail feathers. One child's coloring book with an inscription that reads, 'Little Bibo, nineteen thirty-seven.' " Popov's eyes peer over the top of his pince-nez. "The Flag Holder was in Spain then, I think. Sssssssss. Where was I? Ah. One sheet of Czarist stock certificates. One rear cover from a silver Audemars Frères pocket watch, with an inscription that reads, 'For F.M.R., from his loving parents, on his graduation from Bucharest University, June twenty-fifth, nineteen twenty-four. *Magna est veritas et prevalebit.*' " Popov looks up, seeing nothing through the tears welling in his eyes. "That means, truth is mighty and will prevail." He smiles weakly. "Perhaps that was so in nineteen twenty-four. It was a very long time ago and I don't remember. I used to have a motto. My motto was, '*Nulla dies sine linea.*' That means, not a day without a line. That was before they . . . before they . . . that was before they destroyed all my . . . all my . . ."

Octobrina reaches out and gently rests her hand on Popov's arm.

"Where was I? Sssssssss. Ah, the watch cover" — he looks around like a child who is afraid he has disappointed his listeners — "was my last but not least."

15

"It was very moving," Valyo tells Popov. "Really it was."

"I hoped to have a poem ready . . ." Popov is visibly upset. Octobrina squeezes his hand. "But your lists *are* poems."

"Do you think so?" Popov asks eagerly. "Or do you just say that?"

"Of course I think so," Octobrina promises him. "Everyone thinks so. Isn't that right, Valyo? *Isn't that right, Valyo?*"

Valyo quickly nods. "Certainly it's right."

One of the soccer stars across the room laughs at a dirty joke, but he stops abruptly when Gogo catches his eye. The Dwarf, trailed by three of his Hungarians and Dog, pushes through the crowd at the door.

"Coffee," he tells Gogo. As usual the girls cluster around the counter eyeing the pastries. The Dwarf takes the Racer by the arm and pulls him into a corner. "The bastards are started," he rasps.

"How do you know?" Tacho glances through the window at Trench Coat, who is sunning himself in front of a barber shop across the street from the Milk Bar.

"Kovel — he seen it with his eyes. Not one of them death papers is left to tell the story. All them others are still up there on the walls, but the Flag Holder, he been scraped off — "

"But if they're denying the" — the word doesn't come easy to Tacho — "the immolation . . . they had to do that."

"More." The Dwarf is impatient. "His photo gone. From Krimm. From Hotel Balkan. From War Museum — I seen that myself. From lobby of Central Committee building."

"What do you mean gone!"

"Gone, goddamn. You understand word. Gone. Jesus, Tacho, sometime you give stupid question. Gone is gone. In Krimm, in Central Committee building, they hanged other pictures in place. In War Museum, in Hotel Balkan, they just gone. Hook still there. Wall all clean where picture was."

"My god," moans Tacho. The full weight of what is happening hits him.

"More," insists the Dwarf. "Kovel got a daughter, and the daughter she been sent home from school this morning to bring history book back to school. She says they all of them been ordered return history books. She says it's Party people, not school people, that's doing the collection."

"The Flag Holder's photograph is in that book."

"In front, before all the writing been started."

"It's not possible . . ."

"It possible." The Dwarf's face twists into a grin. "If they do it to him, they can maybe do it to me. But I not ever let them." He tilts his head and looks curiously at the Racer. "You still thinking on that idea of yours?"

"I'm thinking." Tacho notices Octobrina casting worried glances in their direction. "Don't say a word about what I told you to the others," he warns.

A short while later, Octobrina, the Dwarf, the Racer and Popov pile into Kovel's taxi, which is double-parked around the corner from the Milk Bar.

"That dumb Tomato," snorts Kovel, glaring through the windshield at the policeman directing traffic at the intersection. "He's the one what tried to give me a ticket."

"The thing to do," Valyo ventures, "is to yell back at them. That way they know you are important and leave you alone."

"I tried that," Kovel asserts.

"What did it cost you?" demands Valyo.

"Fifty leva," Kovel replies with a smirk.

The Dwarf taps him on the shoulder. "Cemetery," he orders.

"Flower market first."

Dog farts, and those nearest the windows rush to open them. Kovel rolls his eyes, and the Dwarf strokes the dog's deformed head soothingly. "He only doing that when he upset," he apologizes.

"I do the same when I'm upset," quips Kovel.

"You'll have to get a smaller dog, or Kovel will have to get a larger taxi," Valyo says, but his effort at humor falls flat.

The flower market is a splash of color against the gray side streets of Sofia. Kovel double-parks, blocking the narrow street.

Horns blare behind him but Kovel turns and stares at the drivers until they stop. Octobrina hurries back with an armful of rust-colored chrysanthemums.

"Fall flowers are the most beautiful," she sighs. "They have an inner life" — she smiles thoughtfully — "a still life. Spring flowers are brighter, but their brightness is superficial. They have an outer life. A restless, gossipy life."

"There's an old Russian poem about fall flowers," Popov says. He rubs his forehead with his thumb and forefinger. "I can't seem to remember how it starts."

Kovel parks alongside the iron gate of the cemetery and settles down to read the sports page. The others make their way past row upon row of graves.

"This is right," calls Ocrobrina, in the lead and cradling her bouquet. "I remember passing that statue. Doesn't she have a demonic smile? Whoever honored her certainly didn't like her. Here, this way. Maybe the headstone will be up."

They come to the part of the cemetery that borders on lush farm fields. Octobrina looks around, confused. "But I could have sworn . . ."

"It was over here," Tacho observes grimly. He looks down at the gravestone of a mother and child, both of whom, according to the legend, died in childbirth. The stone, which is weatherworn, is dated January 12, 1942.

The Dwarf calls to a gravedigger weeding in the next row of graves. "We bury some person here, old man — "

The man — bending the way the peasants do: from the waist — straightens up. "You must be makin' a mistake," he replies coolly. "That there's been 'round long as I been 'round."

"How long is that?" Tacho demands.

"Long enough."

Tacho kicks at the soil, which is freshly turned, with the toe of his boot. "This is a new grave."

The gravedigger shakes his head. "You can see from the stone it ain't no new grave. It was me what turned the earth this mornin', if you're a-wonderin' about that dirt there."

Tacho notices Green Socks leaning against a gravestone four or five rows away. It is hard to be sure at that distance, but he appears to be smiling, as if at some private joke.

Octobrina touches the gravestone with her fingertips; the flowers she brought dangle from the other hand. "They're . . . trying to turn him into a nonperson," she says, hushed. "As long as we're around, they won't be able to do that, will they?"

She studies their faces, one after the other, for confirmation. Finding none, she slowly clamps her hand over her mouth.

"Oh!"

16

"WHY ME?" Kovel whines. "I keep my nose clean. I don't never say nothing political. What did I do to deserve this?"

He casts a long fearful glance toward the back seat, where the Dwarf's dog, Dog, is curled up in a silky brown tangle. (In the shadows, there is no way to tell head from tail.) "And what in god's name am I going to do with a dog that farts all day?"

"Dog's the least of our problems," the Racer tells him absently. Totally absorbed, he stares out the front window of the car, focusing on the raindrops running down the glass. Kovel reaches into the glove compartment for the windshield wipers and climbs out to put them on. When he gets back in, he runs them three or four times. As the world comes back into focus, Tacho snaps out of his reverie.

"How did the Dwarf know they were coming for him?" he asks.

"Someone telephoned — one of his circus friends, maybe," Kovel guesses. "He got a lot of friends, you know. He slammed down the receiver and dumped that damn dog of his in my arms and pushed me out the door and told me to watch the house from the next block and if anything happened to find you."

"Well, you found me," Tacho mutters glumly. He reaches back and feels the dog's shirred flesh stir warmly under his touch.

Kovel runs the windshield wipers again. "He said for me to give you a message."

"What message?" the Racer demands. Kovel chews on his lip and Tacho shakes his elbow impatiently. "*What message?*"

Kovel peers into the Racer's face. "Run."

"That's all — just *run?*"

"He told me to tell you to run," Kovel repeats softly.

The Racer thinks for a moment. "How long after you left did they come?"

"Twenty minutes maybe. Twenty-five on the outside. Three

cars and a paddy wagon. Oh sweet Jesus, them poor little girlies started bawling like it was the end of the world when they seen the wagon waiting for them."

"I wonder if Angel warned — "

"He never came out, you know."

"What do you mean he never came out?"

"He never came out." Kovel's eyebrows arch up. "I passed an ambulance coming up the hill when I was going down."

Tacho collapses against the window. "He said he would never let them do that to him," he remarks weakly.

On the corner a horn sounds. Tacho looks around. They are parked on a side street off Don Dukov, which is clogged with morning rush-hour traffic. "I've got to try and warn the others," he says urgently. "Wait here."

Oblivious to the rain, which is light but steady, Tacho crosses the street to a workers' lunchroom with a bank of telephone booths along one wall.

"The trouble is I never like nothing from Column B," a middle-aged man is yelling in the first booth. "Can you hear me now?"

A young woman is reading from notes in the second booth. "Disintegration of the ozone layer. Right. Thickening of the polar ice cap. Right. Drying up of the monsoons. Right. Slowing down of the earth's — "

In the third booth, an old man is studying a pocket chessboard. "Bishop to rook three," he says. "Same time tomorrow?" The old man smiles savagely as he hangs up, and tells Tacho happily:

"He was expecting probably pawn to queen's knight five! Ha! Life is full of its little surprises."

The Racer settles into the booth, leaning against the folding glass door as he tries to collect himself. All around the telephone are scribbled numbers: "Zlatarov 90.25.14" and "Kitka 38.16.16" and "GG 24.12.56" and "Airport Inter 27.27.07." He dials Valyo's apartment. There is a strange clicking noise, and then nothing. The same thing happens a second time. Tacho retrieves his coin and dials the Flag Holder's number. A man answers, and Tacho hangs up immediately. An old woman taps impatiently on the glass door with a coin, but Tacho turns his back on her and tries Octobrina's number. The phone rings four, five, six, seven times. He is about to hang up when Octobrina answers.

"Octobrina," Tacho blurts out, cupping the mouthpiece with his hand.

"They're here," she tells him with measured dignity, "they're on the earpiece, so don't say where you — "

Octobrina gives a sharp cry of pain and the phone clicks dead. The old woman is tapping on the booth again, and Tacho turns on her, trembling. *"What do you want?"* he yells, his face livid, and she backs away in fright.

Tacho frantically dials Octobrina's number, but there is a busy signal. He tries again, and again there is a busy signal. On a hunch, he dials his own number. On the first ring a man answers.

"Yes?"

"Who's this?" Tacho demands.

"The Racer," the man says casually. "Who's this?"

"This is the Flag Holder," Tacho replies, and he chops down with his forefinger to sever the connection.

The old woman with the coin is still there as Tacho emerges from the booth. "What do you want?" she mimics. "What do you want? What I want is to use the phone, what do you think I want?"

Tacho brushes past her without replying, and she follows him onto the street. "Rude is what you are, all you young people," she shouts, her voice rising hysterically. "Rude, rude, rude." People turn to stare at Tacho. "You're nobody," the old woman flings after him. "You think you're somebody, but you're nobody."

At the taxi, Kovel waits nervously, both hands gripping the steering wheel. "Did you get anyone?" he wants to know.

Tacho slides in, ignoring the question. "There still may be time to find Atanas," he says. "He was supposed to work the morning shift — he may be on the streets."

They begin cruising the side streets off Hristo Botev near the Russian Monument: Mihailov first, then Hadžidimov, then Blagoev. As they swing into Hristo Botev again, Tacho touches Kovel's elbow.

"Slow down," he orders. "Look — next to the cinema."

A uniformed militiaman is on duty in front of the Lamplighter's print shop, and two workmen in overalls are boarding up the plate-glass window, which has been splintered. People on their way to work stare curiously, and the militiaman motions for them to go on about their business.

"Maybe Popov's gone home already," Kovel ventures after a while. "Maybe — "

"Pull up," Tacho yells excitedly, and before the taxi comes to a stop he bolts from it and dashes back to the corner they have just passed to look down Košut. A garbage truck, surrounded by three or four police cars, is blocking traffic halfway down the block. Popov stands with his back to the truck; his hands, manacled at the wrists, droop in front of him. A militiaman is grilling him harshly, but Popov, who wears the uniform of a garbage collector, stares back at him with great serenity. Tacho is suddenly sure that he has turned off his hearing aid. Another militiaman kneels nearby, inspecting the contents of a small canvas sack; he lifts each item and lays it on the sidewalk. There is something made of stained glass, a rolled-up canvas, a stuffed bird, an oval picture frame, a toy airplane. A civilian looks down at the collection, touching with the toe of his shoe each item as he checks it against a list in a pocket ledger. Women with their hair in curlers lean from the windows of the surrounding apartment buildings (daylight arrests are rare; they will have something to tell their husbands) until a detective looks up at them; instantly the heads retract and the windows slam down, the shades right after them.

"What did he do with all that junk he collected?" Kovel asks — he has come up behind the Racer to see what is going on.

They turn and walk back to the taxi. "He made lists of what he found and read them to us every day . . . Octobrina said he was taking inventory of his epoch."

"Inventory of his epoch," Kovel snickers, "that's a laugh."

"It's no joke, friend. His lists were his poems. They destroyed his real poetry during the period of the cult of the personality. After that, Atanas wasn't able to invent images, so he rummaged for them in garbage cans. The things he collected he brought to his apartment. Octobrina said he had a whole wall papered with pages from some old bankbooks he found. He was a beautiful, brave, lost old man."

"What are we going to do?" Kovel asks once they are back in traffic. He himself is calm now, almost resigned.

"Take me up to Vitoša," Tacho tells him, looking toward the mountain. "Then you go to militia headquarters and turn yourself in. You weren't involved with us, and they'll probably go easy on you."

"Oh, Jesus, you think so?" Kovel grasps the straw eagerly. "You think they'll understand I'm only just a taxi driver with a yearlong fare?"

"I think they'll understand, yes," Tacho reassures him. To his own ear, he doesn't sound very convincing.

Kovel drives down Hristo Botev, then turns into Aleksandâr Stambolijski. Behind them police sirens wail. Kovel casts a frightened look into the rearview mirror. As the taxi turns onto Avenue Vitoša, the first police car screeches to a stop in front of the Hotel Balkan. A crowd is gathering at the foot of the steps leading to the hotel, and the militiamen have to shoulder their way through it to the entrance.

Trapped in the great revolving door with the corroded brass handles and the gold lettered "BAL AN" in English on the glass is the Mime. His white pancake make-up is flaking off; patches of pink skin appear like freckles. Faces press in on him from either side of the glass. One of the militiamen hefts his handcuffs. The Mime reaches up and starts slapping his palms against the glass as if to see how far it extends. His eyes grow panicky. His hand motions become quicker. He searches wildly for an opening, a door, a window, a crack, but there is nothing but solid glass. Eyes bulging in terror, he scratches at it with his nails. His fingertips begin to bleed. Backing into the narrowest corner of the door, the Mime opens his mouth and screams a silent scream that makes the faces pressing in on him wince.

"You need money, clothes — " Kovel says.

The taxi is parked at the end of a dead end street high on Vitoša; according to a nearby billboard, garden apartments will be constructed here as part of an intensification of the state building program.

"Hey, wait a minute," Kovel yells excitedly. He races around to the trunk compartment and pulls out a bag full of sweaters. "I got them from a guy who got them from his wife's sister, who works in a sweater factory. Here" — Kovel holds one up against Tacho's chest to check the size — "I got to get rid of these before I go to the militia anyhow."

Tacho takes off his jacket and pulls the sweater over his head. Then he puts the jacket on again. When he reaches for his wallet, Kovel grabs his hand by the wrist. "Listen, no, wait a minute," he exclaims, shaking his head in embarrassment.

The Racer offers his hand to Kovel. "We won't meet again. You have been a friend to all of us. For that, thank you."

Kovel accepts Tacho's hand. "You really think they'll understand?" he asks again. He is anxious to be rid of the Racer, and afraid to see him go, so he holds on to his hand for a moment.

Tacho nods and backs off a step. "Doviždane." He waves, and turns into the fields. Before he is lost from view, high up at the tree line, Kovel can see that he has started to run.

17

EXHALING on his fingertips, the Racer sinks down against a sapling on the edge of a long sloping hill high in the Rila range. Below, far below, a narrow rutted Tarmac road winds through a gorge parallel to a silver stream. Every now and then a wooden footbridge arches across the stream from the road: to an old Turkish cemetery, to a shed full of firewood, to a village clinging to the side of a scrub hill with its tractor cooperative and clucking chickens and muddy streets and wooden homes with garlands of red peppers strung like laundry from the windows.

Where the road curves around the lip of the mountain, overlapping white-painted tires set in cement serve as a guardrail. For a long while the road is lost in the trees, which look like Octobrina's palate before her "white" period — dried rusts and browns mixed with dirty yellows and every conceivable shade of green. Where the road comes back into view, as if emerging from a tunnel, it is clogged with an enormous flock of sheep winding down from the mountains for the winter. A shepherd with a drooping knapsack and a wooden staff leads the way, another brings up the rear, and three or four dogs dart around the rim snapping the stragglers back into the flock. An ancient tourist bus with valises stacked on the roof appears to be aground, high and dry in a sea of sheep. Suddenly they scatter, and a few seconds later the Racer hears the faint beep of a horn. When the sheep are clear, the bus starts down a straight stretch of road lined with evenly spaced trees, the bottoms of which have been painted white. ("We are the only country in the world," Tacho remembers Mister Dancho quipping, "where an automobile can hit a tree and the tree is considered to be at fault.") A few minutes later the bus pulls up in front of the high stone walls of Rila, the fortress-monastery that was the jewel of the Bulgarian kingdom six hundred years before.

Tacho climbs stiffly to his feet and pulls the sheepskin coat around him. To the west, above the crest of some mountains which sprawl over into Yugoslavia, the sky is streaked with a washed-out sunset — "color with too much water" is how Octobrina once described a similar sunset, Tacho remembers. To the east, a cold metallic full moon is rising over Mount Musala, the highest peak on the Balkan peninsula. Tacho remembers Musala from the war: many a time they camped around its base, and once even they climbed beyond the snow line to escape German patrols. In those days the comrades already called it Mount Stalin, a name that was to stick until Nikita Khrushchev put an end to that particular cult of the personality. What had been Musala for centuries became Musala again.

Tacho pushes aside the past the way he pushes aside pain when he rides. "I must concentrate," he mutters out loud, "on the present ridiculous." Placing his feet sideways because of the steepness of the slope, the Racer starts down toward Rila. Where there are no roots to hold on to, the earth, stirred by his footfalls, runs away in rivulets. Tacho reaches back with his hand to steady himself; the ground feels colder now that the sun is gone, but he is grateful to be close to it.

"You smell just awful." Her nose wrinkles up in mock disgust.

"It's the coat," he assures her.

"Where did you get it?" she wants to know — she wants to know everything, but she is afraid to ask.

"I bought it from a shepherd in the hills; I traded him my jacket plus twenty leva. He said he had never seen twenty leva all at once. And he was an old man."

"What did he want your jacket for if he was a shepherd?"

"He said it was for his son, who might one day go to the city. He said . . ." Tacho sees that she is not paying attention, and lets the sentence trail off.

The girl studies the ground for a moment. "I wasn't sure you would come," she ventures softly. "I wasn't sure you *could* come. I'm . . . I'm . . " Looking up, she fumbles for the right word, the right tone. "I'm very happy to see you again," she declares, and Tacho is reminded of the Flag Holder's way of confronting emotional moments with a defensive formality.

The Racer nods quickly, as if accepting the greeting — the part spoken, the part unspoken too. Then, embarrassed at the sudden emotion between them, he plucks at her sleeve. "Come," he orders, "I'll show you the monastery."

"I've seen the monastery," she protests. "I've been here for days."

"I'll show it to you anyhow," he insists. "That tower there is called Hreljo's Tower. It was built by a flag holder, the feudal lord Hreljo, who was later strangled in it. See here" — Tacho's fingers trace an inscription on the tower's base. "It says, 'Thy wife sobs and grieves, weeping bitterly, consumed by sorrow.'"

"What happened in Sofia?" Melanie lifts her eyes to study his face. "You must tell me. How is it with Octobrina? How is the one you call the Rabbit — how is Elisabeta?"

Tacho turns away from her. An old priest with a stringy gray beard emerges from the church and begins knocking a stick against a hollowed-out piece of wood. From the far side of the monastery, other priests slip out of their cells and drift like shadows across the courtyard. A group of German tourists crowds into the church behind them. A single bell rings. An owl hoots. Tacho steps inside the church. It is heavy with gold-crusted icons and incense. The priest who has summoned the others stands before a gold crucifix, swaying back and forth as he chants from a thick book which he glances at only occasionally. His black hat keeps slipping forward on his head and every few pages he pauses to push it back from his eyes.

"You are a Communist," the girl whispers to Tacho. "Don't you say that religion is the opiate of the people?"

"Violence is the opiate of the people," the Racer retorts, thinking of Georgi in his hospital bed with its hospital corners and mucus stains on the starched pillow case.

Outside the church, the girl asks Tacho if he has registered for a room.

"I haven't — "

"You haven't or you can't?"

"I can't," he concedes.

"What has happened?" Melanie is pale and close to tears, but he turns away again.

"Have you eaten?" she asks, but she doesn't wait for an answer. "I can see you haven't eaten — why do I ask such a foolish question. Go to my room" — she indicates a door on the top row of cells — "and wait for me."

She is back twenty minutes later carrying a plate of *kebapčeta*, some slices of peasant bread wrapped in a paper napkin and a bottle of Mavrud.

There are two iron cots in the small cell; one is made up for the night with rough peasant blankets, the other has only a straw-filled mattress on it. Tacho sits on the unmade bed, but the girl places the tray on her bed and motions for him to join her.

After he has eaten, the girl clears away the tray. "Now you will tell me what happened," she insists calmly.

Tacho breathes deeply and begins to tell her: of the funeral, of the arrests, of Octobrina's cry of pain on the telephone, of the ambulance climbing the hill toward the Dwarf's house, of the Mime trapped in the revolving door, of his escape. "I came over the mountains," he recounts, "staying clear of the roads. I made my way through woods where the light slanted in so thickly it looked like mist. I drank from streams. The peasants gave me food. I tried to pay for it, but they wouldn't take money. Our peasants are like that: in the mountains, they will share their last crust of bread with a traveler."

"Didn't they ask questions, ask where you were going?"

"They never ask questions — that's not their way. But I told them I was tired of the city and going back to my village in the mountains. The men would smile when they heard that and look knowingly at the young ones, as if to say: 'See, here is one who has experienced the city and rejected it. Learn from him.'"

"You like mountain people, don't you?"

"I am a mountain person."

"You're going to try and cross the border, aren't you?" she wants to know.

Tacho nods.

"But how will you cross?"

"I'll cross," he evades.

"There are patrols in the hills, and dogs."

"I'll cross at the official crossing point," Tacho tells her, "right under their noses."

"How can I help you?" Melanie asks.

"You can take me to Melnik."

The Germans, who have been drinking boisterously in the canteen below, troop noisily up the wooden stairs to their cells.

"*Mein gott*, it's cold," a woman whispers excitedly as she passes Melanie's door.

"My tool will shrivel," her companion snickers, "if I don't get into something warm soon."

"What did you have in mind?" the woman leers.

"Do you speak German?" Melanie asks the Racer, her lips pressed against his ear.

"A little," Tacho acknowledges.

"What did they say?"

"Nothing important."

"But what?"

"It was something . . . dirty."

"You're a prude," she states flatly.

"Why do you say that? Because I won't tell you what they said?"

"Because you didn't look," she chides gently, "when I took my clothes off. You turned your head to the wall."

"I thought you would appreciate some privacy," he explains.

"You *are* a prude, you know," she insists triumphantly. "Nakedness always attracts men."

"It's not the nakedness that attracts them," Tacho corrects her, "but the vulnerability that goes with the nakedness."

Melanie props herself up on an elbow. "Do you think I'm thin?" she inquires archly, talking down at him in the darkness.

"You're not thin," he assures her, "you're fine," and he pulls her down and covers her breast with his palm.

"I'm flat as a board," she challenges stubbornly. "Once, when I was sixteen, I think, I bought a bra filled with water. It did wonders for my sex life. The boys flocked around me like sheep, brushing my new breasts with their elbows or the backs of their hands whenever they could. At the first school social, my date pinned a corsage on me and pricked the bra. Water leaked out all over my dress." In the pitch-darkness, she blushes at the memory.

From the courtyard below comes the hollow sound of the stick being beaten against a piece of wood. "It's the Klepalo again," Tacho tells her. "That's what they call the old priest who summons the others to prayer."

"When do they sleep?" Melanie marvels.

"When we all do," Tacho shoots back, "between prayers."

"You sound almost religious." There is a hint of astonishment in her voice.

"I'm a Communist," Tacho reminds her.

"You say that as if you're trying to frighten me," she reproaches him. "It doesn't, you know. You don't."

"Don't what?"

"Frighten me — you don't frighten me. Whatever you are, it's good." She presses her body against his. "Are you cold?"

"I'm warm," he replies, "warm and tired and sick at heart."

He thinks she has dozed off when she suddenly props herself on her elbow again. "How did you like it — the lovemaking with an American?"

"My god!" Tacho rolls away from her. "Our women don't ask that kind of question. How did you like it?" he mimics.

"Are you asking seriously?" she taunts.

"I wasn't — but I am now. How *did* you like it?"

"You're sure you want to know?" she warns.

"I'm not sure, if you put it like that," he fires back, "but tell me anyhow."

She moves close to him and talks quietly, seriously, to his chest. "I was engaged once, to a boy from Brazil. He deflowered me when I was twenty-three. The first time in bed he forced my head down to his crotch. Oh, how I hated it. Ugh. It smelled of urine, his thing. He was really very nice about it; he kept reassuring me I'd grow sexy once I lived in the warm climate of South America. But I figured if it was like that the first time, it would always be terrible, so I called off the wedding. I stayed away from boys for a long time after that. They made me very nervous: I'd sweat so much I could never wear the same dress again. Then I fell in love with someone quite a bit older, an American who knew my father. They had come over together from Russia at the start of the war. Our sex life consisted of him coming off against my stomach." Melanie smiles. "All that's changed now, of course. I don't lie to you, Tacho, *ever*. I like lovemaking, but I don't love it, not the way men seem to love it. I'll tell you something I don't tell everyone I sleep with: everything I've wanted in my life, the wanting's been better than the getting. Sex very much included. The irony is that once you learn this, once you learn the wanting's better than the getting, it takes some of the pleasure out of the wanting."

"The first time I saw you, that night in Club Balkan," Tacho confesses, "I got the impression that whatever you wanted, you could wait to get it."

"That's close for a first impression," she concedes. "I can wait to get what I want, because the getting of it ends the wanting, and I enjoy the wanting more."

He is drifting off when she curls herself around his body. "I must know more about you before I can love you properly," she tells him seriously.

"Go to sleep," he mumbles.

"I can never sleep when I sleep with someone I've never slept with before," she complains. "Are you afraid of death?"

When he doesn't answer she prods him in the ribs. "Answer, you," she insists. "Are you afraid of death?"

"I'm lucky," Tacho says quietly. "I have always had to confront the possibility of dying before I was old enough to fear death."

"Have you always felt like that? Did you feel like that when you broke the speed record?"

"I never knew I felt like that until this moment," Tacho admits thoughtfully. "That's one of the things that bothers me a great deal. I learn what I believe when I hear myself say it."

"But it's the same with everyone," she says.

"Well, it makes me feel I don't have any control over what I believe. You ask something, and I answer off the top of my head with the conviction that can only come from months of thinking about that very thing. The funny part is I really do believe the things I hear myself say."

"For instance?"

"What I just told you about death, for instance. Or" — he lowers his voice — "I dialed my own apartment before I left Sofia. Even now I don't know why I did it. I was trying everyone's number, so I tried my own. A man answered and said he was me. He asked me who I was. Before I could think of what to say, I blurted out that I was the Flag Holder. And as soon as I heard myself say it, I realized I thought I was. I still think I am."

"You're like him in many ways," she remarks. "You hold part of yourself back, the way he did. You do that with me, you know. You're doing it right now — holding part of yourself back."

"I don't trust you with my emotions," he admits.

"You trust me with your mistrust!" she snaps angrily. "Oh,

Tacho." She clings to him, and he becomes aware of her nipples pressing into his chest.

"You're getting hard," she notices. "Would you like to make love again?"

"Would you?"

"Yes, thank you," she agrees with a laugh.

The Racer gropes for her in the darkness and, guiding his penis with his hand, thrusts inside her. She cries out softly.

"I'm hurting you." He hesitates.

"No, no," she assures him, and pulls him toward her. "Oh, dear Tacho," she cries, "you don't hurt me."

18

"Slow down," Tacho orders, leaning forward in the passenger's seat expectantly. "The turnoff is after the curve."

"Will this one be paved?" the girl asks hopefully.

"Not unless they've paved it in the last few months," Tacho tells her. "Here — just before the sign."

The sign reads "Bistrica," but someone has written "The Village of" in paint above it.

"Civic pride," Tacho comments dryly. "Look down there" — he points to the main highway threading its way through the valley; a river runs alongside it, twisting and turning with every twist and turn of the highway — "that's the Sturma. It flows all the way to Greece. The border crossing is actually a bridge over the Sturma."

"How do you know all these back roads?" Melanie asks.

"From the war," Tacho explains. "We owned the hills up here, the Germans owned the road down there. Every once in a while they would come up to shoot at us; every once in a while we would go down to take a shot at them. I know the hills from the war."

"You make it sound like a game," she remarks.

"Those were our days of innocence."

"Innocence!" the girl explodes. "How can war be innocent?"

"Compared to today, it was. We knew right from wrong; we knew which of the wrongs to right, and how to right them; we knew we were on the side of the gods. Now you can never be sure."

Melanie glances quickly at Tacho. "The Flag Holder, you, Mister Dancho, Popov, the Dwarf, Valyo, even Octobrina — all of you lived in the past," she says passionately, almost angrily. "*In the past, and off the past.*"

Her vehemence makes him defensive. "I've always regretted that the greatest moment of my life came when I was nineteen. It's true, what you say — I have been living off it, the way someone lives off capital instead of income. But that's over with."

They are silent for a long time. Then, out of the blue, the girl says:

"Oh, Tacho, why did you wait for Czechoslovakia? You should have taken a stand long ago, when taking a stand might have changed something."

"It's not too late," Tacho says grimly.

They pass another village, a relatively new one with red brick buildings instead of wooden ones, and then another with two new concrete apartment houses.

Melanie concentrates on her driving. Suddenly she demands:

"You know whom I liked the best — present company excluded? I liked Octobrina the best. I had the feeling that if a live ember from one of her cigarettes ever fell on her, she'd go up in a wisp of smoke, like those leaves you see crackling away on a damp fall day. Tell me something, was she ever married?"

"She had two great passions in her youth — Communism and someone with whom she had a great love affair. Her lover died in prison during the period of the cult of the personality."

"What was he like?"

"It was a she."

"Oh."

On the rise before the next village, Tacho has her pull the Deux Chevaux over to the side of the road. "There's a militia road control ahead," he explains, starting to get out of the car. "After you pass it, you'll see a gasoline station on your right. Fill up there. Just beyond the gas station, on the far edge of the town, is a restaurant. Park in the lot behind the restaurant. Eat slowly; it'll take me an hour at least to skirt the town on foot. If you think of it," he adds, "put some bread in your pocket for me."

By midafternoon, they have passed two more militia checkpoints and are well into the Pirin Mountains, twisting around S-curves on obscure back roads, some of them paved, most of them graded but unpaved. Twice the Deux Chevaux overheats from the strain of climbing. They pull over until the radiator water has cooled enough to put a finger in it, after which Tacho tops it off from the icy mountain streams that flow all about them. Near a waterfall that cascades down from a low cliff, Tacho points out a historical marker cemented into the side of the hill. It commemorates a battle between the outnumbered Rila partisan detachment, led by Colonel Lev Mendeleyev, known as the Flag Holder, and a Gestapo unit, on August 24, 1944.

"We were on that side of the falls," Tacho reconstructs the battle, "over in the woods there. The Germans came up a goat path from a village which you can't see from here. They seemed to know just where they were going. We held them for a while, and fell back up the slope when we started to run low on ammunition. There where the boulders are, the Flag Holder held them off with our machine gun. The gun overheated and jammed, and they swarmed up the hill and captured him. I saw the whole thing from the crest, where that tree is. The one we call the Minister was next to me; I remember he seemed more concerned about the loss of the machine gun than the loss of the Flag Holder. The Germans looked up the hill, laughing and making obscene gestures, and started down with their prisoner. We lost six dead, including a cousin of mine named . . ." Tacho raises his eyes to the mountain. "I can't . . . I can't seem to remember his name," he fumbles.

They have been driving for a while when the girl asks:

"Is it far to Melnik?"

"Not very," Tacho replies. "You will know we're close when you see vineyards. Melnik is wine country."

Gradually the hills flatten out and the first vine fields appear on the slopes that border the road. Soon every meter of land is covered with vines, long rows of them held up by wire strung between two poles and weighted at the ends with stones. At dusk, they enter a small village with wide dirt streets and a large néon " **Б К П** " sign over the only building made of brick.

"What does the BKP stand for?" Melanie asks. She is tired and squinting into the dimness.

"Bulgarian Communist Party," Tacho answers. "There's a very big wine cooperative about a kilometer down the road, so they put a Party headquarters here to keep tabs on it."

They pass the wine cooperative, a sprawling prefabricated building with production posters peeling away from the corrugated walls like skin that has had too much sun. Tacho spots Bazdéev's picture on an old circus poster on the side of the cooperative. "Angel used to boast he had been to every village in Bulgaria with a population of more than ten," Tacho remembers. "The first time I saw him perform, I —"

Tacho stiffens in his seat.

"What do I do?" Melanie whispers.

A wooden barrier is stretched across the road, and a militiaman with a rifle slung across his back stands before it, swinging a lantern.

"I'll do the talking," Tacho says as the militiaman starts toward the Deux Chevaux. "What's the trouble, comrade?" he calls, half out of the car.

The militiaman, a young peasant with a jutting jaw, is chewing tobacco. "Rock slide," he replies. "Blocking the road down a piece."

"It's a rock slide," Tacho tells the girl, forgetting she understands. He turns back to the militiaman, who is holding his lamp up and shading his eyes so he can get a better look at the car.

"We were going to Melnik," Tacho says conversationally.

"Double back to the crossroad 'bout three kilometers before the village, take a left to the macadam, then the next left and follow your nose."

"I don't have a ten-kilometer permit," Tacho remarks casually. "The militia won't let me pass."

"Militia knows 'bout the slide — they'll let you pass if'n you tell 'em you're headin' for Melnik. Say, what kind of a contraption is that anyhow?"

"French car," Tacho tells him. "The girl is the daughter of an important member of the French Communist Party. I'm her guide."

"Mighty nice," the militiaman allows, kicking a tire with his boot. "What's she go for?"

Tacho lets a hard note creep into his voice. "Our Russian comrades construct cars that are just as good."

"Wasn't saying they don't," the militiaman replies quickly, suddenly alert to the pitfalls of such a conversation. "If'n I had a choice, I'd take a Russian automobile every time, if'n I had a choice."

Another car pulls up behind the Deux Chevaux. "Now that there's a car for you," the militiaman exclaims, advancing toward the Russian-made Moskovich sedan.

A young man emerges from the driver's seat. "What's up?" he calls cheerily.

"Rock slide's blocking the road," Tacho tells him. "Where you headed?"

"I'm on my way to Melnick," the young man advises.

"That's a beauty of a car you got yourself," the militiaman says loudly.

"You can say that again," the young man declares proudly. "And she's every inch mine, she is. A black beauty. That's what she is, and that's what I call her."

"Sure wish I could lay my hands on a black beauty like that," the militiaman says.

The young man smiles broadly. "Take you better part of four years, working as a waiter. That's how long it took me. Been away four years in the German Democratic Republic. But she's all mine."

"Listen," Tacho interrupts, "would you mind if I trail you to Melnik? I'm not familiar with the roads around here."

"Sure thing," the young man agrees. "I know the way blind-folded. You stick on my tail and I'll take you right to the macadam. After that, it's straight on." He hesitates, "Say, you sure do look familiar." He takes a step in Tacho's direction, tilting his head quizzically. The militiaman looks from one to the other. "You put me in mind of somebody," the young man observes carefully, "but I'll be darned if I can remember who."

"Why do you want to follow him?" Melanie asks when they are under way again. "You know the roads as well as he does."

"We're not permitted to travel within ten kilometers of the frontier without a special permit," Tacho explains. "The macadam curves inside the ten-kilometer zone, which means there'll be a militia checkpoint somewhere out there. That boy's going to tell me where it is."

The boy driving the Moskovich slows down and turns into a dirt road. A few hundred meters further along, he signals another left and swings onto a two-lane macadam.

"Keep him in sight if you can," Tacho orders. "That's good. When he comes to the checkpoint, you'll see a jeep's lights flash on. Slow down, but whatever you do, don't stop."

"You'd better switch this light so it doesn't go on when the door opens," Melanie advises.

Tacho smiles at her in the darkness. "You learn fast," he says admiringly.

About ten minutes later the brake lights on the Moskovich flash on. "He sees something," Tacho snaps. Suddenly the Moskovich is pinned in a high beam playing on it from the side of the road. Melanie slows down, using the engine. Tacho opens the door. "When you're past the checkpoint," he tells her, "pull over and turn out your lights and wait for me." He slips out of the car and is lost in the night.

The militiamen are finishing up with the Moskovich as the Deux Chevaux breaks to a stop in the headlights of the jeep parked on the side of the road.

"*Dokumenti*," snaps the militiaman, looming up next to the driver's window. Melanie can see he has a submachine gun slung over his shoulder. The Moskovich driver beeps his horn and starts down the road. Melanie slides her passport through the window. The militiaman walks around to the front of the car and examines her photograph in its headlights. Melanie squints at the jeep, but its headlights blind her. The militiaman hands her passport back through the window.

"*Graničen viza*," he demands.

The girl forces herself to smile. "Tourist," she fumbles, pointing to herself. "Melnik," she says, pointing down the road. "Rockslide," she says, imitating as best she can with both hands rocks tumbling down a mountain.

"Melnik?" the militiaman asks.

"Yes, yes, Melnik," Melanie agrees, nodding and smiling.

"Melnik," the militiaman calls across to the parked jeep, and a voice floats back:

"*Razbiram.*"

"*Dobăr păt*," the militiaman salutes, and motions her forward. Suddenly he grins. "Happy trip," he says in English. He pronounces the "H" as if he is going to spit.

The headlights on the side of the road fade off. Melanie starts to shake all over. "Thank you," she stammers in English. "Thank you very much." She starts off down the road.

Beyond the first curve, she cuts her engine and lights and coasts to a stop. She waits tensely in the darkness, straining for sounds. Fifteen minutes go by before she hears what she thinks are footfalls. An instant later Tacho slips into the seat alongside her. She takes a deep breath and leans across to kiss him.

Nodding, he rests his palm against her cheek.

19

THE DEUX CHEVAUX threads its way through the silent streets of Melnik. The headlights play over elaborate carved wooden shutters, the empty Moskovich parked under the overhang of a house, lanes that narrow and twist up and away, as if squirming out of your grasp, to disappear amid a tangle of footbridges and back alleys and fenced-in gardens.

"It's hard to believe anybody lives here," Melanie tells Tacho. "It's hard to believe you lived here."

"Born and reared," he observes. "I rode my first bicycle on the flat stretch at the bottom of the hill; when I was a boy, it was the only pavement in town."

Melanie guns the car up a steep slope and stops with a jerk when the road suddenly narrows to a footpath.

"I have the feeling I'm in a bowl," she declares nervously, jumping into the street and peering at the bulking blackness that seems to press in on her from all sides.

"You are," Tacho confirms. "We're surrounded on four sides by sand cliffs. The only way to see the sky in Melnik is to look straight up. Here" — Tacho gropes for her hand — "be careful crossing this bridge. The hotel's down a bit on the other side of the river."

The door of the hotel is locked, and Tacho bangs on it with his fist. After a few moments, he bangs again. A voice, muffled by the thick wood of the door, calls:

"Can't you see we're closed — it's past eleven."

"It's me, Petar. It's Tacho."

Fingers fumble with the lock inside and the door is suddenly thrown open.

"Tacho!" roars Petar. He limps forward and catches the Racer in a bear hug, then thrusts him back and plants noisily formal kisses on both his cheeks. "What in hell are you doing in Melnik? Here, come in out of the night."

Petar catches sight of the girl behind Tacho. "You are not alone then," he remarks.

"Melanie, meet Petar. He was my trainer in the days when I rode. Petar, meet someone who has been a friend to me. Her name is Krasov. Melanie Krasov."

"Krasov," Petar repeats the name thoughtfully. "Wasn't there a Krasov — "

"He was my father," Melanie acknowledges.

"He was an American," Petar remembers.

"So am I," the girl says.

"I've never met an American before," Petar notes. "So far, it's been painless. Do you all speak Russian?"

"Only the ones with Russian fathers," Melanie smiles.

"Are you alone, Petar?" Tacho looks into the restaurant. The only one in there is a teen-age boy curled up in front of a roaring fire.

"I'm alone," Petar says, steering Tacho and the girl toward a table in front of the fire.

"What about the boy?" Melanie whispers.

"He's retarded," Tacho explains quickly. "He's Petar's grandson."

"Oh, I'm terribly sorry. I didn't mean — "

"No harm done," Petar tells her. He prods the boy gently with his cane. The boy opens his eyes and squints up unblinkingly at his grandfather.

"Be a good boy and tell Blagoi to put a light under the *guveč*," Petar instructs him. The boy's head jerks, and he skips off toward the kitchen. Petar lays out three tumblers and a bottle of *slivova*.

"Lower than the grass, quieter than the water," he toasts, and downs the glassful in a smooth swallow.

"Lower than grass," Tacho repeats, and follows suit.

Melanie sips at hers tentatively, sputters, then sips again. The two men smile at her.

"What news from Sofia?" Petar demands. "How did the Flag Holder react to the Czechoslovak business?"

Tacho downs another tumbler of *slivova*. "The Flag Holder is

dead" — Petar's mouth sags open — "he . . . took his own life
. . . killed himself . . . to protest against the invasion."

Melanie rests her hand on Tacho's. Sapling branches crackle
in the fireplace.

"So that's how it is," Petar remarks quietly. "I will tell you
honestly. I never liked him the way you liked him, but I honored
him. And he was one hell of a driver!" It suddenly dawns on
Petar why Tacho is here. "Of course, they are arresting the others."

Tacho nods. "They are trying to turn him into a nonperson.
The only way they can do that is to take us out of circulation."

"Which means you're running."

"Which means I'm running."

"You'll be safe here for a while."

"I've come for my bicycle, Petar," Tacho says.

"Your bicycle! What are you going to do, ride across the frontier?" Petar's eyebrows, tufts of gray, arch up and he looks sharply
at the Racer, toying with the idea that has just entered his head.
"It's possible," he concludes cautiously. "How many days until
the race?"

"They should cross tomorrow — probably late afternoon, about
dusk."

"Have you been riding? Can you keep up with them?"

"For short distances, yes."

"Putting on racing tires and rims is no problem. But I'll have
to take off the big gear and install a sprint gear." Petar is thinking
out loud. "I'll get Blagoi to give me a hand. We should be able
to do it before morning if we work through the night."

"Thanks, Petar — I knew you would help."

"What bicycle are you talking about?" Melanie interrupts impatiently. "What's going on?"

"They turned one of the empty rooms in the Party building into
a museum and put my bicycle in it — the one I used when I set the
speed record. Petar here is more or less the custodian."

"Our Tacho is something of a hero," Petar explains. "Local
boy makes good."

"Lay off," Tacho warns.

Petar enjoys his little joke. "What about the girl?" he demands.

"She will drive across the border tomorrow morning like any
tourist on her way out of the country."

"I'm not crossing until you do," Melanie declares vehemently.
"You'll cross when I tell you to," Tacho lashes back at her.
"You'll cross when I tell you to," he repeats more reasonably.
"There is no other way."

Blagoi, a shepherd's second son who is learning to be a cook,
comes in with two plates of *guveč* and a basket of peasant bread.
Petar brings two bottles of Melnik wine and some clean glasses.
Tacho and the girl attack their plates ravenously: Tacho eats in the
peasant style, sprinkling salt on the bread from his palm and using
the bread to scoop up the *guveč*; Melanie eats more sedately, cutting
the meat into small pieces, then shifting the fork to her right hand,
American style. Blagoi stands over her shaking his head, baffled.

"I have seen the tourists eat that way," he acknowledges, "but
I do not arrive at seeing the logic of it."

Blagoi has just put two cups of Turkish coffee on the table when
they hear the pounding on the front door of the hotel. Melanie
looks quickly at Tacho.

"Who knows you're here?" Petar demands.

"No one," Tacho declares.

"Wait here."

Petar limps out of the dining room to see who it is. There is a
blast of cold air as he opens the front door.

"So, you are again serving after eleven," a voice booms. "Don't
insult me by denying it. I can smell the *guveč* from the bottom of
the hill. Your man Blagoi puts too much garlic in it, as always."

The visitor tries to shoulder his way into the dining room, but
Petar blocks his path and pulls the door closed with his cane. Their
voices come through the glass panes, which are covered with lace
curtains.

"They are not clients," Petar tells the other man. "They are my
guests."

"They are always guests," the first man sneers. "So were they
guests, those hikers last week. So too were they guests, the Greek
businessman and his wife the week before that. The regulations
under which we function specify we are to close at eleven" — the
man's voice turns shrill with anger — "but you, Petar, go your own
way. Don't think I don't know why, because I do know why. You
make it appear as if your restaurant is more productive than mine.
But the only way you can do that is by serving after eleven. Well,

you are not going to get away with it. I am going to report you
this time."

"Do as you like," Petar scoffs. "Do whatever will make you feel
a man."

"You, Petar, dare say that to me," the other man challenges in a
hurt voice.

"I say that to anyone who tells me he is going to the militia,"
Petar tells him.

"Who said anything about going to the militia?"

"You spoke of turning in a report," Petar reminds him
caustically.

"That was a figure of speech," the visitor maintains. His hands
shoot out, palms up. "Are you so thick, then, you don't recognize
a figure of speech when you hear one? I have come here to discuss
with you, man to man, the feeding of clients after the regular
closing hour of eleven. Where is the crime in that?"

"And I have told you, man to man, that I am not feeding clients.
I am feeding my guests."

"I have your word on that?"

"You have my word, yes."

The visitor starts toward the door. "You understand, Petar, I
am merely looking after my interests. Your restaurant has fewer
tables than mine, and greater income. The District Secretary is
certain to start asking questions. What do I say to him when he
asks these questions?"

"Say to him," Petar advises, "that I feed customers after the
obligatory closing hour of eleven. That way, he will issue a warning to me, and be pleased with both of us — with you for keeping
your eyes open, with me for surpassing my quota."

"You consent to my saying such a thing, then?"

"Of course say it," Petar urges. "We will have the last laugh."

The two men shake hands warmly, and the door closes behind the
visitor.

"How is it," Tacho asks Petar when he returns, "you do more
business than he does if you have a smaller restaurant?"

"Simple," Petar confesses, pouring himself another full glass of
red wine. "He weighs out each portion according to the instructions from the Party — seventy-five grams of chopped meat, one
hundred fifty grams of sliced tomatoes, two hundred grams of boiled

potatoes. Christ, when a Communist makes love, he is only permitted to expel twenty cc's of sperm! I beg your pardon, American
lady, but that's how it is with us."

"And you don't weigh your portions?" Tacho inquires.

"We don't even have a scale!" Petar boasts. "Isn't that right,
Blagoi?"

From behind the bar Blagoi smiles wickedly.

Later, in an icy hotel room — there is no central heating, only
more blankets — the girl undresses with the light on. This time
the Racer props himself up on an elbow and watches her.

A donkey brays under their window, waking them before the
cocks crow.

"Get up," Tacho shakes the girl. "I have something I want to
show you."

Tacho puts on a pair of hiking boots and some work clothes that
Melanie has not seen before.

"Where did you get those?" she wants to know.

"Petar," the Racer says.

It is warmer outside than in, and Tacho leads the way up a narrow
footpath that runs parallel to the river. The houses of Melnik are
of a style Melanie has not seen before — sprawling two-story
wooden structures, with the second story hanging over the first.
Every house has something to distinguish it: carved shutters, a
colorful weathercock on the sloping roof, delicate lace curtains on
the windows, a fist carved out of wood which serves as a door
knocker. Huge piles of cut logs are stacked under the overhangs of
the houses. Chickens peck the ground near a garden of tomatoes
planted late and no longer ripening on the vines.

"I see what you mean about the sky," Melanie announces. The
sand cliffs, carved into exotic contours by centuries of wind and
rain, loom around her, over her.

Tacho turns the corner of one house and spots the boy with the
Moskovich from the night before. He is stumbling up the steps of
a house with his arms full of boxes. The boy's wife, a chubby girl
wearing a new pair of high-heeled East German shoes, totters uncertainly along behind him with another armload. Her father
brings up the rear. He is carrying an electric iron, an electric

blender, an electric heater and an electric toaster. A neighbor flings open her shutters across the path and leans out.

"So he's back from where he went," she observes, eyeing the boxes in the old man's arms.

"Yes, he's back," the old man allows. "He has come by automobile, of which he is the owner."

"A Russian automobile," the daughter calls over her shoulder excitedly.

"A Moskovich," the boy corrects her, emerging from the house empty-handed.

The old woman takes this in. "Aren't many in Melnik what owns a private automobile," she notes, obviously impressed.

"Aren't any," the boy corrects her, blushing with pride, "less you count the co-op van and the hotel pickup."

The higher the Racer climbs in the village, the closer the houses get to the river until finally, near the limit of the village under the cliffs, the upper floors hang over the river itself. Beyond the last house, Tacho pauses to look back at Melnik, which tumbles away from him, like the river, toward the main road far below.

They continue to climb the cliffs until Melnik is lost from view. About twenty minutes later the path flattens out, the river narrows and shallows and the land becomes greener and softer underfoot. Presently a kind of miniature valley opens before them. In the middle of the valley, some thirty or forty peasants are lined up before a brightly painted one-room cottage which has been constructed on the edge of the river.

An old woman with coarse skin and a bristly mustache sits on a sturdy chair before the front door, her head cocked, staring through sightless eyes. Baskets of food are piled behind her chair.

"The peasant Slaveykov," she calls. Her Adam's apple bobs when she talks, and her voice sounds like the croaking of a bullfrog.

A heavyset peasant with knee-high boots and an embroidered cape steps from the line and approaches the woman. She holds out her hand and he places something in it.

"Money?" Melanie whispers.

"Sugar cubes," Tacho says. "She is the Witch of Melnik — member I told you about her the first time we met?"

The Witch turns the lumps of sugar in her thick fingers, licking and sniffing them for a moment.

"The child your wife carries will be stillborn," she croaks. "Plant maize. Enlarge your flock, for you will lose half of it come spring to a disease the name of which no one will know."

The peasant Slaveykov grasps the Witch's hand and kisses it.

"The tanner Stojanov," the Witch summons the next person. A thin man with a bushy mustache steps from the line and hesitates, but his wife pushes him forward. He advances warily, and drops two sugars into the Witch's outstretched palm as he would into a cup of coffee too hot to touch.

"You don't believe," she cackles, and communes with the sky: "A nonbeliever."

There is a murmur from the other peasants in the line.

"No difference," the Witch mumbles, and she begins licking and sniffing at the sugars. "Your son Panchu will walk again — the bone was well set."

Stojanov glances at his wife, shaken; she sinks to her knees and touches her forehead to the ground.

"The investment your godfather invites you to make is a good one. The winter will be mild and the harvest will be prosperous. Stay away from electricity."

The tanner Stojanov kisses her hand, but the Witch pulls it back and rises slowly to her feet, where she stands silently, her head cocked, listening to the river.

"All honor," she croaks, "to the one from Melnik — the Racer Abadzhiev."

Tacho steps from the line. The peasants turn to look at him, whispering excitedly to each other.

"Don't stand for me, old woman," Tacho says, approaching the Witch.

"Have you then become a man of movement?" she challenges, settling back into her chair.

"I am becoming," Tacho replies. He reaches in his pocket for the sugars he put under the pillow the night before. The Witch fingers them for a moment, then licks them and raises them to her nostrils.

"Even so," she says vaguely, as if the sugars merely confirm what she already knows. "Beware of a Greek appearing to bear a gift," the Witch declares carefully, articulating each word. "Do you see it?"

"I'm not sure," Tacho stammers.

"You will lay the foundation of a house that your sons will build and your grandsons will live in," the Witch intones feverishly. "Do you see it?"

"No," Tacho whispers.

"No matter," the Witch cackles, "I see it. Ha, ha, ha, ha, ha, ha, ha."

Limping painfully on his bad leg, Petar meets them halfway up the sand cliffs. His grandson walks alongside, holding his hand. Blagoi struggles along behind them carrying the bicycle over his shoulder.

"It is done," Petar says, motioning to the bicycle. The grandson settles back on his haunches and stares up at the Racer. Petar breathes with difficulty because of the climb. "Five gears," he says, "closely spaced, with a full two hundred and twenty-five centimeters on the bottom one. Remember to let some air out before you ride to increase traction."

Petar hands the Racer a small shepherd's knapsack, which he hangs over his shoulder. "The uniform is in here." Tears well up in the old man's eyes. "I never thought you would ride that bicycle again," he admits. "I never thought . . ." He shakes his head, unable to say more.

Wordlessly, they embrace.

Tacho turns to the girl, whose face is contorted. "Let me have your wristwatch," he says.

She hands it to him. It is a man's watch, with a sweep second hand. "It was my father's — he used to time himself with it. It has a stopwatch. To make it start, you press here. To stop, here."

"I'll give it back to you in Greece," Tacho tells her.

Melanie starts to look around wildly.

"Listen to me," Tacho tells her. "I have always been intrigued by two things in my life: bicycle riding and politics. Now they have come together — bicycle riding has become a political act."

The girl fights back tears. Tacho leads her a step away from the others and talks to her quietly, quickly. "There is a poem by the

Russian Mandelstam called 'I Have Studied the Science of Parting.'
Atanas read it to me many times. As for me, I have never studied
parting before today — I had no one to part from, and no place to
go. Now you have given me the gift of both."

Tacho kisses her formally on both cheeks, and then on the lips,
and embraces her. For an instant she clings to him.

Blagoi leans the bicycle against a rock and, with a wave, starts
down the path toward Melnik. Petar takes his gandson's hand
and follows him. Tacho gently pushes the girl away. She looks
into his face, her eyes wide with fright.

"What did the Witch mean?" she asks. " 'You will lay the foundation of a house that your sons will build — ' "

" 'And your grandsons will live in,' " Tacho finishes it for her.
"I don't know yet what it means."

Melanie nods once, and hurries down the hill after Petar.

20

THE RACER recognizes the spot from the war (and a hundred dreams): the clearing where they buried the grade-school teacher from Blagoevgrad, the old forestry trail sloping down through heavy timber to join the main highway just after it twists, in an almost perfect U, around a hairpin curve. They had come across it while combing the countryside for an ambush site, the Flag Holder, the Minister, Mister Dancho and the Racer. It was a serious business, the selecting of ambush sites; your life could depend on it. They inspected several possibilities, mulled the advantages and drawbacks of each and settled on this one as the most promising; the forestry trail especially interested them because it offered a convenient route for the getaway. At the last moment the Minister, pouring over the map, raised an objection: the gunfire could be heard at the frontier post, he said, which meant they would have to terminate the ambush quickly before help had a chance to arrive. The Flag Holder didn't agree. It was the very nearness to the frontier, he argued, that made the spot so attractive; the Germans, knowing they were so close, would never suspect an ambush here.

In the end, the Flag Holder was right: the first German to die, the machine gunner on the open mount of the lead truck, had taken off his helmet and was sunning himself atop the turret when the burst of gunfire caught him in the face. The partisans then blew up two trucks which were supposed to be full of tank treads (they didn't stop to confirm this) and retreated up the old forestry trail into the Pirins on the run, carrying the only one among them to be wounded — a nearsighted grade-school teacher from Blagoevgrad. He had blown off his own leg with a clumsily handled grenade, and was bleeding to death from the stump despite the belt that Mister Dancho had tightened around it.

In the clearing, they scooped out a shallow grave near a dead oak and waited impatiently for the grade-school teacher to die. Tacho wet his lips with a damp rag. The grade-school teacher licked the moisture with his tongue, which had swollen to twice its normal size. He turned his head and saw the stony-faced partisans squatting on their haunches next to the grave, fidgeting nervously, fingering the loose earth, worrying about whether the gunfire had been heard at the frontier.

"I'm trying to hurry," the grade-school teacher said thickly. And as soon as he decently could, he died.

The clearing has not changed much in twenty-four years. All traces of the shallow grave have vanished, and for a moment the Racer is tempted to hunt for it, to turn up the earth near the dead oak and see if the bones of the grade-school teacher are still there. It sticks in Tacho's mind that the grade-school teacher came from the Valley of the Roses. He remembers the Flag Holder telling him, just before he set the speed record, how the peasant women harvested dew in the rose fields. It comes to him now: Lev had the story from the grade-school teacher. Tacho would like to put a rose on the grave — if there were a rose around and a grave to put it on.

There is the scar of a campfire in the center of the clearing; several people have eaten here, and slept here afterward. Poking through the debris, Tacho finds some empty cans and a broken can opener which he recognizes as being of Russian manufacture.

"One can opener, broken, manufactured in the Soviet Union and popular with Bulgarian housewives in the early nineteen fifties," Tacho says out loud — in his mind's eye he can hear Popov delivering the day's inventory. "Four empty, rusted cans, apparently opened with this very same can opener. One spoon, rusted, apparently used to eat the food that came from the cans opened by the Russian can opener. One shoelace, black, of the kind used by hunters or frontier patrolmen. One razor blade, rusted, origin uncertain. They say that shaving is the only thing that separates men from monkey. So they say. Sssssssss."

Tacho feels a great emptiness, which manifests itself as a tightness in the chest. With a conscious effort, he forces himself to concentrate on the ride ahead of him. He sits cross-legged on the ground and methodically eats the food Petar has put in the knapsack: chunks of cured ham, small pieces of dark peasant bread. His throat is dry and he has difficulty swallowing, so he washes down each bite with a mouthful of water from a canteen.

Afterward, his hands burrowing deep inside the pockets of his sheepskin coat, his eyes fixed on the ground, he starts down the forestry trail toward the highway, one hundred forty meters away, kicking aside branches and stones as he goes. He inspects it again on his way up to the clearing, then coasts down on the bicycle to memorize the contours of the trail. He climbs to the top with the bicycle and strips off the sheepskin coat. Selecting a gear, he leans the bicycle against a tree at the top of the trail and takes up a position on the side of the clearing that overlooks the highway to the north.

"Ready, set, go." He punches Melanie's stopwatch and dashes for the bicycle, leaps on and starts down the trail, picking up speed as he goes. The trees flash by with only the faintest view of the road between them. He dips onto the hard surface of the highway and stops the sweep second hand in the same instant. It reads nine and eight-tenths seconds.

The Racer makes three more trial runs before he is satisfied that his timing is accurate — for accurate it must be if his plan is to work. If he comes out onto the highway too soon, the other riders will see him; too late and he will never catch up with them and be spotted at the frontier.

Ten seconds to get down the forestry trail. In ten seconds, Tacho calculates, the four Bulgarian riders, pushing uphill in third gear toward the hairpin curve, will cover one hundred twenty meters. Tacho paces off one hundred twenty meters down the highway and ties his handkerchief to a twig on the side of the road to mark the spot. When the last of the four Bulgarian riders reaches the handkerchief, he will dart for his bicycle and ride down the forestry trail and come out — god willing — right behind them. Then it will be just a matter of keeping up.

In the clearing again, Tacho strips off the hiking boots and peasant clothes that the Trainer provided. From the knapsack he pulls his old riding suit, the one he wore so many years ago in the Valley of the Roses — black riding shoes, red shorts and a green T-shirt with the number eight in red on the back. It is the same uniform that Tacho has designed for the four riders.

He packs his hiking clothes in the knapsack, and wraps the knapsack in the sheepskin coat and hides the bundle behind some bushes
in the woods. He looks at Melanie's watch — half an hour to go
— and forces himself to urinate. Then he checks the bicycle
again. He is about to lean it against the tree when he remembers
the Trainer's warning about the traction, so he lets a small amount
of air out of both tires. That done, he takes up his position on the
edge of the clearing overlooking the highway. The Trainer has
left some rock candy in the pocket of his shorts, and he sucks
noisily on a piece. After a while he feels chilled — nervousness,
he thinks — and begins to run in place to keep warm.

He is still running in place when the truck with the loudspeaker
and the big sign in front ("Pull over — bicycle race in progress")
hauls into view. A police car follows close behind it. Five
minutes later two motorcycle policemen come along, and right
behind them Tacho spots the four Bulgarian riders, with big Sacha
riding point. As the last of the four riders glides by the white
handkerchief, Tacho spits out the rock candy and dashes for the
bicycle.

"Any time now," the male secretary whispers discreetly in the
Minister's ear — he knows, from long association with him, that he
is very bored. They are standing in the middle of the bridge that
spans the river that marks the frontier with Greece.

"We greet you," the Greek Colonel intones, "at a moment
when the friendship between our two neighboring countries is
ripening — "

"Could you start again, please, Colonel," a man with earphones
yells. "The voice level wasn't right."

"We greet you" — the Colonel smiles toward the camera at
exactly the same point in his speech — "at a moment when the
friendship between our two neighboring countries is ripening into
a bud that will flower in this fertile — "

The Minister signals the translator, who is muttering in his
ear, to stop and listens to the voice drone on in Greek. When his
turn comes, he speaks briefly, modestly, about the historical roots
that bind all Balkan peoples together, about Bulgaria's desire for
friendly coexistence with its non-Communist neighbors, about the
bicycle race now in progress being a first concrete step in that

direction. Then the Colonel and the Minister shake hands for the cameras.

"The truck," one of the border guards on the Bulgarian side is shouting. Its arrival is the first exciting thing that has happened since he was transferred to the frontier post some weeks before, after having had the misfortune to witness a minor disturbance while he was on guard duty in front of Dimitrov's tomb. "The truck is here."

The news spreads to the people on the bridge. Civilian functionaries and military aides from both countries crane on tiptoes for the first glimpse of the riders. Suddenly the border guards on the Bulgarian side cheer wildly. An instant later the team swings around a bend into view.

"They're ours!" the Minister's male secretary cries. "Our boys are ahead."

"How very interesting," the Minister murmurs coolly, amused at all the commotion being made over some bicycles. Barely visible in the gathering dusk, the Bulgarian riders dip down an incline past a wire-mesh frontier gate that is wide open and pedal onto the bridge.

"We congratulate you," the Greek Colonel yells in the Minister's ear; he is obviously disappointed, but determined to play the good loser.

"He congratulates you," the translator repeats, cupping his hands and yelling into the Minister's other ear, but the Minister is not paying attention, the Minister is watching the riders and frowning.

"I thought there were four riders to a team," he shouts to his male secretary.

"The newspapers did say four — "

The five Bulgarian riders, arched gracefully over their handlebars, their wheels almost touching, their shirttails whipping around their waists, flash by the Minister and pull for the Greek side of the bridge.

"Stop them!" the Minister stammers, starting into the roadway after them. "STOP THEM!" he screams, but his voice is lost in the uproar that the riders leave behind them like a wake.

As they touch Greek soil, the first four riders put on a spurt of speed, but the fifth rider, no longer pedaling, drops back, gasping for breath. Coasting past the red-and-white-striped crossing gate, he thrusts his right fist deep into the sky as if the race has ended. Flash bulbs pop around him. A girl runs toward him and flings her arms around his neck, pulling him from the bicycle. People mill around them, puzzled. Soldiers shout. A siren wails.

On the bridge, an officer dashes up and whispers something in the ear of the Greek Colonel. He glances quickly at the Minister — it is difficult to tell from the Colonel's face whether he is annoyed or embarrassed — and hurries off without saying goodbye.

21

EVERYONE is unfailingly polite: the Greek boy who raps quietly at his door, the night porter who operates the ancient elevator, the policemen who accompany him through the deserted streets to the building with the Greek flag hanging limply over the door, the civilian who leads the way up the creaking staircase to the dimly lit room, the bureaucrat who sits behind the desk tapping his finger impatiently on the polished mahogany.

"Ah, here is our fifth racer," he says in fluent (though accented) Bulgarian, rising with a smile and gesturing Tacho to a seat. "Can I offer you something: a Turkish coffee perhaps, or an infusion; I don't drink it myself, but I am told they make a really splendid herb tea in this region."

"Coffee, thank you."

The bureaucrat motions to an aide and in an altogether different manner snaps at him in Greek. Then, smiling again, he turns his attention back to the Racer.

"It is my hope you will excuse the earliness of the hour; I am only just arrived from Athens, and I am obliged to return as soon as possible. It was my thought that we could" — he purses his lips — "hold a conversation . . ."

"Yes, of course," Tacho agrees readily. He shifts in his chair; the clothes he is wearing are too large for him and make him feel uncomfortable. "What is it you would like to know?"

The aide, who Tacho now sees is in military uniform, places a cup of coffee on the desk. The bureaucrat, who is dressed in a dark business suit and has close-cropped hair, glances at a single sheet of paper on the desk.

"Your name is listed here as Abadzhiev, Tacho. Am I pronouncing it correctly?"

Tacho indicates he is. "To whom am I talking if you please?" he inquires.

The bureaucrat smiles innocently. "But you are talking to me."

"I would like to know your name," Tacho persists.

"My name." The bureaucrat looks around the room and Tacho, following his glance, notices for the first time that there are six or eight men, most of them in uniform, lounging in the shadows against the wall. "My name," the bureaucrat advises Tacho, "is of no importance. It would mean nothing to you. You would not remember it later, for it is difficult for a foreigner to pronounce." As an afterthought, he adds:

"If it would make you feel more comfortable — and by all means we would like you to feel more comfortable — you may address me as Major John."

"Are you a representative of the Greek government?"

"In a manner of speaking, yes."

"I think I understand," Tacho says hesitantly.

"I was confident you would," the bureaucrat declares good-naturedly.

Tacho reaches for the cup of coffee and sips it. He finds it difficult to swallow and does so only with an effort. He turns his head, almost as if he is looking for a way out of the room, and notices a thin man with glasses bent over a writing desk near the window.

"Is that man making a transcript of our conversation?" Tacho wants to know.

"He asks if you are making a verbatim," the bureaucrat says in Greek. Some of the men along the wall snicker. The man making the notes says:

"Tell him I am doing sums."

"In response to your question," Major John advises Tacho, "yes, he is making a verbatim. Can I assume you raise no objection?"

"Would it make a difference if I did?"

"Only to you. You would feel frustrated, inasmuch as you would be unable to do anything about it."

The bureaucrat is tapping his finger on the desk again, as if he is calling the meeting to order. "Down to business," he says.

"By all means," Tacho agrees, "let us get down to business."

"I am informed that you are the possessor of an international sporting reputation. Bicycle racing, I believe. Of course, bicycle racing" — Major John pats his forehead in self-depreciation — "that was how you came across the border. Bravo. Bravo." He claps his hands together slowly. "Ingenious, I have had" — he hesitates over the word, and then draws it out — *"conversations* with quite a few people who have crossed the frontier, but I do not remember anyone accomplishing it on a bicycle. Yes indeed, you have my unrestrained admiration." Traces of a smile linger on Major John's thin lips as he leans forward and asks:

"What is it you require from us?"

The question shocks Tacho only because he thinks the answer is self-evident. "Why, political asylum is what I want from you."

Major John slaps the table happily. "Exactly what I said you would want." He addresses the men leaning against the wall. "Didn't I say what he would want?" To Tacho he holds out his hands, palms up, as if something were in them. "I offer it to you, this political asylum, as a gift."

Beware of a Greek appearing to bear a gift!

"I accept," Tacho tells him cautiously.

"Good, good. Then it only remains for me to remind you that in this remote corner of Europe, it is the custom to respond to a gift."

"Respond how?"

"Why, with another gift, of course."

The two men eye each other across the polished expanse of desk.

"What is it you want from me? What have you come all the way from Athens to get from me?"

Major John leans back in his chair, which creaks under his weight. "What is it you have to offer?"

Tacho takes a deep breath. "On nine September, during the parade marking the twenty-fourth anniversary of our liberation from German occupation, before the tomb of Georgi Dimitrov, under the eyes of our Party leaders and tens of thousands of Party cadres, Lev Mendeleyev poured gasoline . . . poured gasoline over . . . he poured gasoline over his clothes and set himself on fire to protest against the Soviet suppression of Socialist Humanism in Czechoslovakia." Tacho is speaking very softly now, and the men against the wall strain forward to catch his words. "No news of this . . . immolation was permitted to be published in my country. Not one word. The authorities instead undertook to turn Lev Mendeleyev into a nonperson and obscure the reasons for his suicide. In order to accomplish this, his close friends, all of whom are well known abroad, were arrested. I fled in order to testify that there was one in the Socialist world who — "

Major John stops the Racer with a raised palm. "I beg your pardon, but who is Lev Mendeleyev?"

"Why, he was our Flag Holder." Tacho's pulse pounds in his temple. "He led . . ." His voice peters out.

"Mendeleyev was a big-shot partisan," the man making the transcript explains. "He drank too much and never made it into politics."

"He was very respected," Tacho bridles. "He was a national hero — "

"He was an alcoholic," the male secretary sneers. "He got roaring drunk and shot himself in the mouth when he discovered he had terminal lung cancer. There was a small obituary in the Party paper day before yesterday."

"They're lying," Tacho cries angrily. "It's a lie."

"Even assuming your version is the more accurate of the two," Major John intervenes, "the information you offer is of no use to us."

"How no use to you? Surely the Americans could make use of it to embarrass the Russians."

"Surely the Americans could use the material," the male secretary mimics in Greek.

One of the men against the wall snickers. "That's very humorous," he says in Greek.

"Do you follow?" Major John inquires.

"I don't understand Greek," Tacho says.

"My colleagues ridicule the idea that the Americans could use the material you offer. I tell you frankly: I have many American friends in Athens more or less in the same line of work as all of us here. I know how they think, these Americans. I understand their requirements. If I could help them, I would. But I strongly suspect, and I urge you to believe, that the last thing in the world they want to do is to embarrass the Russians over Czechoslovakia." Major John taps his finger again on the desk. "Between us, the Americans are not at all disappointed with the way things turned out. They are supposed to have opened a case of champagne at the embassy when they got word of the — " He looks inquiringly at his male secretary. "What is the delicate expression?"

"Intervention."

"Yes, intervention will do nicely. They opened champagne when they heard about the intervention." Major John shrugs. "You are obliged to do better."

"Unfortunately, I have not brought with me any secret codes or blueprints," Tacho confesses cynically. "I possess no military or diplomatic secrets. I know only one person in a position of high authority, and he would have me arrested if he laid eyes on me."

"Then let us hope, for your sake, he never lays eyes on you."

"Let us hope," Tacho agrees stiffly.

"Perhaps there is something . . ." Major John purses his lips thoughtfully, as if he is trying to decide whether to make the effort. "Yes, perhaps there is something you can do for us after all." He rises to his feet and moves around to sit on the front of the desk, looking down at Tacho. "There are some in my country who seek to normalize relations with our Communist neighbors — this silly bicycle contest was organized by such people. There are others, in whose ranks you will find myself and my colleagues, who feel more comfortable with the status quo. Now, the fact of the matter is that those who prefer the status quo could make good use of an internationally known sports star who risks his life in a dramatic escape from his motherland *in order to discredit Communism.* In short, we are prepared to make you a gift of political asylum if you, for your part, are prepared to make us a gift of your anti-Communism."

Tacho sees through the window that it is beginning to get light outside; the girl, he thinks, will be pacing the floor of their room in the small hotel, waiting for him to return. "Don't go," she begged when the boy woke them up with the knock on the door. Did she have some sixth sense, Tacho wonders? "Or at least wait until they print your photograph in the newspapers."

"Take your time," Major John smiles down at Tacho.

"I am not *anti*-Communist," Tacho says quietly. "I am a Communist."

The men around the rim of the room exchange knowing looks. One of them clears his throat. The secretary stops writing and screws the cover back on his fountain pen. Major John walks crisply back to his seat behind the desk.

"Someone open the damn window," he orders irritably. An officer leaning against the wall jumps to a window and throws it open. To Tacho, Major John says coldly:

"Obviously there is some confusion here. How is it you can be a Communist when you have escaped from a Communist country —"

"Bulgaria is not a Communist country —"

Major John's eyes narrow. "What is it you understand yourself to be when you describe yourself as a Communist?"

"I can't put it into words," Tacho responds evasively.

"Try."

"I am not equipped —"

"*Try.*"

"Communism," Tacho attempts slowly, "is the name I give to the belief that there must be a better way, for the existing ways are intolerable."

Major John taps his finger on the desk again. "I too have made a study of Communism. In a sense, you could call it my profession. In a sense" — he laughs as he corrects himself — "you could call it my obsession. It it my conclusion that Communism deals, albeit not so efficiently as Capitalism, with ways of acquiring things —"

"Things!" Tacho cannot keep from crying passionately. "My god, we will all drown in *things,* gasping for air and proclaiming with our last breath what a great big abundant world we live in. Communism — real Communism, which is Socialist Humanism — is a way of life in which things are a means to an end, and not an end in itself."

"Yes or no?" someone demands impatiently from the wall.

"Will he or won't he?" the male secretary wants to know.

"Are you or aren't you?" Major John insists.

Tacho looks from one to the other. "You're bluffing. You can't send me back and you know it. There were dozens of people at the border. There were photographers. I saw the flash bulbs go off. I felt their heat. My photograph will be in the newspapers —"

Major John removes a shoe box from a desk drawer and angles

it so that Tacho can look inside. It contains rolls of undeveloped film.

"It is said," he informs Tacho tonelessly, "that a tree falling in a wood makes no sound unless someone is there to hear it."

"I believe that someday people will hear all the trees that have fallen," Tacho retorts. "They will cover their ears, the noise will be so great. They will feel the ground shake under their feet from the crashing down."

Major John rises. The men leaning against the wall straighten up. The male secretary scrapes back his chair.

"You Communists always deal in the future," Major John observes distantly. "When will you learn there is no future. There is no past. There is only now."

Tacho is strangely persuaded by the things he hears himself say. "There is no now" — the syllables sound on his ear like the delicate ticking of bicycle spokes — "there is only a past and a future. Now, if it exists at all, is merely a bridge between what was and what can be."

In the lobby, they stare in embarrassment at their shoes as they wait for the truck to be brought around.

"Do you have the time?" Tacho looks up.

"I am not authorized to give you information," one of the officers who attended the conversation replies.

Somewhere down the street a store owner winches open a steel shutter. The screeching sends shivers down Tacho's spine. He turns and notices a large mirror on the other side of the lobby. Nothing moves in it, and for an instant Tacho imagines it is the mirror at Krimm. He reaches up to adjust his collar, and glances to his right expecting to see Octobrina cocking her head to one side to present the profile Mayakovsky admired.

A soldier trots noisily down the stairs. Tacho catches sight of him in the mirror. Then he steps closer and sees himself too.

The town is pitted asphalt and potted plants and cheap store-fronts with elaborate gold lettering on dirty plate-glass windows. Tacho sees it all through the tunnellike rear flap of the covered army truck in which he is riding. They pass the small hotel and he catches a flash, almost subliminal in its brevity, of the girl inside;

the window has fogged with her breath, and she seems to be wiping it clean with the lace curtain.

"We cleanse our souls the way we clean our windows," he recalls Popov reciting, "with the curtains already hanging on them."

"I remember that it was very lovely," Octobrina comforted him when he wasn't able to repeat the line.

The topsoil in the fields outside the town is thin, and the rows of cabbages meander, as if planted by the wind. They pass an old man with knee-high rubber boots shoveling manure into a wheelbarrow; he doesn't look up as the convoy speeds by. Beyond the town, beyond a large billboard that announces the spectacular achievements of a government irrigation program, the fields are bone dry and the topsoil swirls up with each gust. The wind cuts through the canvas sides of the truck, bringing with it the smell of snow, and the smell folds back the memory of other winters, and the memory sucks a smile to the Racer's lips.

"He smiles," observes the soldier sitting next to Tacho.

"Not for long," laughs the soldier sitting across from him.

The truck stops with a jerk, the tailgate drops and Tacho jumps down. He walks around the side of the truck and sees the bridge that marks the frontier. Nearby, a soldier holds his bicycle.

A boy — Tacho guesses he is fourteen or fifteen — shouts excitedly and runs over to the bicycle; his wide eyes take in the polished gears, the thin tires, the leather saddle, the graceful sweep of the handlebars.

Tacho takes the bicycle from the soldier and holds it out to the boy, who steps back and looks around in bewilderment.

"He gives it to you," Major John explains.

The boy blinks in confusion.

"Go ahead," Tacho encourages him gently, "take it."

"Take it, damnit," Major John repeats in Greek.

The boy hesitates an instant more, still unable to believe his good fortune. Then he flings a leg over the saddle and coasts off down the road toward the town, looking back from time to time to see if anybody will stop him.

Nobody does.

"Idiot," Major John scoffs as he walks with Tacho toward the bridge.

"Him or me?"

"The both of you — you don't know a good thing when it is offered to you. You place me in an awkward position, I will concede it to you. I am a democrat, and being a democrat implies a certain — how shall I put it so that you won't mock what I say — *solicitude* for people."

Across the river, a covered truck is backing up to the wire-mesh gate. Two soldiers with machine pistols jutting casually from their hips advance onto the bridge.

"What I am attempting to say to you is that you can still change your mind," the Major tells Tacho.

When Tacho makes no answer, Major John stops in his tracks. "Do you know what it is you do?" he calls after the Racer.

Tacho turns toward him. "I think so," he says slowly. "I have been told I am laying the foundation of a house that my sons will build and my grandsons will live in."

"You there, Abadzhiev," the Major yells as Tacho starts toward the bridge. "My name is Xanthopoulos. Epaminondas Xanthopoulos."

The Racer calls over his shoulder:

"You were right — it is too difficult to pronounce. I won't remember it. Nobody will remember it."